Haven

The Last Humans: Book 3

Dima Zales

♠ Mozaika Publications ♠

Copyright © 2016 Dima Zales and Anna Zaires
www.dimazales.com

Published by Mozaika Publications, an imprint of Mozaika LLC.
www.mozaikallc.com

Cover by Najla Qamber Designs
www.najlaqamberdesigns.com

Edited by Elizabeth from arrowheadediting.wordpress.com and Mella Baxter

e-ISBN: 978-1-63142-167-9
Print ISBN: 978-1-63142-168-6

CHAPTER ONE

I'm brimming with contentment as I walk down the beach, Phoe's slender fingers wrapped in mine. The highlights of our activities flash across my mind's eye: frolicking in the sun reading books, listening to music, watching movies, swimming in the warm ocean, eating Phoe's exquisite culinary inventions, and many intimate activities that residents of Oasis would see as beyond obscene. We've spent what feels like weeks doing all of the above, here in the beach paradise Phoe constructed. I'm currently an uploaded mind—a backup that she animated—but that doesn't make our fun any less real. In all this subjective time, only a few minutes have passed in the real world of Oasis, where my biological body is sleeping in his bed.

In theory, we could do this all night long, which would equal to many years here. This gives me pause, and I ask, "Will I feel groggy in the morning if I spend the whole night here? Or does my body get sleep regardless of what this version of my mind does?"

"You'll feel rested." Phoe's voice is as serene as the foamy surf around my feet. "This will feel like the longest dream anyone's ever had."

"Cool," I murmur, and we walk another couple of miles down the shore. I focus on the pleasurable feel of my feet touching the sand, the pungent smell of kelp, and most importantly, the sensation of Phoe's delicate hand clasped in mine.

As I gaze at the never-ending ocean, all our recent troubles seem far away. It's hard to believe that the horrors of the IRES game and Jeremiah torturing me happened only three days ago. It's even harder to process all the insanity of Birth Day. My ploy to

Forget Phoe to fool the L.ns of Truth, flying the disk to the black building, enduring that horrific Test—all that seems incredibl. distant at this moment. Even learning that Council members don't die, but ascend to a place called Haven—an existence similar to the virtual world I'm enjoying—feels like something that happened long ago.

The tension in Phoe's hand bursts my daydreaming bubble, and I turn to look at her.

She's stopped walking, and there's a strange expression on her face. Before I have a chance to ask her what's wrong, she jerks her hand away and grabs her head protectively, her features contorting in agony as she backs away.

My pulse leaps. "Phoe?" I take a small step toward her.

She continues backing away, cradling her head between her palms. "Something is happening," she says through gritted teeth. "It's Oasis-wide—"

"Hello," a strange, gurgling voice interrupts. "I should have no problem destroying you here, in this little environment, as easily as anywhere else."

I look around frantically.

No one else is here, but I do recognize that voice.

It's a younger version of Jeremiah's, though it sounds as if he's under water.

"Theodore," he says in that odd voice. "I have to say, I'm surprised to see you collaborating with this soon-to-be nonentity."

"What's going on, Phoe?" I think, fighting a sudden bout of dizziness. "Is this a joke?"

Before Phoe can answer, the sand to my right shimmers and rises up, as though a powerful wind is blowing upward from underground. The sand forms a small dune and morphs into a murky, thick, liquid-like substance. I recall reading that glass is made of sand, and for a moment, I wonder if that's what I'm seeing—some sort of molten glass. Whatever the substance is, it begins to congeal, taking form.

"This is so bad," Phoe whispers in my mind, and I get the feeling that if she spoke out loud, her voice would be shaking.

"Why?" I try not to panic. "What is this—"

A rustling to my left catches my attention. I turn and see that the same sand-to-liquid process is happening over there.

I'm about to repeat my question when I hear another rustling to my right and see the same morphing action occurring there as well.

My heart hammering, I glance at Phoe. She's looking at the liquid stuff behind me with alert determination bordering on terror.

I follow her gaze and have to blink a few times.

It's now possible to make out the rightmost liquid shape for what it is—not that "what it is" makes any sense. The dune is much bigger now, and instead of molten glass, it reminds me of a jellyfish. There's a vague outline of a human face on top of the amorphous blob, and it's somewhat recognizable as Jeremiah's—though if I hadn't heard his voice, I might not have realized that.

The being starts to wave from side to side, seemingly trying to move forward. Where the abomination touches the sand, that sand turns into the same viscous, clear protoplasm that the creature is made of. Frantically, I look around. The same process is happening all around me, though the Jeremiah-blob behind me is in the early stages of its gelatinous development.

"Phoe, did you create this?" I ask in desperate hope. "Is this your idea of fun—making a Jeremiah that got crossed with a giant amoeba?"

"No, I didn't create this." Phoe's tone is full of anxiety. "And rather than comparing this to a bacterium, it might be more accurate to say it's a virus."

"A vi—"

I'm interrupted by Phoe's sudden movements. She gesticulates and an object appears in her hands. It looks like a cross between an ancient vacuum cleaner and a bazooka.

She points it at the rightmost—and largest—Jeremiah-blob and pulls the trigger.

With a yelp, the strange creature is sucked into Phoe's weapon. As soon as it's gone, Phoe points the weapon at a spot of sand a few feet away and squeezes the trigger again. In a stream of disgusting liquid, the creature half flies, half pours out onto the sand, splattering bits and pieces of itself along the way. Wherever a droplet of the protoplasm falls, a new blob congeals. Now that I know what to look for, I see Jeremiah's face forming in all of them.

Phoe grabs my hand squeezing it hard as she drags me through the patch of sand that she just cleared with the bazooka vacuum cleaner. The Jeremiah amoebas—or viruses, if Phoe is correct—slither after us like gigantic slugs. As they crawl, I notice to my horror that the sand behind them shifts into more of them.

Phoe drops her weapon and raises her hands, palms up, to the sky. A blinding flash follows the gesture. I'm momentarily blinded, and when my vision clears, I notice two extra people on the beach. Both of them look identical to Phoe. The two pixie-haired women examine the slugs approaching them.

The original Phoe picks up the bazooka-like weapon and uses it on the blob crawling right behind us.

"Don't touch that substance." Grabbing my hand again, Phoe hurries down the quickly diminishing untainted sand, dragging me along.

I can't help but glance behind us. The two Phoes raise *their* hands in the same gesture my Phoe used to create them. I look away, but the flash, twice as bright as the last time, stings my eyes anyway. As soon as the light fades, I look back. Not surprisingly, there are now four Phoes. Then the four Phoes raise *their* hands to the sky. I avert my gaze and squint, but the flashes nearly blind me anyway. The four Phoes are now sixteen.

My guide jerks my hand, and I pick up my pace. A slug-blob is an inch away from my leg when my Phoe, the one with the vacuum cleaner in her hand, uses her strange weapon to remove the thing from our path.

"It's futile," Jeremiah's voices say in unison. "You know you're just prolonging the inevitable. I've cleaned up enough of you to prove this, haven't I? Or does this humanoid instantiation make this part of you dumber?"

I look back and see those sixteen Phoes respond by raising their arms to the sky. After a supernova-bright flash, they multiply yet again. Given that each new batch was a square of the prior one, I assume that there are now 256 Phoe duplicates, and eye-balling it, I see about that many. If they do the maneuver again, there will be sixty-something thousands of them.

The virus, or whatever it is, must've done the same math and is determined not to allow it. As one, the hundreds of instances of Jeremiah throw themselves at the multitude of Phoes.

It's painful to look at. Wherever the slime of the attackers touches a Phoe's skin, that skin turns into the disgusting slimy substance, and from there, that Phoe quickly starts melting into clear protoplasm. What's truly horrific is the end of that transformation. That unfortunate version of Phoe inevitably turns into another instantiation of the Jeremiah-slug-thing.

The rest of the Phoes don't wait to join their sister's fate. They gesture, and bazooka vacuum cleaners appear in their graceful hands. They use the weapons to push back the wave of Jeremiahs.

The Phoe holding my hand looks back, and her eyes widen. Urgently, she says, "I won't last much longer. I've written this version of myself—with memories of you—into the DMZ, or Limbo. If I ever recover from this attack--"

The world shudders.

I follow Phoe's petrified gaze but don't comprehend what I'm seeing.

What I've been thinking of as the ocean is no longer made up of salty water, but of the horrible

Jeremiah ooze that surrounds us. If my heart wasn't a simulation, I think it would've stopped. The whole ocean begins to form into a shape. Hurricane-loud laughter rumbles in the distance, and a mountain-sized tsunami hits the beach, bringing with it millions of gallons of the disgusting protoplasm. It covers the barely struggling Phoes and then rushes toward the last Phoe and me.

She steps in front of me, bravely facing the tsunami, and yells, "I'm writing you back into your sleeping mind."

As soon as the meaning of her words registers, my consciousness turns off.

CHAPTER TWO

Through the haze of sleep, I hear a siren-like noise.

With vivid clarity, I recall the events on the beach, and my grogginess vanishes. Before I open my eyes, I forcefully think at Phoe, "Was all that a dream? And if it wasn't a dream, then what the hell was that?"

Phoe doesn't respond. Instead, the siren-like noise grows louder.

"Phoe?" I subvocalize.

She doesn't answer, but the alarm, or whatever it is, blasts even louder.

"Phoe," I whisper and open my eyes.

Flashes of red light assault my eyes, forcing me to blink a few times.

"What did you just mumble?" Liam asks.

My friend's voice is right next to my ear. I flinch, rolling away. It could be my confused mind playing tricks on me, but Liam sounds frightened—an emotion I didn't think him capable of feeling.

My eyes adjust, and I make out Liam's features as he bends over my bed. His eyebrows are drawn together in his signature "forehead caterpillar" look, and the flickering red lights give him a strange glow.

"Some kind of alarm is going off," Liam says as I push myself up into a sitting position. "I've never seen anything like it."

"Weird," I mumble, swinging my feet down and gesturing for the mouth cleaning.

Nothing happens.

I gesture for Food and water—nothing.

In the middle of my attempt at a mental command, I hear Liam say, "If you're trying to bring up a Screen, or anything else for that matter, it won't work. It's like the Witch Prison in here."

To confirm his words, I gesture to bring up a Screen.

"Told you," Liam says when nothing appears. His breathing sounds heavy.

I attempt—and fail—to mentally summon a Screen.

"Phoe, what the fuck?" I say out loud and get up.

Liam looks at me in confusion, and Phoe doesn't answer despite my saying her name out loud—the final confirmation of what I already know.

Something has gone terribly wrong. The question is: what?

Without my usual footwear, my feet turn into icicles when they touch the chilly floor. Ignoring that, I walk a lap around the room, trying to make sense of the situation. The flickering red light is coming from every direction, replacing our usual white illumination.

"Did you check to see if the door is unlocked?" I ask Liam and follow up with a mental shout at Phoe: "Where are you? What the hell is happening?"

Phoe still doesn't answer. Liam walks over to the door and gestures, but the door doesn't respond to Liam's command.

"Try opening it manually," I suggest in desperation and subvocalize my plea at Phoe again.

She's silent.

Liam pushes the door by hand, and it opens into the hallway. The alarm continues to blare. I wonder whether it's some kind of fire drill or the real deal. The air inside the room certainly feels musty and unusually still.

Liam's breathing seems to confirm the latter supposition. His chest is expanding and contracting in a quick, labored rhythm. Of course, that doesn't have to be carbon monoxide poisoning; it could just be fear.

"Attention," Phoe says in a staged, super-loud voice. "Attention, please."

"Phoe," I yell mentally, but then notice that Liam is standing at attention, as if he heard her too.

"Oxygen production and circulation compromised. Evacuate the building immediately," Phoe's booming voice orders.

"Is this a drill?" Liam asks.

My eyebrows rise. "You heard that?"

Liam cocks his head, his forehead pinched. "Dude, a deaf person would've heard that."

"Oxygen production and circulation compromised. Evacuate the building immediately," the voice repeats, and I realize that though it sounds like Phoe, it isn't exactly her. Now that I'm paying closer attention, it sounds like a recording of Phoe's voice delivered by one of those ancient automated phone systems. There's no emotion, and the diction is slightly off.

Liam steps out into the hallway, then returns a second later. "We should go." His voice is unusually raspy. "Everyone else is getting out."

As if to emphasize his suggestion, Phoe's mechanical voice repeats its command for us to evacuate.

"Okay," I say. "Let's go."

In the hallway, the red lights are brighter, and the sinister announcement is louder. The Youths Liam saw earlier are gone, leaving the corridor completely empty.

Feeling increasingly uneasy, Liam and I start sprinting down the hallway. As we run, I consider the distance we have to cover and curse my younger self. Back when we were choosing our lodgings, it was *my* idea to take a room on the top floor and in the farthest corner of the Dorms. In my younger self's defense, I didn't think emergencies ever happened in Oasis. To some degree, I still can't believe an emergency is happening.

"Phoe," I yell mentally. "Phoe, if you don't answer me, I'm never speaking to you again."

She doesn't respond—unless one counts the robotic announcement as a reply.

When we turn the corner, I see a couple of disheveled Youths running toward the stairs. They have a huge lead on us.

Liam's breathing is audible now, which concerns me. The optimist in me hopes Liam is breathing this way because he's neglected his cardio, but I know that most likely, Liam is having a hard time breathing because the oxygen has stopped flowing in the Dorms and he's experiencing asphyxia—a condition I've only come across in books and movies.

I examine myself and realize my own breathing is completely normal. That stumps me for a moment, but then I recall the Respirocytes—the nanomachines Phoe enabled in my bloodstream a couple of days ago. This technology serves the same function as red blood cells, only the Respirocytes are a few hundred times more efficient at carrying oxygen than the little biological guys. When she first did this to me, I tested it out by running while holding my breath, and the effort it took was a joke. I also used the Respirocytes to survive a Guard choking me.

My selfish introspection is interrupted when I see Liam struggle to open the staircase door.

"Let me," I say.

When he moves his hand away, I pull on the door. The door opens so easily that I worriedly marvel at Liam for struggling with it at all.

We dash down the stairs. I can't help but notice that Liam's breathing is growing more frantic, and his speed is decreasing with every step.

"Dude, do you want to lean on me as we walk down?" I ask him when his dash becomes a careful walk.

"Me, lean on *you*?" Liam says with a wheeze. Though talking is clearly difficult for him, Liam's somber expression brightens a little. He thinks I'm kidding since he was always considered the stronger one in our crew. "Right. That's happening. Now shut up. Oxygen is low, and we're wasting it by talking."

"It's just that the climb down is easier for me," I say. "There's a reason for it, and I'll explain when we get outside, but just trust me when I say you should let me help."

Stubbornly shaking his head, Liam starts walking down at a faster pace. His burst of energy doesn't last, though. As we approach the second floor, he falters, and to stop himself from falling, he slows to nearly a crawl. A few moments later, even walking slowly seems beyond him, and he clutches at the handrail, wheezing.

"Okay, that's it. You're letting me help." Without waiting for him to object, I grab his left arm and drape it around my neck. Once I have a good hold on him, I move as fast as I can.

I thought Liam would complain, but he gives a grateful grunt and leans on me as we make our way down. I press my index finger to his wrist and sneakily check his pulse. His heart is beating frighteningly fast. I look him over, keeping my expression neutral to mask my worry. It's hard to tell whether it's a side effect from all the red alarms, but Liam's eyes look bloodshot and his face has a blue pallor. On top of that, the veins on his forehead and neck look swollen.

Half a staircase later, my back is hurting from stooping to accommodate Liam's shorter height. On the bright side, I don't feel any effects of oxygen deprivation.

"Phoe," I shout mentally. "You don't even have to answer. Just enable Liam's Respirocytes, please."

She doesn't respond.

Liam leans more heavily on me, forcing me to slow down. We're only one floor away from the ground, but once we reach the main floor, we still have five long corridors to traverse.

Halfway down to the first floor, Liam begins wheezing harder and clutching at his throat.

I grit my teeth and ignore my back screaming with every step.

Twenty steps to the bottom.

Fifteen steps.

To distract myself from the strain, I focus on counting the stairs and ignoring the biting cold seeping into my bare feet. I also listen to Liam's quick, gasping breathing.

Then a new development shatters my concentration. Liam's frantic breathing ceases—or slows to barely audible. At the same time, he slumps, putting all his weight on me.

We're ten steps away from the bottom, but we might as well be on top of Mount Everest.

No. I'm getting Liam out of the building.

My heart starts beating like an ancient power tool as adrenaline blasts through me. I tighten my grip on Liam, and in a haze of ripping muscles, I get us down a step.

One step conquered, nine more to go.

Ignoring the pain in my back, I drag Liam down another step, and then another.

The last seven steps go by as though I'm in a trance. All I see is red; all I hear is the blaring of the announcement. I no longer feel my muscles straining or feel my spine aching.

Only when my foot touches the flat ground does the weariness hit me with full force. Instead of giving in to it, I carefully lay Liam down, then grab him under his arms and begin dragging him out of the building.

Twenty feet later, my arms feel like I have lead coursing through my veins. I also catch myself breathing heavily, though I'm not sure if it's from the lack of oxygen or the exertion. Not that it'll matter to Liam soon.

I can tell that my muscles will fail in a matter of seconds.

CHAPTER THREE

"Phoe," I scream, straining to be heard over the blaring alarm—as though volume ever mattered in communications with Phoe. "Help me. Please."

There is no answer.

I try to quell my panic. Phoe is gone, and I need to come to grips with it. The attack on the beach must be related to what's happening here. The Jeremiah-blob virus has something to do with Phoe's silence, as well as the oxygen problem in the building, but how it all fits together, I'm too overwhelmed to work out. It's best if I clear my mind of everything and focus on dragging my friend to safety.

I move my left foot, followed by my right foot, over and over for what feels like hours, though rationally I know only minutes have passed. My muscles almost tearing with effort, I drag Liam another half corridor. As I go, I notice I'm slowing down.

No. I can't slow down. If I do, Liam will die.

Suddenly, there's a blur of movement as someone joins me at the intersection, and Liam's overwhelming weight is made incalculably lighter. Dazed, I stare at the Youth who caught up with us and grabbed Liam by his legs, helping me carry him.

It's Owen—the closest thing to a nemesis Liam's had in his sheltered Oasis life. Owen—the person I knocked out yesterday when he was acting like an ass, and whose head, according to Phoe's retelling of the story, adorned the manifestation of my worst nightmare as created by the anti-intrusion algorithm of the Elderly's Test.

"Thank you," I manage to say, fighting off my shock. "I don't think I could've carried him much longer."

Owen bobs his head, the movement making him look like a rescue dog. Instead of speaking, he purses his lips and nods at the alarms, the message clear: "Don't waste oxygen, dumbass, and don't force me to do the same."

Emboldened by the help, I increase my pace to the point where I feel as if I'm dragging both Owen and Liam out of the building. The rest of the journey is a foggy blend of red lights and Phoe's mechanical announcements.

I'm almost shocked when we reach the entrance.

I let go of Liam to manually open the door to the Dorm building, and when it opens, the air feels a modicum fresher. I can tell Owen is breathing a little easier, though Liam's chest is still motionless.

We rush out of the building and push our way through a crowd of disheveled Youths.

"Make room," Owen yells.

"Move the fuck away," I echo.

Youths aren't used to hearing that kind of language, and it shocks them into motion. They clear the area, and we set Liam on the ground.

I lean down to check my friend's bulging neck vein, and my insides freeze.

Liam's pulse is barely detectable, and he's not breathing.

Owen says something before rushing away, but I don't register his words. 'm too busy trying to recall what I know about first a d. What was that technique the ancients used in these types of situations? CPR?

Doing my best to copy what I've seen in old movies, I move closer to Liam's torso and place the heel of my hand against t e center of his chest.

Something doesn't fee quite right, so I put my left hand over my right and i terlace my fingers.

"Okay, this looks li e what all the people in movies do," I think at Phoe, then recall she isn't there.

Positioning my shoul ers above my hands, I use the weight of my upper ody to push down. Liam's chest presses inward. I re ease the pressure, wait half a second for his chest o bounce back, and then repeat the compression.

Nothing happens.

"Try breathing into is mouth," a female voice says. I instantly recogni e it as belonging to Grace, though I didn't notice her approach. "It's more effective in combination," she adds when I glance up at her.

My hands shaking, I perform another set of compressions and say, "I'm not sure how—"

In a flash of red hair, Grace kneels on Liam's right side and puts her hand on top of mine. I stop my compressions and watch as Grace carefully pinches Liam's nose closed and puts her lips on his, creating a tight seal. She then breathes into him, and I feel his chest rise once, then twice.

"Now you," Grace says.

I do two dozen compressions before she stops me and gives Liam more air.

We alternate for another couple of rounds. I compress Liam's chest, and Grace relentlessly forces her breath into his lungs. The air around me is cold, but sweat is pouring down my face. Not all the moisture on my face is solely from sweat, though; some of it is from the burning tears streaming from my eyes.

"Liam," Grace says after another round. "Liam, can you hear us?"

Fighting the chill of fear inside me, I stare at Liam, but he's still comatose.

"He's breathing on his own," Grace says, answering my unspoken question when I glance up at her. "And his heart rate is more stable."

I move my hand on Liam's chest to the left, and my breath whooshes out n relief.

She's right. His heart i beating steadily.

"You don't need o do the compressions anymore," Grace says. "V e just have to wait for him to regain consciousness."

Even in my dazed s ate, I have to wonder at Grace's unusual compet nce. "How did you know how to—"

"I want to be a Nurse ne day, remember?" Grace says with a slight disappo ntment in her voice.

As soon as she says i , I recall her talking about that when we were very young, back when she was friendly with our crew. I ven recall her going by the Nurse's stall on that Birth Day.

"I thought you might've changed your mind by now," I mumble in an eff rt to cover up my faux pas. The icy panic inside me is receding slightly. "It was more than a decade ago."

Grace opens her mout 1 to reply when, with a gasp and a grunt, Liam open his eyes. "Grace?" he says faintly. "What are you doing in my room at this time of n—"

He notices me then and falls silent, his gaze moving slowly from side to side. I turn around and, for the first time, notice the Youths around us, their faces pale and worried.

"There was an emergency, and we got out of the Dorm," I say, turning back to Liam. "You might've blacked out a little toward the end."

Liam closes his eyes, furrowing his caterpillar-like eyebrows. Then he says, "Oh yeah. We were going down the stairs when—"

"I'm sorry to interrupt," Grace says. "But I have to go."

"Wait, what? Where are you going?" My question comes out a little too forceful. More calmly, I say, "What if Liam loses consciousness again?"

"Now that he's outside and conscious, he should be fine," Grace says. "I just spoke to Nicky." She nods toward a white-faced Youth about twelve years of age. "He evacuated the Middle-Grade Dorms for the same reason we evacuated ours. Their alarm went off even earlier."

She looks at me as if that explains everything.

I rub my temples. "So ry, but I don't see why that means you have to run of . My mind is—"

"It must be all the adr naline," Grace says. "I need to go because I'm worr ed they might've had the same oxygen issues at tl e Elementary Dorms." She glances in the directioi of the forest, where the cylindrical building in qu estion is located. "The little ones might need help."

"She has a point," Li m says and attempts to sit up. "We should go help."

"You need to lie here i or a bit," Grace says sternly, kneeling to push him b ck down. "But you, Theo, could be useful."

"I don't know," I say, my hesitation at the idea of leaving my just-rega ned-consciousness friend fighting with mental ima es of little kids suffocating. "What about—"

"I'll be fine," Liam say . "Go help Grace."

I scan the faces of he Youths around us for someone to volunteer as irace's helper in my place. I spot Kevin, a Youth we don't know too well. We make eye contact, and I v ave him over.

"No, it should be you ," Liam says when he sees the Youth approaching.

I'm about to voice a counterargument when it occurs to me that with my Respirocytes, I probably *am* the best person in Oasis to deal with any kind of rescue operation involving limited oxygen conditions. In contrast, pretty much anyone can look after Liam at this point.

Kevin stops next to me with an expectant look, so I say, "Can you please look after Liam? He's not feeling well, and I want to make sure he recovers. Did you see the CPR stuff Grace and I performed earlier?"

"Yes," Kevin says uncertainly.

"Can you do it if he loses consciousness again?"

"I won't," Liam interjects.

"He really won't," Grace assures.

"Okay," Kevin says. "Go help Grace. I'll take care of Liam."

I get up and tell Nicky, "Help Kevin if he needs it."

Nicky nods.

Grace gets up and makes her way through the crowd of Youths, and I follow, trying to block out the deafening din of hundreds of voices. Some Youths are panting and wheezing in the aftermath of their oxygen deprivation, so1 1e are shouting questions about what's going on, and many are weeping or telling each other reass ring lies about this being only a drill.

As we navigate our way through the human obstacle course, a few o dities stick out to me. For one thing, everyone is hoeless and wearing night clothes. Some Youths ai e even half-naked. All this makes them look like a ack of lost puppies in the red glare of the sky—wh :h is the next oddity.

The sky is not sunset r ed, but rather blaring-alarm red, like back at the D)orms. It's as if someone painted the Dome with r d, luminescent paint. More than a few Youths are s aring up at the sky with a mixture of horror and ascination. I presume this means the Augmented Reality has malfunctioned, though it's possible the ky is supposed to look like this in case of emergencies.

Thinking of Augm nted Reality brings my attention to a third, m ore subtle oddity. All the statues and many of tl e hard-to-reach trees and vegetation are gone, givii g the environment a barren look that's only enhanced by the red hue of the sky.

It's Oasis as none of us have seen before: a place about as far from serene green paradise as one can imagine.

As we walk, Grace checks on several Youths who are lying on the ground. It seems Liam wasn't the only person who ran out of air. Some of these Youths also managed to bang their heads when they passed out—at least judging by the bruises on one girl's head. None of them are in dire condition, however, so Grace leaves them and proceeds to the edge of the crowd.

As Grace and I get farther away from all the Youths, I realize the cacophony of voices was masking a different sound. I can now make out a new message that the omnipresent, mechanical-sounding Phoe is delivering.

"Habitat heating functions compromised. Oxygen production—"

An ear-splitting alarm pierces the air. It's so loud it drowns out the rest of the announcement.

A chill travels up from my icy feet and spreads through my body—a coldness that has nothing to do with the heating malfunctions and everything with the location of that new alarm.

It's blaring from th: Elementary Dorms, the cylindrical building a few hundred feet in front of us.

Grace was right to hu ry here. What happened in our Dorms is about to ha pen to little kids.

CHAPTER FOUR

As one, Grace and I start sprinting toward the building. When we're halfway there, the first wave of kids bursts through the doors. Even from this distance, I can tell that they're the older kids. Then more children run out, with the older kids leading out the younger ones.

A boy of about ten intercepts us near the building. "I had to leave two girls behind," he says, desperately gulping in air. "Her roommates." He glances down at the first grader whose tiny hand he's holding.

"How do we find th it room?" Grace asks, her voice taking on an Adult like air of authority.

"It's room 405, second on the right if you take the eastern staircase to the t)p floor," the boy explains, panting, and we hurry to vard the building.

As we make our w ay through the horde of shivering, half-asphyxiat d younger Youths, I curse under my breath. Whoe\ er caused this situation has a lot of explaining to do.

"Grace," I say when w e reach the entrance. "Why don't I go and you stay 1ere? I might have a better chance at—"

Ignoring me, Grace ri shes into the building. She was always stubborn, so I m not surprised. Of course, she doesn't know about ny Respirocytes, so to her, my statement might've so unded like a boast.

Pushing my frustratio 1 aside, I run after Grace. In the glow of the alarm lights, her red hair looks sprayed with blood. The mechanical voice repeats the same words as in our dorm: "Oxygen production and circulation compron ised. Evacuate the building immediately."

When we almost reac t the eastern staircase, I see a Youth my age in the distance, carrying a small child. As we get closer, I make out who it is and realize that this is where Owen ran off to. He must've had the same idea as Grace. I nod at him solemnly. He rolls his eyes at me, which is typical, but then he gives the little girl in his arms a worried look and continues hurrying toward the exit.

Grace and I keep running, and as Owen disappears from sight, I realize that I can't help viewing him in a new light. I expected Grace to play the hero, but not Owen. Then again, it's hard to predict how a person will react in a catastrophic emergency. Some cower in fear—I saw plenty of examples today—while others embrace the situation and step up. Sometimes people can pleasantly surprise you.

My reverie is broken when Grace stops near the first door and stares at a new figure.

It's a Guard, only he's not wearing his helmet.

I'm even more shocked than Grace. For a Guard to show up in the Youth section without his reflective helmet, with signs of aging on display, things must be dire indeed. This particular Guard isn't too old, but I can still see the red light reflecting off his graying temples. I'm not sure Grace will notice it, though. Then t hits me: I actually know this guy.

It's Albert, the Guard who objected to Jeremiah torturing me.

"What are you doing here?" Albert asks, audibly sucking in air.

He's cradling a tiny boy in his right arm and gripping the hand of a slightly older girl with his left hand. The girl peeks at us from behind the Guard, her huge eyes wide and her bottom lip quivering.

"We're heading to room 405," Grace says. She also sounds out of breath.

"We're trying to save some kids there," I say to spare Grace from speaking. "What are you doing here? Why are you not wearing your helmet? What's going on?"

The Guard just shakes his head. "No time," he wheezes out. "I had to take off the helmet because all the Guards' visors went berserk—"

Albert stops because the girl behind him starts sobbing loudly, tears dripping down her cheeks. Albert sucks in another breath and says to us firmly, "You're not going anywhere. Here"—he hands me the boy—"take him. And you"—he gives Grace the hand of the girl—"take her. I'll go check that room. 405, right?"

I cradle the little boy in my arms and in a single breath rattle out, "Yes, it's the second door on the right if you take this staircase to the top."

"Go," Albert orders, and I dash down the hallway, Grace and her charge on my heels.

As we run, I try to feel for the kid's pulse but have a hard time detecting it. He's not breathing either. Even worse, the little girl's breathing is growing more labored with each second.

Half a corridor away from the building's entrance, the girl stumbles and clutches at her throat, wheezing audibly.

"Grab her legs," I command Grace as I secure the boy in my right arm, mimicking Albert's earlier hold. With my left hand, I grab the girl under her armpit.

All I hear in response is Grace's shallow panting, but she grabs the girl by the legs, and we carry her the rest of the way outside.

The moment we come out of the building, we lower the girl to the ground and Grace looks around. "You there." She motions at a lanky girl who looks to be around nine or ten. "Watch me and learn what

I'm doing." She then ch cks the girl's vitals. "She's breathing. You can't d CPR on someone who's already breathing," she ells her designated helper. "You might stop their he rt."

The recruited little nu se-to-be looks like a bunny in the jaws of a rabid wo f, but manages a small nod, showing Grace she under tands.

I'm still holding the li tle boy, so I put him down, and Grace swoops in, erforming CPR while her student observes her.

"Anyone else have fi ends unaccounted for?" I yell over the frightened li tle voices. "Please speak up if you know of anyone wl o's still in the building."

A boy of about seven ears of age raises his hand, and I make my way thro gh the crowd to speak with him.

"Jason is still there," t e boy says in a shaky voice as I stop next to him. I e hugs himself and begins crying, mumbling, "I she uld've woken him up. He's my friend. I'm sorry."

"Where's his room?" I ask, trying to sound as authoritative as possible vithout frightening the kid.

"On the second floor, he says and hiccups. "On the side of the western st ircase. Room 204."

"Thank you," I say and hurry back to Grace.

"He's stable, but I need you to stay here and watch over him," I overhear Grace tell her newest assistant. "Theo and I are going—"

"I can do this on my own, Grace." The fact that she didn't hear about Jason might improve my chances of her complying.

Her blue eyes gleam in the red light, and I know my hope was futile.

"Stop wasting time, Theo," she says. "I'm going. You might need my help."

"Fine," I say and hurry toward the building.

Before we walk in, I tell Grace where we're heading, and once inside the building, I don't speak. I don't want to pull Grace into a conversation that would cause her to run out of oxygen faster.

I see the outline of a Guard as we turn toward the western staircase. It must be Albert with the kids from room 405, unless he already brought them out through another exit and is saving someone else.

I ascend the staircase in a single breath. Grace starts to drag slightly behind. Pushing the door open, I exit the staircase, and in two leaps, I make my way to room 204.

"Jason," I shout as I nudge the door open. "Are you in here?"

No one responds, but I see a tiny body lying by the farthest bed.

Like his friend, the unconscious boy looks around seven. I reach out to check his pulse, but then I hear Grace walk into the room. I look up, noticing how quickly her chest is rising and falling under her nightgown, and how much the veins on her slender neck stand out.

"Grace, I can carry him," I say, starting to pick up the boy. "He probably only weighs—"

Without wasting oxygen uttering a single word, she walks up to the boy and grabs his legs. Unwilling to delay her exit by arguing for even a second, I grab the boy by the shoulders and lift him.

Grace was probably right to insist on helping me. Together, we're moving a lot faster than I would have on my own, which is good for the boy. The problem is that Grace's breathing is getting more ragged with every step.

We make our way down to the first floor and turn into the first corridor. The sound of someone crying reaches my ears.

Grace and I exchange a glance and pick up the pace.

When we turn the corner, we see a body lying on the floor with a very small girl standing next to it, half-crying and half-panting for air.

The body is Owen's. It looks as though he lost consciousness while trying to save the crying girl.

"Let go of Jason's legs," I tell Grace.

She complies gingerly, her breathing rocket fast.

I grab Jason by his waist and put him over my left shoulder like a sack of potatoes. As soon as I have the boy secured, I carefully bend down and weave my right arm under Owen's shoulders. My muscles are already beyond tired, and as I strain to lift him off the ground, I wish I took more of an interest in sports—especially deadlifting.

"You take her," I order Grace, nodding at the little girl.

Grace grabs the now-quiet girl by the hand, and with her free arm, she snakes her arm under Owen's knees, helping me lift him.

With monumental effort, I take a step, then another. It feels like my muscles are tearing.

A thousand mighty efforts of will later, we're almost at the exit. In the silence between the announcements, I can hear Grace's shallow wheezing. To suppress the fear gnawing at me, I picture us succeeding in leaving this building. I picture the air tasting less stale and the red Dome above my head.

The full weight of Owen's body plunging into my arms rips me out of my fantasies.

The little girl is wheezing-crying again, and Grace is on the floor, clutching at her throat.

CHAPTER FIVE

"No," I yell. "No, Grace, you can't do this to me!"

Grace's convulsions begin to subside.

I'm faced with a terrible choice. There's no way I can carry the boy, the girl, Owen, and Grace. It's physically impossible. I'll have to tell the girl to walk on her own and choose between Owen and Grace.

In ancient times, rescue workers, such as firemen, probably had to make choices like this all the time. I don't know how they managed it, because I'm paralyzed with indecision. I know inaction will result in an even worse outcome, but I can't make myself move.

This is what those moral dilemmas in the Test must've felt like.

"Phoe," I shout in desperation. "I really need your help."

Nanoseconds pass at the speed of thought, and I make a decision. Only I'm afraid my bias, rather than logic, is influencing my choice. Would logic even help in this situation?

The little girl stops crying and looks over my shoulder.

"Dude," Liam says, startling me. His voice is the most welcome sound I've ever heard. "Why are you just standing there?"

I don't have time to berate him for putting himself in danger again so I say to the little girl, "Can you walk?"

She looks at me like I'm a creature from her worst nightmare but nods, almost imperceptibly.

I take that as a yes, and say to Liam, "Hold her hand. If she has trouble walking, put her over your shoulder like I did with the boy. Now grab Grace by her shoulders. Hurry."

Liam grabs the girl's hand. I expect her to cry out, but she keeps quiet. With a grunt that makes me cringe, Liam puts his arm under Grace's armpits and starts dragging her around the corner of the last corridor.

I lead the way. If I thought my burden was heavy before, I was wrong. Owen's full weight feels like a sack of bricks, and Jason seems to have been secretly replaced by a human-shaped ice sculpture. My back feels like it's about to break, and my heart threatens to jump out of my ribcage with every step I take. Despite the Respirocytes, the stress is turning my breathing fast and shallow, and even my vision is blurring.

Step after step, I try to focus on anything but the enormous strain in my muscles. I think of music and art, but even that doesn't help. The music in my head is heavy metal, and the art that comes to mind is a piece by a famous ancient Russian painter that depicts eleven men struggling to haul a barge through a river.

"We're almost there," Liam wheezes from behind me. "Just a little farther."

Hope renews my stre gth, and I pick up my pace, walking at a whopping s eed of a step per second for the remaining length of t e corridor. When I'm a few feet away from the entr nce, I manage to speed up more, dragging my charg s the remaining distance.

As soon as I'm outsi le, I kneel down, lowering Owen to the ground and arefully place Jason next to him. Then, sucking in gu ps of air, I look for Grace's CPR trainee.

Our gazes meet, and I vave at her. "Come help!"

The girl and a couple f other Youths rush over.

I jump up to go b ck for Liam, but at that moment, he comes out o the building.

I run over to him and lelp him lower Grace to the ground. As soon as she' on her back, I crouch and prepare to perform CPR.

Under any other circ mstances, putting my hand so close to Grace's breast and touching my mouth to hers would be awkward, ut right now, it's clinical. I finish my presses and br athe air into her lungs. All my thoughts are concent ated on helping her breathe again.

"Please, Grace," I thin desperately. "Breathe."

As though she heard my mental plea, Grace gasps. Her long eyelashes flutter open, and she stares at me, her blue eyes bloodshot but alert.

"Owen," she gasps out. "Did he make it?"

My pulse lurches. I've been so focused on saving her, I've all but forgotten about Owen's equally dire circumstances.

I jump to my feet and am about to rush over to Owen when I see Grace trying to get up. Bending down, I offer her my hand, and she takes it, her palm cold and clammy in my grasp.

Together, we hurry over to the girl I left in charge of Owen. She's frantically breathing into Owen's mouth as Liam waits to resume the compressions.

Grace kneels down next to Owen and touches her hand to his neck as I stand, watching helplessly. A visible shudder ripples through her; then she says in a choked voice, "Move over, both of you."

Grace proceeds to feel for pulse in Owen's wrist, then his chest.

When she looks up, her eyes are brimming with tears.

"No," I say numbly. "No, he can't be…"

Grace starts perform ing CPR on Owen, her expression grimly determ ined.

"Phoe," I scream in m mind. "Phoe, come on! He can't be dead."

There's no response. In a haze, I watch Grace perform several rounds of CPR. By the time she stops and looks up, st e's shaking and tears are streaking down her cheel s.

"I think it's too late," s te says, her lips tinged blue, but I barely hear her tl rough the cold numbness paralyzing me in place.

Next to me, Liam star s at her wide-eyed, and the helper girl looks as if sl e's about to sprint for the edge of Oasis.

In theory, facing dea h should be easier for me than for the others. Afte all, I've faced it repeatedly in the last few days. Yet my insides are burning up despite the cold, and th back of my throat spasms uncontrollably.

I'm brought out of ny anguished daze by the realization that Grace is maniacally pacing around me, muttering somethin; morbid. Liam is rubbing his arms, and Grace's he per is hugging her knees to her chest, rocking back a d forth.

I search for something soothing to tell them, but before I can come up with the words, Grace shakes her head violently and darts off toward the building. As she runs by, I catch her mumbling, "I have to make sure no one else dies…"

The surrounding Youths go silent, wary of Grace's shouting and erratic behavior, and in the resulting quiet, I hear a new warning: "Habitat's oxygen levels abnormal. Habitat's nitrogen levels abnormal. Life support functions out of balance—"

The kids all start talking and crying at once, preventing me from hearing whatever else the ship-wide intercom system is saying. On some level, I know the message is troubling, but I'm too dumbfounded by Owen's death and Grace's reaction to process it fully. I can't think about anything but the fact that she's going back into that deadly building.

My legs are wooden as I stumble after her. "Wait, Grace."

She either doesn't hear me or ignores me as she disappears through the doors.

Cursing under my bre th, I start to give chase, but someone grabs me in a ear hug from behind with sweaty, trembling hands.

"Don't go in there," .iam mutters into my ear. "You'll die."

"Dude, I'll be okay," I say, pushing him away. "More okay than her."

"Then I'm—"

"Don't you dare fin sh that thought." I spin around to glare at him. "I you go anywhere near that stupid building, I will kno ck you the fuck out."

Liam blinks at me, hi face contorting as though he's bracing against my tl reat.

I don't wait for him to recover and run inside the building. Grace is nowhe e in sight.

The corridors zigzag nd the red light blurs my vision as I hurry from h llway to hallway, searching for Grace.

"Grace," I scream ov r Phoe's mechanical voice. "Grace, where are you?"

I enter a room and ins inctively gesture to dismiss the abandoned beds. Wh en the gesture fails, I bend to check under each bed. The room is empty. Then I enter another room and another—all empty.

Adrenaline is messing with my sense of time. I have no clue how long I've been searching the building, but I'm confident I've looked inside every room on the first floor.

I go up the nearest staircase toward the second floor. A door slams shut somewhere above me.

"Grace!" I shout and take the stairs three at a time. "Is that you?"

Albert is walking down the stairs toward me. He's straining under the heavy weight of his burden. Over his right shoulder, he's carrying a boy, and over his left, he has Grace.

"Let me help." I hurry to his side.

"No," Albert wheezes. "Get out of here."

I step in front of him. "You can barely walk. Don't waste oxygen arguing. Give me one of them and let's go."

Albert hesitates for a split second, but then practicality appears to win out. He knows it'll take him twice as long to carry Grace and the boy outside on his own, assuming he doesn't pass out on the way. Carefully, he gives me the boy. With a grunt, I position the kid over my shoulder. His body feels lifeless, and Grace doesn't look much better.

"Go," Albert rasps out

Realizing I'm costing the man precious air, I quickly descend the stairs.

My breathing is frantic, but it's impossible to tell whether I'm suffocating or experiencing side effects from the adrenaline.

Albert's wheezing intensifies; he's running out of air. I'm amazed at his stamina. Older people are usually frail, but then, for an Elderly, he's not *that* old. Also, he must've gone through extensive training to become a Guard—not that the training will be of any help if he can't breathe. He looks like he's barely holding on.

I open the door to the first floor and hold it for Albert. He grunts gratefully as he exits, and I hurry after him.

Either I'm numb from exhaustion or I've developed something like a runner's second wind, because I'm rushing through the corridors with the boy on my shoulder and I don't feel the cold or the strain in my muscles. I don't even hear the alarms.

When Albert's steps falter, I prop him up with my shoulder. He leans on me, hesitantly at first, then more fully as oxygen deprivation takes its toll on him. The numbness blanketing me starts to dissipate, and one corridor later, I realize I might've pushed my body too far.

Every step feels like an ordeal now. If the alarms weren't coloring the world red, I'd be seeing white spots, and even through the deafening noise, I'm pretty sure there's a dull ringing in my ears.

Rationally, I know it's me who crosses the last half of the corridor to the entrance, but it feels like it's happening to someone else.

I regain my wits when I see the Youths outside—though I can't help but notice that unlike before, the air doesn't feel much fresher than inside the building.

Albert lays Grace on the ground, and I do the same with the boy on my shoulder, and we begin performing CPR.

I compress the boy's chest, then breathe into his mouth at least a dozen times before I think to check for his pulse. I can't find a heartbeat. I look over at Albert, and my hopes shatter at the expression on his face.

Albert catches my g ance, wipes the moisture from his face with his v hite sleeve, and shakes his head.

"No." Frantically, I re ume pushing on the boy's chest. "No, no, no."

Albert kneels next to me, pushes me away, and checks his vitals.

"I'm sorry," he says, l fting his head. The look on his face echoes the horro gnawing at my chest. "We did our best."

Ignoring him, I jump up and rush over to Grace, where she's lying still anc lifeless.

Frantically, I check fo her heartbeat.

There isn't one.

Stubbornly, I begin (PR. Her lips are blue and cold as I breathe air in o her, and her chest feels inanimate, like that of a oll's. I perform round after round of CPR, losing t ack of time as I toil over Grace's body.

Someone grasps my ai m and pulls me away.

"That's enough, Theo, ' Liam says when I look up, ready to fight. His voice cracks as he says hoarsely, "We have to face it. Grac is dead."

CHAPTER SIX

I stare at my friend, uncomprehending. The pain in his eyes echoes the agonizing throb in my chest. My grief, or whatever this is, is so overwhelming that I think I zone out for a moment. Over Liam's shoulder, I see the red sky, and I stare blankly at it. Eventually, I notice white text scrolling across the Dome. Maybe it's been there all along, but I haven't noticed it until now. I squint at it and make out part of the messages scrolling past. Most of them are warnings. I spot the same warning about the nitrogen and oxygen being out of whack. I pushed the initial warning out c f my mind, but now that I think about it, the impl cations are dire. It means we're—

Sharp pain brings me out of my daze.

Blinking, I gape at Li m—who just smacked me across the cheek, like an ancient wife with a philandering husband.

"Dude, what the hell?" I rub my stinging cheek.

"You weren't respond ng," Liam says defensively. "I wanted you to snap out of it. We have to do *something*."

I notice he's doing his best not to look at Grace's body or the dead boy—o Owen, for that matter.

I look around for the Guard. "Where's Albert?"

"Who?" Liam follows ny gaze in confusion.

"The Guard who can e out of the building with me. Where is he? He's not insane enough to go back in there, is he?"

"Oh, the Guard," Liam says. "No, he doesn't need to go back into the buildi ig. He said it's clear."

"So where is he then?"

"He headed that way," Liam points toward the forest. "He didn't say why."

I scan the golf course in the distance. The short grass has an odd reddish-black tint thanks to the redness of the Dome, and Albert's white spacesuit is easy to spot.

"We should follow him," I say, a vague plan forming in my mind.

"Why?" Liam asks.

"You wanted to do *something,*" I say. "This is as good as anything, under the circumstances."

"I guess, but I don't see how leaving the group will help."

"I'll explain as we go," I say and begin to make my way through the crowd of Youths. To myself, I mumble, "Assuming I figure out what the hell to do."

Liam looks like a duckling following its mama as he trails after me. I can tell he's not sure about leaving the Youths, but his trust in me—or maybe his general confusion—wins over, and he keeps following me.

When we leave the crowd behind, Liam recovers enough to take the lead, his eyes glued to Albert's figure in the distance.

"Habitat's oxygen levels critically low," Phoe's sky voice announces. "Nitrogen levels critically high.

Carbon monoxide levels rising. Thermostatic modules malfunctioning.'

"What does that mean?" Liam says, stopping so suddenly that I almost walk into him.

"I think it means that what happened inside the buildings is happening outside," I say, trying to ignore the expanding knot of fear in my throat. "It means Oasis's air won't be breathable soon, and we'll all suffocate."

"But how can that be?" The tendons in Liam's neck are standing out. "Is it the red light? Is it messing with the plants' oxygen production?"

"Let's walk and talk," I say. Stepping around him, I explain, "The plants never produced the bulk of the oxygen. There are machines that do that."

Liam follows me, but his gait is uncertain, and his breathing is labored again. "Everyone knows it's the plants that produce—"

"Right." I can't keep the sarcasm out of my voice. "Just like everyone knows that the sky is never red." I look up at the screen-like Dome. "Just like everyone knows we're on Earth, in a paradise, and nothing can go wrong."

Liam gives me a confused look and says, "Okay, let's say machines are at work. Why is it getting harder to breathe so quickly?"

"I don't know for sure." For the millionth time, I hope Phoe will chime in with some scientific explanation, but she remains silent. "It might be the part about the nitrogen," I fib, suppressing a shiver from the chill seeping into my skin. "I read that too much nitrogen in the air can suffocate you, and it might also take oxygen out of the air. If not nitrogen, then maybe the machines are messing up in some other way. It's not hard to run out of oxygen if you stop or slow down its production, since all of us are using it up by breathing. It's not like air can come from outside the Dome..."

"What about thermostatic what's-it-called?" Liam says after catching his breath for a few steps. "What was that about?"

"Haven't you noticed how cold it is?" I say, rubbing my hands up and down my bare arms.

Liam looks at the gooseflesh on his own arms. "I thought it was from the lack of clothes and this being the middle of the night. At least I assume it's the middle of the night. Do you actually have any idea what time it is?"

"No, I don't," I say. The air coming out of my mouth looks like smoke, or more accurately, vapor. This is how the ancients' breath looked when people walked around during winter. I've never seen it in real life.

Liam jams his hands into his armpits. "So what's going to happen to us? What's going to happen to everyone?"

"I'm not sure." I try to keep my teeth from chattering.

"Then where are we going? What's the point of following the Guard?"

As though he was waiting for Liam to ask that question, Albert disappears into the forest.

I pick up my pace. "If we run, we'll stay warm," I explain when Liam glances at me. "Plus, the forest might have more oxygen with all those trees."

Without complaining that I didn't answer his question, Liam runs after me. By the time we reach the tree line, his breathing starts to sound like a broken steam engine.

The forest looks creepily black under the red light, reminding me of an evil, magical forest from a fairytale. I expect Liam to say something about it, but he doesn't—not a good sign.

A mile or so into the woods, Liam stops, and I can tell he's about to ask me why we're following Albert and where we're going. To save him oxygen, I say, "The Guard isn't really our destination. He might know something, but the place we really need to reach is the Adult section. *They* might have some answers."

Liam takes a couple of heavy breaths and says, "But how are we supposed to get through the Barrier?"

"Let's keep moving," I say and grab his ice-cold arm. "I'm hoping if we can catch up with the Guard, he'll get you through."

I don't tell Liam that even if we don't catch up with Albert, there's a good chance that the Barrier will let him through because he's with *me*. I can access any area in Oasis thanks to Phoe's Birth Day hack that fooled Oasis's systems into thinking I'm an Elderly.

The smell of the pine forest, or perhaps the oxygen it produces, reinvigorates me, but the same can't be said for Liam. His run quickly diminishes to a jog, then a walk. By the time we reach the forest's edge, he's barely trudging along.

When we exit the forest, I'm not surprised to find the shimmering Barrier missing. Given that the Barrier is an Augmented Reality artifact and the Screens, trees, and other AU-generated things are gone, it stands to reason—if by reason, one means complete chaos—that the Barrier would also be gone. Plus, since Liam easily passed the threshold where fear should've gripped him, I half-expected *something* to be wrong with the Barrier.

Liam drags himself to the middle of the clearing. When he sees the forest on the Adult side, he gives me a despairing look.

"Another forest," I say. "Hey, that means more oxygen, right?"

Liam doesn't say anything. His whole body slumps, and he starts walking with the same enthusiasm as a condemned man going to the gallows.

"Lean on me," I say and walk up to Liam.

Liam doesn't argue and meekly puts his right arm over my shoulders. His added weight slows me down, but I'm grateful for his body heat. I just wish we could cover the ground faster.

When we reach the Adult section of the forest, I pick up a stick for each of us to lean on. Our improvised canes help for a bit, but when we reach the edge of a small clearing, Liam drops the stick and leans on a gigantic pine, gasping desperately.

I let go of him and step back, not knowing what to do. Then it comes to me.

"I'll walk ahead and find a Disk," I say, half to myself and half to Liam. "The Adults have these flying devices. You can sit on one and—"

"Please," Liam wheezes. His face has a bluish-purple tint under the red light of the dome. "Don't go. Don't leave me alone."

"Of course," I say instantly. Those words must've cost my friend a lot of oxygen.

He nods and inhales deeply, then again and again. With every breath, his eyes get wider, and his face turns a darker shade of purple.

My pulse skyrockets as I watch Liam grab at his throat the way he did inside the Dorm. *No, please no.* Frantically, I reach for him, but it's too late.

My friend slides down the enormous tree trunk, falling to his knees.

His eyes and the veins on his forehead are bulging as he continues to clutch at his throat. He wheezes painfully several times, and then his breathing stops.

"Liam!" I grab his arm just as he collapses to the ground.

CHAPTER SEVEN

My mind scrambles for a plan as I kneel next to my fallen friend and begin CPR.

"Phoe," I whisper in desperation, my chilled muscles jumping under my skin as I compress Liam's chest. "Phoe, please."

She doesn't respond.

My chapped lips tremble as I breathe air into his lungs, and I have the incongruous thought that this is how the ancients must've felt when their prayers went unanswered. I'm shivering all over, my hands, feet, and the pit of my stomach frozen solid as I continue the breathing and the chest compressions.

Nothing.

He's not responding.

Shaking, I check his pulse.

Nothing. The giant tree is more likely to have a heartbeat.

Balling my hands into fists, I compress his chest once, twice, a third time. I'm almost hitting him, but nothing changes. With every passing second, Liam feels infinitely colder to the touch.

No. This isn't happening.

"Is this a dream? An IRES game?" My shout resembles a wolf's howl. "Please get me out of here. Please, Phoe. I'll do anything."

The red sky shines dispassionately in reply.

Liam is still unmoving. Still cold.

I've never felt this powerless, this overwhelmed.

Pushing my fear aside, I continue performing CPR. At one point, I feel Liam's ribs crack. The cold air burns my lungs, my arms are stiff and sore, and my legs are cramping, but I don't stop. Despite the intensifying cold, I feel like I'm burning. My heart is beating like an erratic drum, and a wave of nausea hits me, but I swallow the bile in my throat and keep going.

Some detached part of my mind tells me that continuing to do this is desecrating my friend's dead body, that I'm not doing this for his sake but my own—that I'm using CPR as a way to not deal with the ever-colder reality—but I can't stop.

I don't stop until my arms fail from the repetitive motion.

It's only then that I stand up on unsteady legs. Shivering, I stare down at Liam.

The cruelest result of Oasis's systems failing is that the dead bodies no longer break down into molecules for the nanocytes to recycle, like what happened with Mason and Jeremiah. Liam just lies there the way Owen and Grace did, cold and lifeless.

Now I understand why the ancients buried their dead. I feel the instinct to do the same, but I know it would be folly. The ground is rock hard, as my cold feet—which are quickly losing all feeling—can attest to.

For a second, I wonder if I should be worried about frostbite, then dismiss the ridiculous thought.

If I don't resolve whatever's going on with Oasis's systems, losing toes will be the least of my worries.

Numbly, I say a last silent goodbye to Liam and resume my walk deeper into the Adult section.

If I was pretending to have a plan to keep Liam hopeful, I now know the truth: I'm walking aimlessly. There's a small chance the Adults can do something, but I'm not holding my breath— figuratively speaking, at least.

The cold is getting worse. It feels as if my bone marrow is solidifying, so I do the only action I can think of to warm up.

I run.

Movement provides a modicum of relief. My mental turmoil takes a backseat to the pain of branches hitting my face. As I move faster, something resembling warmth spreads through my body, and a ghostly numbness returns to my feet, which is as close to a feeling as anything my feet have experienced in a while.

As I run, I focus on something that's been circling my brain on a subconscious level since I woke up: What the hell is going on? Some sort of virus attacked Phoe and me. The ancients' computers caught viruses all the time, so could something like this have hurt Phoe? When the computing resources of the ship were utilized for other purposes, such as the IRES game, she was hurt, or at least weakened. So if a virus ate up a ton of resources, it would cripple Phoe. And if the virus messed up enough of her resources, it could interfere with the functions we took for granted, such as the ship's oxygen production. It seems plausible, at least if I forget the bigger question: Where did this virus come from?

The sight of Albert interrupts my speculations.

He's on the ground a couple of feet away from the edge of the forest, unmoving.

Leaving the trees behind, I rush over to the unconscious Guard and check for his pulse. I don't find one. Albert's neck is the coldest thing I've ever touched, his body covered by frost that gleams red in the Dome lights.

With Liam's death, I thought my capacity for grief had been maxed out, but an avalanche of emotions hits me all over again. I didn't know Albert that well, but he seemed like a good man, a kind—

No.

With effort, I pull myself together. If I give in to this, I'll fall next to him and wait to die, and that isn't happening.

A macabre idea arises, and I execute it before I can chicken out.

I take off Albert's shoes and put them on the frozen blocks that used to be my feet. Then I put on his pants and the upper portion of his suit, and slide on the gloves.

I feel even colder when I'm done, but the rational side of my brain tells me it's an illusion. Ripping my gaze away from yet another dead body—this one sadder in its nakedness— I break into a run.

It doesn't take long to confirm my worst fears. There are dead bodies of Adults lying everywhere.

"Please, let it only be on the outskirts," I mumble to myself as I run toward the nearest building.

Even from afar, I can see people on the ground. Hundreds upon hundreds of them. When I get close enough, I verify that they are indeed gone, all bearing the same signs of suffocation.

Shaking, I turn to the noticeably larger building a few hundred feet away.

The desolation is the same there. The dead Adults look as disheveled as the Youths did: no shoes, minimal clothing, and horrified expressions stuck forever on their faces.

I find another mass grave next to the tallest building.

As I walk among the dead Adults, I see some people I know. To my right is Instructor Filomena, frozen in an embrace with Instructor George. I spot more Instructors from the Institute, as well as a number of men and women I've seen at the Birth Day Fairs over the years.

Fed up, I hurry away from the buildings—places where the bodies are clustered. I can't look at all this death anymore.

I head for the walkway farthest from any structure, and as I run, the carnage decreases, but even this is too much to bear.

The cold seems to be getting worse. My ears feel literally frozen. I think if someone were to grab my earlobe, it might break off. Stopping, I take a nightgown from a corpse of an unfamiliar, older-looking woman and wrap the cloth around my head before resuming my run.

The hope I'm holding on to now is fainter than before. It's built upon this vague notion that perhaps the Elderly, the self-appointed rulers of our world, know what's happening.

Trying to recall the exact location of the building where the Council meetings are held, I turn toward the forest that separates the Adult and Elderly territories.

> * *

I see the first dead body almost as soon as I enter the Elderly territory. This skinny old man must've been heading for the Adult section. Maybe he thought the forest would provide more oxygen, or maybe, like me, he was stumbling around aimlessly in his desperation.

This is the most tired and cold I've ever been. I can't remember a time when I wasn't running, when I wasn't cold, when I wasn't feeling like I might die.

There was no Barrier going into the Elderly section, and there aren't any signs that the Elderly were spared the Adults' fate. All the Youths I left behind, even the little kids, must be gone too.

Everyone I ever knew is dead.

Stubbornly, I head toward the Council building. I assume it's the one Phoe and I exited after Jeremiah nearly killed me.

Around all the other buildings, the story looks frighteningly familiar. I can picture what happened: first, the alarms went off in different buildings at random, just like they did in the Youth section; then everyone ran outside, where more alarms went off and everyone eventually suffocated.

Dead Guards are lying here and there. Some are still wearing their helmets, while others, like Albert, took them off. None of them are alive.

The closer I get to my destination, the more bodies I encounter. Soon, I have no choice but to step on the dead, and so I do, dry-heaving every few feet.

"Gravity simulation malfunction," Phoe's sky voice says, and I realize I've grown so used to her other warnings that I've been ignoring them. Before I fully process the meaning of this new warning, I start falling.

A moment later, I understand that I'm not actually falling. I'm floating.

So are all the dead bodies around me.

They're all floating in the air, forming a picture one would only expect to see in a surreal painting by an artist whose mind was ravaged by mercury poisoning.

I thrash my arms and legs for a few minutes, but it's futile. The only thing I achieve is a slight warmth in my frozen limbs.

Still, something is drawing me to that building. I don't know what it is. Maybe I'm hoping to find a neon sign that says 'Goal,' or maybe I'm hoping to meet the Council members and hear them say, "That was a nice set of moral dilemmas. You can now exit the Test."

Maybe I want to see if they caused this, and if so, I want to strangle them, one by one, before I die with everyone else.

Through trial and error, I learn that pushing a dead person in one direction launches me the opposite way, so I insult the dead in a new way. Instead of taking their clothes, I use them to propel myself forward.

I fly through this insane morgue for what feels like a day. When I grab the next body, I recognize the person's face.

It's Fiona, the current Council leader and Keeper of Information.

By now, I'm too numb to feel anything. Yes, this woman was nice to me, and finding her dead body killed my remaining hope, but I can't bring myself to care.

I'm too cold. Too tired.

Tears are frozen on my face.

I push Fiona away, letting the movement propel me toward the big conglomeration of bodies. Once there, I burrow into the center of the pack, hoping they'll shield me from the cold.

Then I close my eyes and float.

My fear of heights is gone. I'm even enjoying this feeling of weightlessness.

I wonder what dying will feel like. Will it be like the time I fell into the ocean of Goo inside the IRES game? I guess that depends on how I'll die. Suffocating seems like a horrible way to go, but I think my chances of freezing to death are higher. I read that you simply fall asleep when you freeze and never wake up, which doesn't sound as scary.

I float for a while longer before I realize the pain from the cold is gone— one of the final stages of hypothermia.

It's becoming harder to think. With each moment, I feel more and more like a disembodied mind floating in a realm of pure thought.

The only sensation I have is that of tiredness.

All I want to do is sleep.

Part of me knows I should fight the drowsiness. If I fall asleep, that'll be the end. But I find it hard to care.

At least I'll die in my sleep.

I stop fighting.

Letting go of my consciousness, I drift off.

* * *

I wake up gasping for air. A frantic wheeze later, I recall that I didn't think I'd wake up—that, in fact, I hoped I wouldn't.

This isn't a reprieve, far from it. I've just exchanged a less horrible death for a worse one.

Just for a moment, I allow myself a fantasy, one in which everything that happened was nothing more than a terrifying dream. I imagine I'm waking up in my bed, hyperventilating because of that nightmare.

Having difficulty breathing because I'm stressed.

When I look around, however, I know that to be a lie.

I'm still a human icicle. I'm still floating in the middle of a cloud made up of Elderly corpses.

The cold lulled me to sleep but didn't have time to kill me.

Cold sweat freezes on my skin, and my heart pounds audibly in my ears as I fight to pull air into my screaming lungs.

All the oxygen must be gone. As efficient as the Respirocytes are, once there's no more air for them to carry, they're useless.

My body instinctively fights for more air. My neck muscles spasm, and my diaphragm feels like it might tear.

Screaming for help doesn't work, so I mentally shout for Phoe—probably for the last time. She doesn't reply.

My spasmodic thrashing sends corpses floating in every direction.

I clutch at my bulging throat. My eyes feel like they're about to pop out of my skull. Weakness starts to overtake me. My brain must've run out of oxygen. My pulse slows as scenes from my life play out in my mind.

My heart stops, and the redness that became my world changes into a tunnel of white light.

I die.

CHAPTER EIGHT

I'm floating on the brink of consciousness like a bodiless ghost.

Given that I died, really died, any form of consciousness, even this ephemeral kind, is a good development, though I don't understand how it came about.

I ponder my existence. For how long, I don't know, because I have no sense of time.

Am I a ghost? A spirit? A soul?

Were the ancients right when they invented those fanciful concepts?

My memories are fuz y. I don't remember who I am, why I'm here, or whe re "here" is. Is amnesia part of the afterlife? A way to make sure I don't miss what I left behind? The only concrete and unshakable memory I have is the knowledge that I'm dead. I also have this conviction that I have some important choices to make.

Ah, yes. Though ever thing else is still hazy, the choices I have are like slands of clarity. The first choice is what my wings should look like.

Before I question this —as one would an illogical dream—a vision of rows of different wings assaults me, which is odd for many reasons, but mainly because I don't have any eyes. But even without sight, I see all these wii gs in all their variety and beauty.

Ancient legends con e to mind again. Is this heaven? Am I about to turn into a winged angel with a halo above my head? Is hat why I need wings?

As though spurred on by this theory, countless stereotypical angel wings spread out in front of my mind, each a variation on the dove-feathered appendages and in varying shades of white.

This is one choice among millions.

Other options appear to my inner eye: dragon wings, bumblebee wings, bat wings, rows upon rows of insect, bird, reptile, and gliding mammalian wings. There's even a row of wing-like fins similar to a stingray's. Without knowing how, I know that if I 'zoom in' on a specific type of wing, countless variations of that theme will be presented to me as the next step in the selection process, similar to the way the angel-themed wings appeared.

Some choices aren't rooted in reality. For example, there's a myriad of abstract shapes, which I find fascinating. In response to my interest, choices upon choices of these surreal wings present themselves to me.

I don't know how long I take to decide, but in the end, I choose a set of wings that look like they're woven out of wisps of fire arranged in strange mathematical patterns. They look like someone froze one of those fractal music visualizations mid-design.

My fuzzy mind finds something vaguely humorous in that; my new wings are the exact opposite of the heavenly design I started off with. They look like an abstractionist's vision of a fire demon's wings.

Actually, these wings lso remind me of that fiery bird from ancient lege ds, a creature called the phoenix. Thinking of tha stirs some emotions in me that I can't quite place sc I just float mindlessly until I realize I have more choi es to make.

The next one is much easier: I have to decide what my face will look like.

I'm presented with ev ry version of a human face: some younger, some ol ler, some cute, and some handsome. Some are m re masculine, while others are gently feminine. Eve y face type can also have a variety of features, such is eyes, which can come in every color, shape, and si e imaginable.

I'm drawn to a part cular set of faces straight away.

When I lay my metap ysical eyes on this group, I choose one face almos instantly. My choice is guided by aching famil irity. Something about its handsome features, blue eyes, blond hair, and the expression of curiosity in his gaze touches something forgotten inside me.

I choose a body just is quickly, despite the fact that the choices here are just as varied.

A sense of completion spreads through my sluggish mind. There are more things I can choose, but they're optional and can be adjusted later. Still, almost on autopilot, I decide that yes, I want to wear clothes, specifically pants, and that yes, I'd love to have weapons too. Fiery swords would go nicely with my wings, so I choose two blades in the katana style. Other features are chosen for me at random, such as the sound of my voice and the glow of my skin. I gladly accept those options.

The whole process reminds me of the start of a video game, where the player has to create his character before he can begin his virtual journey.

"You don't know how close to the truth you are," a familiar female voice says in my mind. "I wish you hadn't made yourself—"

I don't get a chance to learn who spoke in my mind just then, or how or why she spoke because the selection process is now officially over and I feel myself streaming somewhere else, regaining memories and becoming whole as I go.

* * *

I come to my senses with a violent shiver. I remember falling asleep for the last time because I was freezing to death. Somehow that's not what happened, since I'm awake.

Instead of floating in the subzero temperatures of Oasis, surrounded by a pile of frozen corpses, I'm standing in a warm, open space, surrounded by beautiful winged people who are speaking to one another in melodious, otherworldly voices.

Something nags at my awareness. Between freezing to death and this place, I had a dreamlike experience. In it, I made myself look like these figures—wings and all.

I recall my theories that this is some kind of life after death, and those ideas don't seem as foolish as they did in my dream state. But these people aren't angels. I've seen similar creatures before: the two Envoys—the one who spoke to Jeremiah back when the old man was still alive, and Jeremiah after he died and became the new Envoy.

Would rooms like this exist in the afterlife? I guess it's possible. The space does remind me of a cathedral, which has a religious connotation, though it's even more reminiscent of an ancient museum.

The ceilings are at least a hundred feet high, and the distance from wall to wall is probably double that. Giant mirrors cover every surface, giving the room a wide-open feel and reflecting the winged people walking and flying around the space.

Ignoring the beings around me, I walk toward the nearest mirror. This is when, without much surprise, I realize that my dream-like wing selection was real.

As in, the wings are real.

As in, the wings are attached to my back.

Aside from the wings, my face looks subtly different from how I remember it. It's as though someone cut it out of marble and polished out any imperfections and asymmetries. My reflection looks slightly older and taller, and my naked upper body is noticeably buffer. To top it all off, I'm somewhat luminescent—not as shiny as some of the others in the room, but noticeably so. I vaguely recall this being part of the choices in my dreamlike state.

"The fact that you chose your own face is a problem," Phoe says as a voice in my head. "I tried to speak to you during the selection phase, but by the time I got through, it was too late. Nice wing choice, by the way."

I now recall that she c id speak up toward the end of the selection, only ba k then I didn't know who she was. Then I recall th most important part: how she *didn't* speak during those fateful hours when everyone around me wa dying. Horrific memories flood my brain, and I sh ut out loud, "Phoe! Where the hell have you been? Where the fuck am I? What the fuck—"

"I know dying can l e disorienting," a melodic female voice says from behind me—a voice that doesn't sound anything l ke Phoe. "But do you have to use that kind of langu ge in front of your peers? I didn't expect that vile f word to ever be uttered in Haven."

Everything falls into place at the mention of Haven, but I don't have t me to dwell on it because I come face to face with a winged, nearly naked female of such beauty that I st re at her curves in open-mouthed awe.

"Stop staring at Fion like that," Phoe says with more than a hint of j alousy. "Don't give her a chance to realize that you re not one of the—"

"Who are you?" t ie woman—Fiona—asks. "You're not part of the C uncil."

My mouth snaps shut. This is Fiona, the last Keeper of Information. She's also the old woman whose corpse I saw before I died.

"Maybe he's a Forebear," a male voice cuts in. "Maybe they finally decided to explain what we're doing here. What happened in Oasis? Why did we all die? Why—"

"Calm down, Vincent," Fiona says, her beatific voice sounding exactly like the soothing notes of a harp. "Let the man speak."

"I, err…" My voice also sounds different, reminding me of a trumpet. "I don't—"

"You're the last one to ascend. There are thirteen of us now. You have to be the last Council member, but I don't recognize your face," Vincent says, his large eyes narrowing. "Start with how you got here and your name."

"Don't tell them your real name," Phoe commands in my mind. "It's bad enough that you decided to look like your own handsome—and recognizable—self."

"What do I say then?" I ask Phoe mentally, wishing we had time for me to ask her about a million other questions instead.

"Say you're—"

Phoe doesn't finish her thought because the large cathedral doors open, and bright light floods into the huge room.

"Finally," Vincent says and heads for the door.

Everyone joins Vincent by the entrance, blocking some of the light pouring in from outside.

"Fly up," Phoe thinks at me. "Now."

"How do I fly?" I respond.

"Using your wings might be a good way," Phoe says. "I doubt thinking happy thoughts will work, though you're welcome to try, as long as you also flap your wing muscles."

"But how—"

"Just do it. Pretend you know how," Phoe says. "They're already inside."

Using my wings for the first time is one of the oddest sensations I've ever experienced. It's as if I grew an extra pair of arms and had to learn how to use them separately from my original arms. At least with spare arms I'd have a point of reference, but my wings are completely foreign. Yet without any effort and as if I've always known how, I spread my fiery wings and leap upward.

With a powerful downward stroke, I fly toward the ceiling, leaving embers and heat haze behind me.

"Your wings don't just look like they're made of fire," Phoe explains. "They actually interact with our environment the same way—"

I fly higher, fear making me miss the rest of her explanation. It seems my new wings did little to quell my problem with heights.

"Yeah, your fear of heights is now even less rational," Phoe says, attempting—and failing—to soothe me. "Winged creatures shouldn't be—"

A big, muscular man with giant, dragon-like wings enters the cathedral with an entourage of similarly beefy specimens.

"Dear new arrivals," he says, his voice booming like a war drum. "I'm Brandon."

He pauses with the air of someone who's used to having his name recognized and respected. But I've never heard of him, and it doesn't seem like any of the others have either.

Unperturbed, he goes on. "It saddens me to inform you that you will not be joining the society of Haven. Our enemy may have contaminated you, and letting you leave this quarantine cathedral is a risk we are not willing to take. I truly am sorry. You will be dispatched back to Limbo. I'm confident we will meet again, under more congenial circumstances."

His eyes are mournful as he looks around the cathedral. With poorly concealed regret, he gestures with both hands as though he's pantomiming holding a baseball bat.

A large two-handed medieval sword appears in Brandon's hands. The blade has a bluish tint, and its sharp edge glints in the bright light of the chandeliers. Without another word, he swings the sword, severing the head of the two winged Council members nearest him.

Everything slows.

My wings feel weak, and I wonder if I'm about to plummet to the floor.

The severed heads begin falling.

CHAPTER NINE

The heads never touch the intricate mosaic on the floor, and the headless bodies never fall down.

Instead, the heads and bodies change shape. That is, they momentarily look like they were ripped apart into square shapes reminiscent of the pixelated images I've seen in the ancient archives. It's as though the bodies turned into tiny cubist paintings. Then, each of the small three-dimensional subcomponents suddenly shines and shrinks in the air until nothing remains. There's an empty spot where two winged being; stood a moment ago. No heads or bodies are left.

"Are they dead?" I thi k, half to myself and half at Phoe.

"They're back in Lim o, stored as mind backups in the DMZ with the r st of Oasis," Phoe replies. "But those are semantic; we'll worry about when we're out of here. For now, I need you to arm yourself. You have to ma e your swords appear. You remember choosing sw rds, right? Will them to appear."

I register her word , but not their meaning because at that moment, Fiona and Vincent scream. Gliding near the ceiling, I look down and see them running away from the c thedral's entrance.

The rest of the surviv rs cry out even louder and scatter like cockroaches.

Brandon doesn't ch ase after them. With a dignified posture, he v alks farther inside, a few winged warrior types beh nd him.

"The katanas, Theo," Phoe screams in my mind. "You'll need them. Spr ad your arms as though you're about to grab two swords and wish you had them. Quick!"

I guess I've been dealing with Phoe long enough that she's conditioned me to do as she says. Spreading my arms palms out, I will the weapons to appear.

Two blades materialize in my hands. They're lighter than I imagined two long pieces of metal would be, but then again, real-world swords don't possess the fiery glow these two have, so I'm not operating under the normal laws of physics. The handles feel comfortable in my hands, as if they're extensions of my arms.

"Tell the Councilors to arm themselves too," Phoe says.

"Arm yourselves," I shout at the frightened people below me.

My command arrives too late for one pale, pudgy Councilor, as one of the armed warriors beheads him.

"Gesture for the weapons you chose on your way to this place," I yell. "Wish for them to appear in your hands."

Vincent—the thin Councilor—looks up at me and nods. He performs the gesture to call forth his weapon, and an intricate scythe appears in his hands.

With it, he looks a lot like the Grim Reaper. As soon as he registers his new acquisition, Vincent swings the giant grass-cutting instrument at his beefy attacker. The winged warrior is caught off-guard. One moment he was chasing an unarmed, pathetic Vincent, and in the next his target is attacking him. The momentary hesitation quite literally costs the attacker his head, and his decapitated parts disappear in that same pixel-by-pixel manner as the bodies did earlier.

"Good job, Vincent," I shout. "Wait—look out!"

Vincent's head is separated from his body, and as he dematerializes, I see Brandon standing there with his giant blade.

"Fighting us is useless," Brandon says in his drum-like voice. "We've trained with these weapons for centuries, while you didn't know you could possess them—until that one told you." He looks at me threateningly, his wings preparing for flight.

I try to make my gaze more baleful than his. He's trying to dominate the environment through psychological warfare, and I won't fall for it. Out of the corner of my eye, I see Fiona. She's approaching Brandon from behind, a rapier in her slim hands.

Instead of metal, her weapon looks to be made of pure light.

"Head for the exit," Phoe orders me at the same time as I think, "We need to help her."

"No, we don't," Phoe says. "Judging by the way Brandon moves, he wasn't lying about his training. You have no chance against him in a fight. Fiona is already as good as back in Limbo."

Phoe's words are like cold water over my brain.

"Can't you take over my body and do something?" I think in desperation. "You should be faster than—"

Before I can finish my idea, Phoe acts on it. The next few seconds are full of the usual paradoxes that happen when Phoe takes control. It feels like I'm acting on my own, but I know I'm not *that* much in control of my fear of heights. It must be Phoe who has me pull back my wings and literally swoop down to the ground.

"I thought you wouldn't consent to my control after my failure in Oasis." Phoe's words distract me from the horror of falling, but when the wind resistance hits my face, terror fills me once again.

Fiona raises her rapier.

Though he's looking at me, some kind of instinct warns Brandon that someone is attacking him from behind. With impossible speed, he spins around, blocking Fiona's strike with such force that she staggers backward.

I'm halfway down when Brandon takes advantage of Fiona being off balance and swings his giant blade. Fiona parries with her rapier, but she might as well be wielding a toothpick. Brandon's blade pushes her elegant weapon aside and continues its trajectory toward her lithe neck.

Instead of splattering on the floor like I feared, I open my wings at the last second and slam my right katana down on Brandon's broadsword, preventing him from decapitating Fiona. Unfortunately, his sword still leaves a gushing wound in her neck.

Instead of red, her blood is luminescent, like the blood of a strange deep-sea creature. She shrieks so loudly that it startles Brandon. I take advantage of his momentary distraction and slice open his left shoulder.

Ignoring the spurting of his blood, Brandon gives me his full attention.

Fiona is clutching at her neck, and I know I'm on my own in this fight.

Brandon thrusts his sword at my chest. I jump away so quickly there's no doubt Phoe was responsible.

Brandon's jaw tenses. He must've expected everyone in here to be an easy kill. His training holds, however, and instead of dwelling on my surprising spryness, he swipes at my legs.

I jump.

He thrusts the point of his broadsword at my right shoulder, and I parry with my left blade. The impact numbs my entire arm, but I don't let that stop me. Instead, I slice Brandon straight across his bicep.

I hear the sizzle of my fire blade searing his flesh, and he yelps in pain, finally revealing that he *can* feel these injuries.

His cry gets the attention of his nearest muscle-bound ally, who stops chasing a bleeding Council member in favor of attacking me.

Crap.

My already-frantic heart is trying to escape my ribcage. Even Phoe can't control my body fast enough to deal with two of these guys.

Then I notice Fiona's neck. It's no longer gushing blood. The bloody wound is bad and must hurt like hell, but it's in better shape than I expected. Healing must work differently in this place. Though I've never seen a sword wound back in Oasis, I doubt they stop bleeding that fast.

Fiona is screaming something, but it sounds unintelligible. Then I see that she isn't looking at me. She must've yelled for help, because a knife-wielding Council woman joins her and they attack Brandon.

Brandon's ally swings his weapons, a pair of long dagger-like swords with two curved prongs sticking out near the handles, and misses.

"They're called sais." Phoe's whisper jars me, and I pull away, narrowly avoiding getting stabbed by one of the guy's sais.

He looks surprised that I dodged his hits, and I—or strictly speaking, Phoe—slice down with my sword.

The guy's arm falls to the floor, and the weapon clatters. The arm doesn't disappear, however. I guess body parts don't dematerialize here until their owner is killed.

"I don't like the term 'killed,'" Phoe says in my mind. "Why don't we call it 'Limbofied,' since people are sent to Limbo? Regarding the lack of dematerialization, it is indeed interesting. When we stop his heart, I want to examine this Limbofication process closer."

Before I can berate Phoe for trying to develop my vocabulary in the middle of a sword fight, my body does something I didn't think it could do. My legs spread sideways, as if I'm an ancient gymnast. When my crotch touches the floor and a sai whooshes by my ear, I swing my sword at my attacker's legs, chopping them off at the ankles. The goriness would usually make me vomit, but I'm not sure this body is capable of doing that. However, I do gag from the smell of burning flesh. As the man falls screaming, I position my right blade where his heart will be, and his torso impales itself on the blade. His severed limbs and the rest of his body dematerialize like every other Limbofied person's.

"That's amazing," Phoe thinks excitedly. "I was indeed able to analyze the dematerialization process.

At the core, it's a data-compression algorithm, which obviously can be exploited. Quick, let's Limbofy someone else so I can intercept the whole process."

As if in answer to Phoe's wish, Brandon makes Fiona's knife-wielding helper disappear with a slice of his sword. The ancients had a saying along the lines of "don't bring a knife to a gunfight," but I think the wisdom applies to a sword fight as well. What's really impressive about Brandon's kill—or in Phoe's terminology, Limbofication—is that he parried Fiona's rapier in the same move he used to kill the woman.

"Crap," Phoe mutters in my head. "I wasn't ready just then. Though I did learn a bit more about the process."

"If we don't do something to help Fiona, you'll get your chance when Brandon turns her into a shish kebab," I think at Phoe. "Or when he Limbofies her, if you really prefer. In case it's not obvious, I don't want that to happen."

Phoe assists in Fiona's rescue by forcing my body to perform more gymnastics. I bring my legs under me and roll closer to Brandon. Brandon's giant sword blocks my strike aimed at his legs, and before I can cut his torso with my left katana, he blocks me in the most unexpected manner—with his wings.

There's a crunching sound as my sword cuts through the wing bones and the smell of burned feathers is disgustingly palatable, but my attacker is still very much alive. With the wounded wing no longer blocking my sight, I see that Brandon has managed to turn this painful outcome into an advantage. With his wings in my way, I lost sight of what he was doing, and I now watch as his sword swings toward my skull.

"This is it," I think for Phoe's benefit. "I'm going to die—again."

CHAP TER TEN

Despite my conviction, I don't die—thanks to Fiona. She thrusts her rapier in the path of Brandon's sword right as it's midway to my head. A painful metal-on-metal clang rings out, which is odd, since Fiona's weapon doesn't look metallic. Her arm ricochets backward with such violence that I'm sure her shoulder is dislocated. What's really frustrating is that her move doesn't even stop Brandon's assault; it only slows it. However, it's enough for me to sidestep before his sword can cleave my head in half.

In a shower of sparks, Brandon's blade strikes the floor next to me.

I jackknife to my feet and perform a ballerina-like feat of dexterity by slicing each sword in opposite trajectories. I bury the right one in Brandon's gut and plunge the left into his eye socket. Bile rises in my throat at the sight of the gore spilling out of Brandon when I yank the swords in a circular motion. Maybe I *can* vomit. Large chunks of slightly crispy flesh fall to the ground and then get digitized and disappear.

"Yes!" Phoe screams—and I do mean out loud. "Yep, I have a voice now," she says in my mind before I can ask. "This is very promising. I got both his memories and a fraction of the resources Haven had allocated to him. This means things are not as bad as I thought, which is all the more reason for you to get out of here. If you go back into Limbo, we're screwed."

"I want to help Fiona escape," I think back. "She saved me."

"Fine," Phoe says. "Tell her to follow you."

"Our only chance is escaping through that door," I tell Fiona, who's dazed y staring at the empty spot where Brandon's body used to be. "Follow me."

I run for the entrance, hoping Fiona heard me and is on my heels. Around me, pieces of Council members keep dematerializing at an increasing rate, which means there are more armed men free to attack me. Two of the nearest winged assholes turn their sights on me. When they're twenty feet away, I launch into the air. The pounding of my wings outpaces my heart rate, which itself was trying to set some kind of a record.

I hear the rustling of wings behind me and assume Fiona has followed my lead.

The two big guys attempt to follow, and as soon as they do, Phoe maneuvers my body in a way that would make a hawk proud. I plunge toward the door as though my life depends on it—which it does, Limbofication notwithstanding. I hear Fiona scream behind me as a sword whooshes by my side.

Just as my legs clear the cathedral's entrance, a terrible pain erupts in my calf.

I glance down at the source of the pain and wish I—or Phoe—hadn't, because there's a dagger sticking out of my leg.

Fiona's situation is worse than mine. Her wings are no longer attached to her body, and she's falling down the mountain that the cathedral is built upon.

My vision goes white, partly from the pain, but mostly from the very bright illumination that hits my retinas. What's odd about the bright light is that there isn't a sun in the sky. The light is coming from all around me.

I try to swoop down to save Fiona, but my body, under Phoe's control, doesn't listen. Instead, I let go of my left sword and rip the dagger from my calf. The pain is so sharp it further blinds me. Despite the pain, I'm still torpedoing away from the cathedral.

My left hand gestures with an open palm, and another fiery sword appears in it.

"I'm sorry, Theo," Phoe says. "I couldn't let you go after Fiona. Remember, she won't die. She'll get written back into the DMZ—into Limbo."

Unsure how I feel about sacrificing Fiona, I glance back.

She's gone, but my pursuers aren't. They're flying after me like two eagles pursuing a mouse.

Channeling my worry into flapping my wings harder, I fly faster, leaving fiery embers behind me.

For the first time, I take a moment to register my surroundings. I'm flying up toward a dome that looks similar to the Dome in Oasis. What's different, though, is the scenery beyond it. In the never-ending cloudy blue sky, a dozen domed islands are floating as if held there by magic. Oasis-like habitats are visible from horizon to horizon.

No, not like Oasis—if the view below is anything to go by. Aside from the mountain bearing the cathedral behind us, there's no greenery at all, just more barren mountain ranges—something we've never had in Oasis.

"I'm sorry to distract you from the tour, but I want you to help me make an important decision," Phoe says. "One that will affect us equally."

"Since when do you ask for my opinion?" I ask out loud, still upset that she didn't save Fiona.

"We don't have time for you to be mad at me," Phoe says. "We need to strategize."

"Fine. What do you want me to help you decide?" I keep my eyes on the approaching dome rather than on the sharp mountaintops below.

"Okay," she says. "Before we can form a plan, we need to Limbofy at least one more person. Two would be better. So the choices are: Do we start with our pursuers, which is risky, or escape and look for someone else?"

Out of all the things I expected Phoe to say, "Let's kill a bunch of people" wasn't among them.

"You should start by explaining why we need to do that," I say. "And if you're ready to explain things, I need you to tell me what the fuck is going on and why you didn't respond when—"

"No time for twenty questions," Phoe says. "The reason I need you to Limbofy a few more targets is because I need more knowledge and resources. When someone gets Limbofied, their memories are prepared to be rewritten into the DMZ, similar to what happens in Oasis when someone goes to sleep. I patched into that process when it happened to Brandon and gained a copy of his memories. More importantly, when he left this system, his Haven resources were de-allocated, so I grabbed as much as

I could. I only acquired a small chunk, since I didn't know what I was doing, but I should be able to get more next time. And before you start again with the whys, even those meager resources allowed me to speak to you out loud instead of as a thought and to speed up the healing of your leg."

As she says that last statement, I realize the pain in my calf is nearly gone.

"Right," Phoe continues. "So to even begin unraveling this mess, I need more resources and more memories. Ideally, the memories should come from someone who knows more than Brandon did, though I guess hunting for someone knowledgeable is phase two of the plan."

I fly in silence for a moment. The idea of hunting down random strangers is distasteful to me.

"Yes, but unlike random strangers, our pursuers are dangerous," Phoe says.

As I think about this, we fly through the dome, which feels like a soap bubble on my wings.

A knife whooshes past my ear, reminding me of my pursuers.

"These assholes are practically asking for it," I say. "Plus, they killed Fiona and a bunch of other people.

We should get your resources from them. It's only fitting."

"Okay then," Phoe says cautiously. "If we're going to face them, we have to dispatch them quickly, before their comrades finish their grisly task and join them. I have an idea, but you won't like it. Though I guess if you keep your eyes closed—"

"Just do whatever it is, Phoe," I say with false confidence. "And I'm not—"

My wings snap shut and I drop.

Below me, my attackers are flying some forty feet away from each other, and the closest one is approximately thirty feet from me. It seems like the smaller one is quicker on his wings.

The fall puts me directly above him. He sees me drop but continues to fly upward. I'm flying down as if he isn't there.

I'm playing another deadly game of chicken, only I can't lose my nerve and swerve away because Phoe is in control. If it were me, I would've chickened out a millisecond ago.

My opponent raises his weapon—a halberd, I believe. It consists of a wooden stick that ends with an axe that has a long, pointy metal tip at the very top. That pointy end is aimed at me.

I hold my right katana in a strange, spear-like grip. The message I'm sending is clear: if my opponent pierces me, I'll slice him in return.

The larger pursuer realizes his friend might need help and speeds up.

The tip of the halberd is an inch away from my chest when its owner chickens out and swerves out of my way, to his right. Phoe must've anticipated this outcome, because a fraction of a second before the guy makes his move, I launch my right katana at the spot he diverges to.

The fiery sword looks like a comet as it speeds toward him, and the guy screams as loudly as I'd expect from someone who has a burning sword sticking through his thigh.

I spread my wings and angle my body to fly close to him before he can recover. He draws back his halberd, but before he can swing it, I cut it in half.

His partner is a leap away.

I grab my right katana from the man's thigh and cruelly turn it counterclockwise. He screams even louder, but his scream turns into a gargling hiss when my left blade cuts his throat.

He breaks into those small fragments and disappears like the others, only in this brightly lit outside world, the usual shine from this process is muted.

"Amazing," Phoe says, and I realize that her voice is no longer disembodied.

Phoe has become a vapor-like outline of herself. No, that's not really true. Unlike her Oasis counterpart, this Haven version has large butterfly wings, and all she's wearing is a tiny thong. Seeing her nearly naked again, even though she's see-through, stirs emotions in me that I know are best kept out of my head for now.

As if to highlight Phoe's incorporealness, the bigger attacker goes right through her.

"You're so dead," the man grits out, saliva spraying from his mouth.

He's holding two curved swords that I think are called scimitars. Unlike real-world scimitars, these are made of ice. I swing for the sword, hoping my fire blade will melt his. He deflects my strike and proves that his scimitars only look like ice; they feel as if they were forged o t of something as hard as titanium. He also prove how good he is with his weapons by using the po t-block recoil to slice at my right wrist.

"Shit. I pulled up B andon's memories of this guy. He's one of the bes swordsmen the Guardians have," Phoe hisses. "We s iould flee."

The sword connects v ith my right shoulder. The combination of burning pain and the unbearable feeling of my joint c unching hits me like a steamroller.

My right katana look like a fiery meteorite as it falls down.

CHAPTER ELEVEN

Through the nauseating pain, I hear Phoe say, "If this is how he wants to play it, fuck fleeing. This guy is going to get it. No one hurts you this badly and gets away with it. I'll try to take the pain away and do all the fighting. Luckily for us, I can leverage Brandon's weapons training against him."

I realize she's talking to distract me from the agony and is partially succeeding in that. Then the pain eases completely, allowing my mind to clear, and I finally notice what my body has been up to: a jerky hacking motion with my left arm.

My remaining sword slices through my enemy's left shoulder. He howls as his whole arm falls off.

A severed arm for an injured shoulder. Close enough to that ancient saying, "an eye for an eye."

To my disappointment, my attacker recovers quickly and swipes at me with his remaining scimitar.

My katana blocks his strike. I try to slice open his side, but he blocks in turn.

He hacks at my throat and I duck under his blow, delivering a deep cut to where his liver should be.

My opponent doesn't disintegrate, which means my strike wasn't lethal. In retaliation, he executes a desperate onslaught of feints and thrusts. I have a hard time following every attack, but Phoe doesn't. Through me, she blocks every strike with mathematical precision. As the fight proceeds, I clue in to Phoe's plan. The man's crazy attacks are tiring him out, and the two bloody wounds aren't helping him either.

My right arm is numb, but at least, unlike his stump, my shoulder isn't bleeding—likely due to Phoe's influence.

"The guys in the cathedral might be on their way," I tell her. "We need to fly away."

Phoe has me execute my own barrage of attacks. If someone were to capture my sword movements with a high-speed camera, I'm sure it would look like a beautiful, fiery work of art. When it becomes clear that the guy can barely block my attacks, I slice at his throat and succeed in cutting it clean through. He begins the Limbofication process and disappears a second later.

Without pausing, I flap my wings and fly toward the point where the dome of the floating island meets its ground.

"We're going to dive under the island," Phoe explains. "This way, when the rest of the Guardians exit, they won't spot us as quickly."

I glance at her as she speaks and realize that her ethereal figure looks more solid, as if she's made out of thicker fog.

"This form is just the beginning." Phoe flies in front of me, showing me the way. "With more resources, I should be able to give myself a real body—or at least as real of a body as I can get in this place."

I remain silent until we reach the edge of the floating island. Once we pass the dome, we fly under the island, passing through thick clouds. I notice that the same kind of clouds seem to cover the bottoms of other islands as well.

We have a clear head start on our pursuers now, so I say, "Okay, now what?"

"Now we get as far away from this place as possible," Phoe says. "Then I'd like you to Limbofy a few more people for me."

"I'm not attacking random people for you—and you still owe me answers. If I didn't know you better, I'd say you've gone evil, assuming you weren't evil from the start. Don't you see how that would explain how everyone in Oasis was killed and why you want me to kill even more people in Haven?"

"We both know you don't believe that," Phoe says, but her ethereal shoulders drop. "Fine, let me explain what I think happened, but keep in mind that there are big gaps in my knowledge—which we'll have to address as a matter of high priority."

"Tell me what you can," I say, my wings flapping even faster.

"First, allow me to do this." Phoe gestures at my injured shoulder, and with a flash of bright yellow light, the gaping wound closes.

The healed shoulder tingles, and I clench and unclench my right hand. It feels as if the shoulder never got hurt. There aren't even any remnants of pain.

"I'm glad that worked," Phoe says, looking at me over her shoulder. "Incidentally, I hope you realize that this feat of healing was only possible because of the resources I pilfered from those Limbofied Guardians."

"Guardians," I repeat. "You called them that before."

"Yes, I got the proper term from Brandon's memories. The others also call themselves that."

"Do you mean you literally know what he knew?"

"I more than know—I can even show it to you. But I know you're dying to learn about what happened in Oasis."

"Yes," I say. "I need to know if everyone is really dead."

She dives down and follows a diagonal path straight to the nearest domed island. This island is greener than the one we left and looks a lot more welcoming, at least from his distance.

We fly in silence for a moment. Though I know what she's going to tell me, I need to hear it. Phoe must realize that and is thinking of the best way to deliver the horrible truth.

"You've already figured most of it out," she finally says, speaking so softly that I almost don't hear her over the wind hitting my face. "That Jeremiah thing on the beach was a virus. I think it originated here, in Haven. I also think the question of who unleashed it, and why, is something we need answered as soon as possible. One thing is for sure: the Jeremiah virus hunted every part of me, every thread, to extinction. Only a portion of me, what I wrote into the DMZ, survived. That part of me was just a static snapshot—an insurance policy of sorts. It was not actively executing on any computing substrate, similar to how the backed up human minds just sit in the DMZ, waiting to be resurrected in a computer world one day. It's like the hibernate function of an ancient operating system. I only know about the horrible events you lived through from your memories. I wasn't around for any of it."

She falls silent for a moment, then continues. "My best guess as to what happened after I was gone is that the Jeremiah virus continued deleting anything that remotely resembled me, including my unconscious processes of gravity simulation, oxygen regulation, and the likes. In its overzealousness to erase me, the virus destroyed the life-support functions of me, the ship. As far as making sure it killed me, it was a good strategy, but as a way of keeping the human population alive... Well, you know what happened."

She stops talking and lets me digest this. Driven by an irrational hatred of Phoe, someone—or a group of someones—was criminally negligent. These people are here in Haven with me, and they're making me rethink my earlier attitude toward violence. They'll answer for all the suffering I witnessed and be held accountable for all those deaths.

Then I realize that though the events were very tragic, no one truly died. There are snapshots of every mind, including Liam's. He's somewhere in the DMZ with Mason and the rest of them.

Theoretically, they could be brought back to life in Haven.

"That's true," Phoe says. "Though I'd like to point out that those snapshots are incomplete, for better or worse. Few will remember their last day in Oasis. As you might recall, the mind backup process starts when you go to sleep, and I doubt many people took a nap in the midst of that disaster. The only reason you can recall what happened is because of your unique circumstances. You fell asleep when you were suffering from hypothermia. If you woke up after that, you lost that information forever."

I shudder. Maybe forgetting something like that is a good thing. Then something occurs to me.

"If you were as good as dead, how did you show up here?" I ask. "For that matter, how did I?"

"I'm here because you're here. Remember that Pi exploit I planted in your head so I could enter the Elderly Test on Birth Day?"

I nod, beginning to understand. Phoe gave me a fake memory relating to Pi. After a certain point in the sequence, the numbers of Pi became the digits that helped her hack into the Test.

"Exactly," Phoe says. "When you enter certain virtual reality environments, those digits in your head are instantiated together with your mind. Once that happens, the numbers become a basic routine meant to create a bootstrap version of me that in turn summons the rest of me to itself. So I got very lucky that you ended up here, in an environment so similar to the Test. With the help of this code, a small shadow of me is once again running. I don't know if it's obvious, but I'm nowhere near my normal self. It's horrible. I'm down to measly human-level intellect."

"Okay, so that explains your presence, sort of," I say. "Except it all hinges on me being here, and you haven't explained that." We're a few feet away from the shimmering dome now, which means we're about to enter the green sky island. "How did I get here? I thought only Council members went to Haven."

"It might be best for you to hear that from the horse's mouth, so to speak, and for that, I'll have to show you Brandon's memories in a moment." Phoe folds her wings and plummets headfirst into the soap-bubble dome.

For the first time sinc our escape, it occurs to me how odd our surroundir gs are. The whole universe looks like a massive sky There's no ground as far down as I can see, not c unting the floating domed islands.

"Do I have to make y u fly down?" Phoe asks as she continues descending.

"No," I think. "I'll fl down by myself—at my own pace."

I don't want her to fo ce me to drop the way she did, so I begin my descen .

Phoe disappears belov the treetops. "The reason there's no ground is beca se Haven is built on top of a virtual reality infrastru ture that is very similar to the IRES game," she expl ins in my mind. "It doesn't need to conform to realit ."

As I listen, I fly slo ver, examining the never-ending woods covering tl e ground of the island.

With the greenery app roaching, even my cautious flight speed feels too fas . Even though I know it's completely irrational l re, my fear of heights awakens with a vengean e, and it's all I can do to keep going.

When I descend below the treetops, I find that Phoe has already landed in a meadow. I spread my wings in preparation for landing, and when my feet touch the ground, I swallow my heart back into my chest.

Phoe smiles at me. "Good job. Now let's walk for a bit. This way, even if one of the Guardians flies by, they won't see us. When we get to the easternmost edge of the island, we'll fly under it."

"Fine," I say. "What are these islands?"

"All I know about them so far is that each one belongs to one of the Forebears—the denizens of Haven, of which you are now one," Phoe says and starts running for the trees on the other side of the meadow.

"Wait." I chase after her. "Does that mean there's an island somewhere that belongs to me?"

"Yes, there is, I'm sure of that. I can even find it for you if you really want, but I think it's useless to us right now," Phoe says from behind a giant oak. "Let's get deeper into the forest, and I'll show you Brandon's memory."

I follow her, thinking that despite what Phoe said, it might be really cool to own an island like this—an island the size of Oasis.

"It's a waste of resources if you ask me," Phoe says after I catch up with her again. "This whole place is an atrocity committed against the ship's computing substrate."

I inhale the fresh air. It smells exactly like a real forest. It looks like a real forest too, but I can't shake the feeling that something is different. Then it hits me: I'm hearing birds chirping and insects buzzing—sounds I'd never heard in the woods of Oasis.

"There's a ton of simulated life here, if that sort of thing impresses you," Phoe confirms. "This island could give the Zoo a run for its money."

I catch sight of something fluffy moving in the bushes. Must be a rabbit or a squirrel. I resist the urge to chase after it like a kid. I still want to get those answers from Phoe, and I can't let this fake nature distract me.

Glancing up at the strange sky, I examine the dozen domed islands floating in the distance. Haven is beautiful in its contempt for gravity.

"All right then." Phoe stops and looks at me. "Why don't you let me walk for you as you experience this?"

"Sure," I respond cautiously. "Experience what?"

Phoe gives me a crooked smile, and the world around me disappears.

I'm standing in an empty, metallic room, and a familiar winged creature is standing next to me. It's the first winged guy I ever saw—the original loincloth-wearing, winged demigod Envoy who gave Jeremiah the Lens of Truth.

The metallic walls of the room are reflective, and I can see myself in one of them.

Only it's not my own face looking back at me. It's the Guardian who nearly killed me with his giant broadsword.

I should've been ready for this, but I still can't believe it.

I'm Brandon.

CHAPTER TWELVE

"You're not Brandon per se," Phoe's thought intrudes. "You're just reliving his memories."

I knew that already, but having her reiterate it helps me come to grips with this strange situation.

Everything about me feels wrong. I'm taller, my feet are planted wider than usual, and I can feel the bulkiness of my muscles. Two streams of thoughts are flowing through my head at once: my thoughts and Brandon's. His are faint and noticeably foreign, but quite accessible. It's eerie.

"This is how I feel when I'm inside your head," Phoe explains. "Pay attention to their conversation."

It's hard to pay attention because there are too many interesting things distracting me. I don't just recall Brandon's memories; I feel his emotions as well, though they're limited to the present. He respects the Forebear he's talking to. The man's name is Wayne. I know this because Brandon knows this, and I make a mental note to remember the name because it's a better moniker than 'the first Envoy I ever saw.' I also know that Wayne is part of the Circle, which is the ruling body in Haven. He, Brandon, is the Leader of the Guardians, which means he doesn't have any guard duties in the Sanctum, the island where the Circle rule from. As a result, he rarely meets with the members of the Circle. The last time Brandon was summoned here, to the basement vaults of the Spike building on the Sanctum, was years ago.

Thinking about the past opens up a floodgate of interesting observations. With little effort, I can recall everything Brandon has done in his life. I remember his life as a Youth, his passion for ancient military strategies as an Adult, and his pride when he first served as a member of the Elderly Council. But I have access to more than just his biographical information. Through Brandon, I know what it feels like to grow feeble with age and eventually die, and I relive his awe upon awakening for his second life in Haven.

"It all began when we received the results from the last Test," Wayne says in his familiar organ-like voice. "Few people know this, but the way a new Council member is chosen is rather simple. He or she is always the Elderly with the highest score on the Test."

Wayne keeps talking to Brandon, but I tune them out. I have my answer, and now that I do, I can't believe I didn't realize it sooner.

"You had no chance to think about it." Phoe imbues the thought with regret. "I'm the super-intelligent being, so I should be the one kicking myself. I didn't realize the Test scores had anything to do with the process of choosing who served on the Council. I think I wanted to shut down the Test so badly that I was in denial. My gluttony for resources blinded me to this possibility."

As Phoe speaks, the full picture starts to form in my mind. She had me reach such a high score on the Test that the testing process nearly took forever, giving me a result no one else could beat and inadvertently making me eligible to become a Council member. Maybe we could've gotten away with it for a bit—if a position on the Council hadn't opened up almost at the same time, thanks to Jeremiah drinking his own poison.

"That's right," Phoe says. "When Jeremiah died and went to Haven, you automatically became a member of the Council. If the Forebears hadn't caught on to your high score so fast, I could've covered it all up, hidden it even from them, but they acted before I knew what happened. They were clever to move so fast with their virus."

I rub my forehead, trying to wrap my mind around the magnitude of our failure.

"You have to look on the bright side," Phoe says. "When you died in Oasis, thanks to the fact that you were a Councilor, you ended up here instead of spending an eternity in Limbo. So what failed us also helped us."

"Yeah." I imbue as much sarcasm into my thought as I can. "Work; out great for you. You've been dying to get your hands on this place, but the Firewall was in your way. Now here you are. I wonder if—"

"Please don't finish that thought unless you truly mean it." Phoe's tone sharpens. "You have no idea how much their virus took away from me. You're pretty much the same person you were in Oasis, with minor changes like these wings, but I'm barely an echo of what I was before the virus attacked me. Parts of me are lost forever, and even if I regain those resources, I'll never be the same person again. I would never execute a plan that involved such a high level of self-mutilation, or one that would cause you so much suffering." In a softer voice, she adds, "I'm sorry I didn't prevent this from happening. You have no idea how sorry I am."

"No, I'm sorry too." Guilt tightens my chest. "I'm sorry that I snapped at you. I don't really think you planned all this. It's just a lot to take in."

"You should listen to what Wayne is about to say," she thinks at me, clearly eager to change the subject.

I try to focus my mind enough to register what Brandon is hearing.

"No, this Youth, Theodore, could not have done this on his own. He's a pawn," Wayne says, his voice hitting deeper organ notes. "We want nothing more than to believe it was the work of a brilliant young man, but we can't ignore the facts. There's been too much tampering beyond what a human being can do. Theodore's age is a good example. He's clearly a Youth, if you look at him, but he's ninety years old in all of Oasis's systems. If any living person pulls up his information, an Augmented Reality illusion will fool them into thinking he's the unaltered age of twenty-four."

Wayne pauses, as if for dramatic purposes, and it works. I feel Brandon's eyebrows rise and the hair on the back of his neck lift.

"Yes," Wayne says. "And that's one example. There are countless others. The Test is no longer running, and there's evidence of mass Forgettings. I could list all the clues, but the conclusion we, the Circle, have reached is rather simple. Only one type of abominable being could manipulate our computer systems to such a degree: the enemy belonging to our deepest fears—an AI."

Brandon swallows thickly as Wayne continues.

"We consulted our ancient protocols, which the eldest among us have had locked away for centuries, and took action," Wayne says. "Without telling the outside world what we were about to do, the Circle struck at the enemy. Unfortunately, our efforts were in vain. No, worse than that. Before dying, in its anger, the AI retaliated by destroying all of Oasis. It suffocated every citizen in the real world."

The terror Brandon feels is so disorienting that I miss Wayne's next few sentences. Once I can push aside Brandon's emotions, I hear Wayne say, "The whole Council, including this Theodore, will soon appear in the Cathedral. We're concerned that before its demise, the AI could've turned those members of the Council against us. You have to send them all to Limbo, especially the one named Theodore."

Questions flood Brandon's head, and, confusingly, there's an even bigger flood of questions in my mind. Unable to cope, I say, "Phoe, can you pull me out of his memory?"

Brandon's thoughts stop, Wayne's too-perfect features frozen in a grimace, and I'm back in the forest, running as I dodge tree branches.

Phoe's see-through form is running next to me.

"I know how you must feel," Phoe says. "When I learned this—"

"I can't believe it was us." I feel like my chest is about to explode from the pressure within. "We're the reason everyone is dead."

Phoe must've returned control of my body to me, because I stumble and almost fall as my foot catches on a branch.

"It was not our doing," Phoe retorts as I right myself and resume running. "That's on the Circle's heads. They unleashed the virus."

"He said it was *you* who killed everyone."

"You don't believe that, do you?" Phoe stops and looks at me with her transparent blue eyes. "Of course he would say that. He's not about to admit that their plan to deal with me backfired so spectacularly. That in trying to get rid of me, they killed everyone in Oasis."

A branch hits me in the face as I stop next to her. The pain of the strike, combined with my turbulent emotions, makes my eyes water.

"Theo, you can't beat yourself up like this," Phoe says, looking at me. "Yes, the way we crashed the Test revealed my existence to these people, which caused them to lash out, but blaming ourselves is like blaming the victim for getting robbed. This virus almost killed me, and your real-world body is dead. It was the Circle that unleashed the virus. Clearly, they didn't understand what they were doing."

I shake my head numbly. "If I never met you, if I never brought up those three hundred Screens, everyone in Oasis would still be alive. Liam would be alive. It wasn't a perfect society, but it was better than none."

"It's not all lost." Phoe places her hand on my shoulder. Though her fingers go through me, warmth spreads from the spot she touched me. "The virus can't penetrate the Firewall or the DMZ area. That means everyone who died is still backed up in Limbo. As long as that remains the case, the deceased are not really gone. If we survive this place, if I regain enough resources, I could simulate Oasis, if that's what you wanted, or I could come up with a better environment, one with more nature and less bullshit. Once that's done, I could bring back anyone you wanted."

I stare at her. I know my friends are stored as backups in the DMZ, or in Limbo, or whatever. We even talked about restoring Mason before. But I also remember that she said bringing him back would be selfish.

"Bringing anyone back before I have enough resources to let them exist beyond a brief time would be selfish. Once I have enough resources, however, *not* bringing them back would be selfish."

"But if you didn't have the resources before, where—"

"Ah, but don't you see that, as sad as it is, the virus created a horde of resources for me to reclaim? It killed everything—every computer program the Forebears ran to keep me unconscious—and made certain costly processing tasks, such as Augmented Reality illusions and life support, no longer necessary. If the virus went away, I'd have more than enough resources to bring the simulated people back."

"But they're dead." I know I'm not being completely rational, but can't forget Liam's purple face. "How real would their resurrected selves be?"

"You tell me," Phoe says. "You don't feel dead, do you? To me, living means experiencing the world with your mind. In that sense, you're still alive and kicking. Liam, Mason, and anyone else you need could have the same life you have now, and in a place of your choosing." She looks up at the strange sky, then starts running again. "If you like what the Forebears created, we can use it for inspiration," she says over her shoulder, "but I suspect you'll want something better for you and your friends."

When I catch up to her, we run for a few minutes in silence. Phoe is right. I feel alive and as real as before, which isn't surprising. I felt real when I was with her on the beach, even though I knew I wasn't alive in that environment. But I had a real-world body as my anchor then, and now I don't. The idea makes my skin crawl. Haven feels like I'm stuck in a video game, and I don't want to feel this way forever.

"You feel like you're stuck in a video game because it's actually not that far from the truth," Phoe says. "Haven was built on a framework technology very similar to the IRES game. That's why choosing your wings and appearance was so similar to the start of a video game. Unlike the environment I would create, this place doesn't model your body exactly, molecule by molecule, and that subtly changes the way you feel. Your wings and the fact that this environment doesn't follow the familiar laws of physics also increase the feeling that this is a virtual space. With time, though, you'd get used to it."

"But it's not real. Even if I get used to it, these birds"—I look up at the distant flock of starlings that form a mesmerizing murmuration—"these trees—all this stuff doesn't exist."

"Now you're getting philosophical on me," Phoe says. "And if you want to play that game, I should point out that everything you've ever experienced in your 'real' life was your brain's interpretation of your sensory inputs. Your mind constructed the world from what your eyes and ears captured through imperfect, ancient, biologically based sensors. Your eyes could only see a sliver of the full range of the electromagnetic spectrum, and your ears could only hear a portion of the sounds surrounding you. Your brain took that incomplete information and created a virtual reality in which you lived. In a way, your reality was a step removed from what's really out there. You *never* had the complete picture. Now there's just an extra layer of unreality added. If we get out of this Haven mess, perhaps I could figure out a way to give you sensors to experience the real world."

I'm glad I'm running through a meadow and don't have to deal with branches hitting my face. In the state I'm in, my dodging skills are probably inadequate. Needless to say, Phoe's words haven't calmed me.

"You feel better when you focus on a plan, so that's what we should do," she says.

I shrug and slow down to walk toward the meadow's edge.

Phoe takes my silence as an invitation to keep talking. "We need to learn whatever we can about this virus," she says, matching her pace to mine. "Once I know how it works, I might be able to beat it and reclaim—"

Phoe suddenly falls silent and looks at the edge of the meadow that's now ten feet away from us.

A tall woman walks out from the tree line of the forest.

She's stunning, as all Forebears seem to be. She's also nearly naked, with only ivy-like leaves covering her private parts. There's a woven basket hooked on her slender elbow, with a bunch of colorful mushrooms inside.

She looks like some kind of wild woman from the forest.

When the Forebear sees me, her eyes widen and she drops the basket, the mushrooms spilling onto the grass.

Her arm twitches, and a large metal stick materializes in her hand. With a graceful gesture, she spreads the object, and I see that it's some kind of metal fan, with blades adorning the tips of the rods that serve as the fan's joints.

"It's an iron fan," Phoe hisses in my ear. "They used this weapon in ancient China and Japan."

The woman lunges at me.

I duck in time to dodge the knife-like blades of the fan.

The contraption whooshes across the crown of my head, slicing a chunk of my hair off.

Unperturbed, the ivy-clad woman gracefully swings the deadly fan at my throat.

CHAPTER THIRTEEN

I pivot back to save my life, but the blades still connect with my throat.

A sharp stab of pain radiates from where the fan scratched me. Stunned but happy to be alive—or still exist, or whatever the proper term is for my state of being—I scramble backward and yell, "Who are you? Why are you attacking me?"

The woman doesn't respond; instead, she executes a somersault.

It looks as though she's doing a handstand that's been recorded and played back at a super-fast rate. By the end of this flashy maneuver, she's beside me.

She folds up her fan so it's a solid stick once more. I begin to gesture for my own weapons, but the woman is faster and jabs her stick into my side.

The pain forces me to abandon my gesture. The metal of her weapon feels so cold that I'm reminded of my last moments in Oasis when I was freezing to death. When I glance down, bile rushes up my throat. Half an inch of her weapon is stuck inside my stomach. She rips the fan out, splashing my luminescent blood onto the grass and redefining what pain really means.

I'm on the verge of fainting. White stardust specks dance across my eyes, and through the haze, I see the woman unfold the fan again.

The sharp points of her weapon fly at my throat.

I suspect Phoe takes over my body again, because I move. Had she left me on my own, I would've curled into a little ball.

With superhuman agility, I dodge the fan and grab my attacker's slender wrist in a white-knuckled fist. At the same time, I slam the side of my other hand into her inner elbow.

The sharp blades of her fan pierce her throat instead of mine.

Not pausing, I punch the handle of the fan, pushing the steel spikes through her throat.

The woman's gurgling scream sounds like someone is using a rusty saw to play a majestic harp. As she falls, her body disintegrates into pixelated blotches and disappears.

Breathing hard, I stare at the upturned basket and the mushrooms on the grass—the only proof the woman was here.

"What the hell was that?" I ask, turning toward Phoe. My eyes widen. "Wow, you have a body now?"

"Yes." Phoe touches my elbow with her very real fingers. "I'm as substantial as anyone else in this place. Jeanine's resources were instrumental in that. As to what happened—well, she attacked us. Since I have her memories, I can show you why, if you'd like."

I check my stomach wound and then my neck. There's nothing there. Not even a scar.

"Everyone heals better here. It's part of the game-based infrastructure," Phoe says. "I just sped up the healing for you again. Now let me show you her memories."

I manage to plop down on the grass before I find myself in a stranger's head again.

I'm walking toward the meadow.

It feels odd because my body is too slender, has curves in all the wrong places, and my gait is completely wrong, with my hips moving oddly from side to side.

My name is Jeanine.

Phoe mentioned this name in passing, but in these memories, it's more than a name.

Like when I was in Brandon's memories, I'm not just aware of Jeanine's thoughts as we're walking; I'm also aware of her entire history and can recall it if I wish. Some of her memories flash through my mind. I remember a little girl back on Earth, boarding a ship that isn't yet the Oasis I know. I remember the illness that took her life and her waking up with the first wave of Forebears in Haven. Particularly interesting, I see Jeanine's entire life here, including the centuries of leisure and pleasures. She knew

Brandon, the man we Limbofied. She knew him so intimately—

"Focus, Theo, or you'll miss what she was thinking when she saw us," Phoe says. "It's what you want to know, isn't it?"

I look through Jeanine's eyes. I'm walking on my island, collecting mushrooms for Brandon's favorite stew. I walk into the meadow and see a new face.

Jeanine's thoughts are frantic. She remembers what Brandon said before departing for the cathedral—the secret he shared about the grim task the Circle gave him—and why.

A quick chain of reasoning fires through Jeanine's mind. This new person must be part of the group Brandon is supposed to neutralize. Yet he's here.

She's in danger. The whole of Haven may be in danger from this person who escaped Brandon and his Guardians.

She needs to act swiftly.

Her heart heavy with worry about Brandon, she summons her weapon, grateful for his lessons.

"I don't want to experience stabbing myself in the throat," I think at Phoe as the memory of the fight unfolds from Jeanine's point of view. "Please—"

I'm back in the mea low, in my body, and my head is spinning.

"She was dating—"

"The big guy we Liml ofied." Phoe squats next to me and hugs her knees. 'It's sad. They really loved each other. You can see it in their memories. In a way, it's almost better tl at these events turned out the way they did. At least they won't miss each other. Hopefully, they'll get r(instated together at some point."

"Wait, Phoe. Let's bac < up. Dating? I saw it in her memories, the taboo thin ;s they did together."

"Not so different fron what we did." Phoe winks at me salaciously.

"But we were breakii g all sorts of rules," I say. "These are Forebears. For them to have sex…"

"I know. It's not the irst time these people have proven to be hypocrites. In this case, I think they'd argue that Haven is a fo m of afterlife, so the rules can be different. From w at I can tell, they look back on their lives in Oasi as a form of extended childhood. The way the] orebears who were born in Oasis see it, you only tru y mature after you've lived a life. If you look at it from their point of view, there's no harm in a two-hundred-year ban on sex when you'll have millenniums in Haven to make up for it." She grimaces. "For the other Forebears, the ones who originally came from Earth, sex was never a taboo. I think they allowed it here because they couldn't live without it, and the Oasis newcomers benefitted—"

Phoe stops talking and looks at the sky in shock—an expression I don't think I've ever seen on her face before.

At first, I think she's looking at the crows flying by, which does seem odd outside the Zoo, but then I see the real source of Phoe's concern.

The clouds that normally float all over the sky have gathered together in one spot, forming a distinguishable shape.

The clouds have become a face.

There is a face made out of clouds in the sky, like something out of an ancient story.

I fight the urge to rub my eyes. Human beings tend to see faces in random patterns. Phoe once explained to me that facial recognition is something human beings are so good at that sometimes the mechanics of it backfire, and we see faces in a patch of dirt or in the ripples of water. However, in this case, since Phoe is also looking up at the clouds, I know it's not a visual self-deception. The face in the clouds must really be a face—which makes as much sense as the floating islands surrounding it.

The face is male. His eyes look wise, and his firm jawline gives him an air of nobility.

The cloud's lips part, and in a voice that booms louder than thunder, the face says, "Haven. Hear me."

The crows scatter, and even the forest looks subdued, as if pummeled by the sound.

"The Circle will speak in an hour," the booming voice continues. "Everyone should gather. We have dire news."

With a theatrical flash of thunder, the face is no longer discernable. The clouds float away, scattering across the sky.

"What the hell was that?" I ask.

Phoe's gaze becomes distant for a moment; then she says, "According to the memories at my disposal, this is the way the Circle calls for rare town-hall-like meetings. Haven's citizens will gather on one of the largest public islands, in a place they call Haven Hall.

This usually happens once every century of existence or so, and involves someone from the Circle giving them a pep talk. This time, I suspect they will tell them what happened in Oasis."

I get up and say, "Okay, how does that fit into our plans?"

"Let's run the rest of the way," Phoe says and gets up. "We still need to make sure the Guardians don't spot us."

As I run, I notice my muscles have completely recovered from my fight with Jeanine. Phoe runs next to me, clearly relishing her new body.

"So yeah, the plan," she says before I even open my mouth to remind her. "You won't like it."

My laugh borders on hysterical. "When have you ever come up with a plan I liked?"

"I know, right? You're a hard man to please." She chuckles. "Seriously, though, this plan is so daring I don't even know if *I* like it."

"Let me guess. You want to go to this meeting," I say, dodging a branch. "Am I warm?"

"Listen," she says, her tone serious again. "To learn about the virus, we need access to the people who unleashed it: the Circle. Unfortunately, the members of the Circle lon't hang around Haven willy-nilly. They stay n the Sanctum, a place everyone's memories dep ct as a rather unwelcoming area for anyone outside the Circle. During this meeting, though, someor e from the Circle will be in attendance." She glances at me. "I won't sugarcoat it for you. I want you to get close to this Forebear from the Circle and Limbofy him or her. My hope is that this person's memories will contain information about the virus."

I stop running, my legs going weak. Phoe stops too.

"So your plan is to assissinate one of the rulers of Haven?"

CHAPTER FOURTEEN

"You make it sound uglier than my actual goal, but sure." She takes a step toward me. "I want to get the son of a bitch."

"And you want me to do this in front of every citizen here?" I step backward.

"No, nothing so suicidal." She reaches for my hand and gives it a gentle squeeze. "I want to attend the town hall meeting in the hope that we'll get the opportunity to do this unpleasant task stealthily."

"Stealthily?" I pull my hand back. "They'll recognize us as strangers as soon as they see us. You accessed the same memory as me. Jeanine knew I wasn't a member of Haven because she knew everyone—"

"I have a solution for that," Phoe says. "If I use all my current resources, I can disguise you as one of the people we Limbofied. I would be reduced to a voice in your head again, but it would be worth it."

"You'll make everyone think they're seeing someone else?" I resume walking.

"No, it would be like shape-shifting from the fairy tales," Phoe says, falling into step next to me. "You'll have a different body. It might be interesting."

I feared that was what she meant but had to check. Taking deep breaths to calm myself, I remember what it felt like when I was in Brandon's and Jeanine's memories; shape-shifting sounds like it'll be similar.

"Exactly," Phoe says. "And I'm thinking it should be Jeanine. Brandon would be a great alternative, because he had access to the Circle, but since some of the Guardians saw you Limbofy him in the cathedral, we can't risk it. I could make you look like Jeff or Bill instead, the two other Guardians we Limbofied, but that's still risky. The other Guardians might ask questions about their pursuit of you and why they didn't come back."

"Why do you even need me to shape-shift? Can't you make yourself look like Jeanine?"

"Not with the resources I have. I'm basically operating on scraps. You, like every other legitimate Haven citizen, have a whole chunk of Haven's computing power allocated to *you*. What I have are some unallocated resources left over from when the system tried to reclaim what belonged to Brandon, Jeff, Bill, and Jeanine. The good news is that I have more than one way I can have you shape-shift. For one thing, I can rerun the selection process you experienced when you entered Haven and guide you to make the choices that would result in a Jeanine-looking Theo. But that might put us on the radar of an anti-intrusion algorithm, assuming this place has one."

I shudder, recalling what Phoe told me about the Test's anti-intrusion algorithm's capabilities.

"I doubt there's one here," Phoe says and turns slightly off our path. "It would be risky for the Circle to employ one, given how far this place has strayed from its original purpose, which, given all the weapons, I assume was entertainment rather than life extension. Still, better safe than sorry, so I'll use the other option and simply tweak your existing body."

She stops walking when she reaches a clear puddle of water. It's too clean to be a rain puddle. Maybe it's an underground spring? Since these water entities didn't exist in Oasis, I'm not sure.

Phoe is looking at me expectantly, waiting for my answer.

"I get your logic for using Jeanine," I say. "But what if I meet someone she knew?"

"Not if, but when." Phoe gestures, and an empty water bottle appears in her hand. "Jeanine knew every single person in Haven, and you'll need to know everything she knew about them, which will be a lot of information to take in. You have to keep in mind how long these people have lived together. Even if time here were one to one relative to the real world, many centuries have passed for most of these beings."

"What do you mean if time—"

"Remember my earlier simulation of the beach?"

I nod.

"Well, similar to that scenario, thoughts occur much faster here, because our minds are simulated, not biological. That means that in a second of real-world time, the citizens of Haven might experience minutes, hours, or even days, depending on Haven's computing resources allocation and the efficiency of the simulations."

She bends down and fills her water bottle with some of the clear water. Despite the seriousness of our situation, I can't help admiring her body in this position.

Straightening, she continues. "Without access to the outside world, it's hard to say what the difference is. Based on Jeanine's memories, it's been a monumental journey. I can't say how much time has passed because there are intentional gaps in her memory, which I don't have enough resources to undo. So yeah, after all this time, she definitely knows everyone. Despite the Forebears preferring to stay on their islands, Jeanine's had plenty of time to get to know every single person in Haven and vice versa."

"Then I'm screwed, because I don't know anyone here," I say and watch Phoe take a small sip from her bottle.

"But we have access to Jeanine's memories." She hands her water bottle to me. "I will set up a link for you, and you'll be able to recall the things you need. If necessary, I'll help too. Though we still have to be careful to avoid in-depth conversations with people who knew her well, since accessing the amount of data that comprises Jeanine's life is computationally challenging. She simply lived too long, and our resources are limited."

"All right." I take a careful sip from the bottle. The water tastes better than any drink I've had in my life. "I guess this idea is not as reckless as it first seems."

"It's pretty desperate, but beggars can't be choosers," Phoe says and disappears. The bottle in my hand also disappears. "Are you ready to turn into Jeanine?" her voice in my head says.

I shrug. "As ready as I'll ever be."

"I'll take that as a yes," Phoe says, and a strong sense of vertigo hits me.

Once the world stops spinning, the sensations are similar to when I was accessing Jeanine's memories, only much more vivid. I stick out my arms; they're slender and feminine, with thin, manicured fingers. I look down and see ivy-covered curves, which makes me panic, so I look forward again. I decide it's better to explore my new body through touch. My soft hands cup my even softer breasts, and the feeling isn't unpleasant. I can't help but touch myself between the legs—for good measure. I quickly pull my hand away. The lack of my usual equipment is terrifying.

Crouching, I look at my reflection in the puddle.

Jeanine's symmetrical face looks back at me, her classical features contorted in fear.

"Phoe?" I say, my voice sounding like a harp.

"You should think at me from now on," Phoe responds as a thought. "It's best if you get used to communicating that way again, since we can't have Jeanine speak to an imaginary friend in front of people. No subvocalizing either—nothing that can draw unwanted attention."

"Okay," I think and rise to my feet. "This is really weird."

"I know," Phoe replies. "Move around and get used to this body. Let's test your proprioception and kinesthetic awareness."

"My what?"

"Touch a finger to your nose."

I do as Phoe says. The motion is smooth and easy, and my nose looks smaller if I focus on it.

"How did you know where your nose was?" she asks.

I shrug, which draws my attention to how narrow and slender my shoulders are.

"The sense that allowed you to touch your nose is called proprioception. Pick up that pebble, throw it in the air, and close your eyes."

I do as she says, but a second later, as the pebble is about to hit me on the head, I dodge it, my eyes still closed.

"As you guessed, it was kinesthetic awareness that allowed you to avoid that pebble," Phoe says. "Proprioception is closely tied to kinesthetic awareness. Let's walk for a while."

I open my eyes. My eyelashes are strangely visible. Must be because they're longer.

I start walking. This time, the movement of my hips doesn't feel odd, even though they're swaying in a way that's unusual for me.

"Try to summon her weapon, but with the most unobtrusive gesture you can," Phoe suggests.

I open my right hand and will the weapon to appear. The iron fan—Jeanine's weapon of choice—shows up in my hand. I half-expected it to be one of my flaming katanas, but I guess this makes sense.

"Yeah, I don't do half-measures," Phoe says. "You should be able to use this weapon by relying on Jeanine's muscle memories. I just made them available to you."

Acting on instinct, I unfold the fan and thrust it at the nearest branch, cleaving it in two. At the same time, I repeat the handstand somersault Jeanine used during our fight, and leap closer to the tree trunk. I slash at the oak, leaving deep gashes in the wood.

"This is going great so far," Phoe says. "You're getting the hang of that body."

She makes me jump, run, dance, and perform a whole range of other tests, all of which I complete to her satisfaction.

"You're very lucky Brandon is dead." Phoe mentally chuckles after I perform a formal bow that everyone gives members of the Circle. "We won't need to worry about you kissing a man—or worse."

Though I'm no longer an innocent virgin, the idea of having to kiss or "worse" anyone as Jeanine didn't enter my mind. I'm still not used to thinking along those lines. Now that Phoe mentioned it, though, I'm grateful we eliminated that possibility—quite literally. I can't imagine kissing anyone but Phoe, and especially not a man.

"I'm so flattered that you can't picture yourself kissing a man over me." Phoe's thoughts brim with mirth. "I think we're ready to get into conscious, long-term memory retrieval. I'll set up the link if you're ready."

"I'm ready," I say and close my eyes, preparing for *something.*

"It's done," Phoe says. "How do you feel?"

I open my eyes. The feeling overcoming me isn't unfamiliar. This happens when I forget a factoid and spend an eternity trying to recall it, even though it's on the tip of my tongue, and then I suddenly remember whatever it was. What makes this different, though, is the sheer amount of factoids.

One example is the smell of forest air. Before Phoe linked Jeanine's memories to mine, the smell was in the background. Now, however, I know that the smell was carefully formulated by Jeanine to be the exact scent of the springwoods she recalled from her childhood on Earth.

Every tree, every bird, and every animal—even the mushrooms—was carefully crafted over the years to make Jeanine feel at home as she strolled through her domain.

"She made this place?" I inadvertently ask out loud. Then I mentally add, "Sorry about speaking."

"The Forebears, including you, can reshape Haven to their will in certain limited ways," Phoe explains. "It's another parallel to how the IRES game operated. Only that game shaped itself based on its user's subconscious fears, but Haven was hacked to reshape itself based on conscious control. I can tap into some of this interface, which is how I sped up your healing. The limitation is that Haven accommodates multiple users at once, and thus multiple wills can clash. You can't walk up to someone and will them to have horns—not unless it's something they desire and other members of Haven don't mind. On their private islands, though, the Forebears' only limitation is their imagination."

I start walking, attempting to hold off the flood of memories as I try to internalize the implications of such a strange setup.

"No time for awe, I'm afraid," Phoe thinks at me. "Now that you don't look like yourself, we don't need to hide in the forest or fly under the island for cover. You can fly straight to Central Island. Can you recall where it is?"

As soon as I think of the island, memories come pouring in. If I fly to my right, passing by the ten closest neighboring islands, I'll reach Central Island.

"Go then," Phoe urges

"Fine," I think and spread my/Jeanine's giant owl wings. "Let's fly."

CHAPTER FIFTEEN

Flying as Jeanine is almost fun, because accessing her experience and muscle memories forged from centuries of flying somehow dampens my fear of heights. The sight of the islands around me triggers memories that further distract me from my anxiety.

To my right is a large island that belongs to Iris. Even from this far, I can see the pink circle of Iris's giant rose garden, a feat that took her three hundred years of calculations and care to develop.

To my left is Caleb's island, with perfect statues that depict every person the man has ever laid eyes on—in precise anatomic l detail.

I pass by the unren arkable wilderness of the island belonging to Sa a, one of my—I mean, Jeanine's—closest frienc s. Sara has spent the last fifty years meditating an l writing poetry in iambic pentameter. Given how lose she was to Jeanine, I recall what Sara looks lik and make a mental note to avoid her, since she mig it know Jeanine intimately enough to pick up on any irregularities I might introduce to Jeanine's bel avior.

As I get closer to C ntral Island, more winged people come into view all headed in the same direction as me. By the ime the giant dome of the island is visible, the trickl of people looks like a huge flock of birds.

I enter the dome anc expertly start my descent, taking care to avoid eve small crowds and anyone who was more than an ac quaintance to Jeanine.

Central Island is huge —at least ten Oasises would fit comfortably inside i —and it's spectacular. It looks as though someon took every major ancient wonder, spruced it up, a id placed it somewhere on the island. I use Jeanine's memories to recall that the structures are themed based on the area of ancient Earth they came from. The Statue of Liberty is near the replica of what can only be the Empire State Building, and the Leaning Tower of Pisa is near the Coliseum.

"It's like the largest theme park ever created," Phoe comments. "Especially given our destination."

She has a point.

The giant castle everyone is flying toward looks suspiciously like the one in the beginning of Disney movies, only scaled up to where the top spire threatens to pierce the island's dome.

I land on the cobblestones leading to the massive castle gateway. The crowd of Forebears is so dense I have no trouble remaining incognito as I enter the enormous hall where the meeting is supposed to take place. I struggle not to let the memories overwhelm me as I recognize the faces surrounding me; if I let every piece of information flood in, my brain will melt from the overload.

Phoe snickers. "Brain melting is a physical impossibility for you now—if it ever was possible—

but your approach is sound. Keep your head down and get as close to the front of the hall as you can."

I carefully push my way through the wings and limbs blocking my path. It's a menagerie of scantily clothed, Youth-looking bodies, and on any other day, my proximity to them would affect me. Today, however, I examine them clinically. No one pays me much attention; they're all preoccupied exchanging theories about this meeting.

"A new member so soon? Jeremiah didn't spend even a day as the Envoy," I overhear a red-haired man say.

"No," says a tall woman. "I think this has something to do with—"

I lose track of their conversation in the cacophony of voices around me. In Oasis, we never had gatherings so large. At the crush of so many people, I feel something primal awaken in me—a fear of sorts. I suppress the feeling, focusing instead on the lush decorations. Based on Jeanine's memories—she was part of the crew who built this place—I knew the hall would be amazing. However, now that I see it with my own eyes, the frescos, the statues, and the intricate glass mosaics are beyond breathtaking.

Eventually, I can't squeeze through the crowd any farther. It's simply too dense. I'm about forty feet away from the stage, and I have to settle for that.

I gawk at my surroundings for a few moments; then the people behind me push me against the Forebears in front of me. The hall is really filling up, with the last people arriving through multiple doors and open windows. Some are even flying down through an opening in the ceiling.

There are too many people to count, but if I had to estimate, I'd say there are a few thousand Forebears here—more than I would've expected. I'm about to comment on it to Phoe when I access Jeanine's memories and learn that not all Forebears originated as Oasis Council members.

"Haven would be a tiny community if that were so," Phoe says.

She's right. In Jeanine's memories, I learn that originally, Haven was seeded by nearly everyone who went on the "great journey into space"—Jeanine's term. I try to recall more about that time period, but I can't.

"It's interesting, isn't it?" Phoe thinks. "Jeanine has a gap in her memories. More interesting still is the fact that she was awa re of that gap. She thought of it as something she i eeded to forget and never worried about it."

I access the memori s to verify Phoe's words. Indeed, Jeanine felt that the gap was part of some larger plan for the greater good.

"I'm certainly curiou ," Phoe says in my mind. "Something must've hap ened in Haven a long time ago—something that g t covered up by Haven's version of Forgetting. Since I can't undo this Forgetting without mor resources, let's hope the Circle members know w iat that gap is about. They are, after all, comprised i i part from former Keepers of Information—peopl who didn't partake in Forgettings in Oasis."

I don't respond becau e my attention is stolen by the crowd's staring at so nething in the front of the room. When I peer over the heads of those in front of me, I see that they'r looking at a contraption Jeanine fondly called "the magic mirror."

The nickname suits the object on the wall, because it *is* a mirror, and it's showing a video stream, similar to the Scr ens back in Oasis.

My mouth opens as Jeanine's memories add context to the beautiful images on the screen. These are the highlights of the biggest accomplishments in art, sculpture, architecture, music, and many other pursuits that Haven citizens care about. The images and sounds are beyond sublime. I'm so entranced by the mirror I don't even notice how the man and his Guardian entourage make it onto the stage.

Once I notice them, I scrutinize the group, especially the person who's about to speak.

Jeanine knows his name: Benjamin. She's heard him speak at these events before. He was already old back on Earth and joined Haven when the first wave of Forebears died. Jeanine and Benjamin had a common interest six hundred years ago. She wanted to master Xiangqi, also known as Chinese chess. Benjamin would play with her when he could get away from his Circle duties, which was rare.

Benjamin's body is more luminescent than any I've seen so far, but his face is less perfect—almost weasel-like. His wings look abstract, as if they're made of tangible smoke. He spreads his wings and raises his hands, palms up. Jeanine's memory tells me that this is his signal for silence.

The crowd quiets down, and Benjamin says, "Citizens of Haven, I come to you with a heavy heart."

The silence in the room thickens. Bad news is never delivered at these meetings.

"I don't know how to say this, so I'll go ahead and say it plainly." Benjamin clears his throat. "The ancient evil we left behind has reawakened. It has taken the lives of every citizen in Oasis. This is what remains." With tears gleaming in his eyes, Benjamin gestures at the magic mirror and images of what's left of Oasis appear.

The mirror shows thousands of bodies floating in the air, still without gravity. They're now covered completely by frost. Even the red lights I remember are dimmed in this more recent image, as if even the alarms are dying.

My chest tightens as I relive the horrible hours before my biological death.

"I'm sorry, Theo, but you can't fall apart," Phoe says. "I think I have a plan of action. Look around you now. It's very important."

I do as she says.

The people around me are showing a full spectrum of emotions, ranging from shock to complete devastation. Some people are outraged, while others look fearful or mournful.

Benjamin recites the bullshit story similar to what Wayne told Brandon. He tells everyone how the Circle learned of a threat and how their valiant efforts to save Oasis failed, leading to the evil AI taking retribution.

Jeanine's long nails are piercing my palms. I guess people who keep their nails long like this have to be careful when they clench their fists.

"I'm going to disguise your voice," Phoe tells me. "As loudly as you can, I need you to say, 'How could you let this happen?'"

"Okay," I think back at Phoe. Then I scream loudly, "How could you let this happen?" My thunderous voice reverberates through the hall with such bass that my insides vibrate.

I look around to see if anyone noticed me speaking. No one is looking at me, but my words had an effect. The crowd turns angrier, their voices growing louder with each second.

"Order," Benjamin shouts. "Quiet down and listen to me!"

His response further aggravates the people around me. They're becoming the type of mob I've read about in ancient media.

"We let the Circle have power, and you failed," someone screams in a voice that sounds like a violin.

"Next, they'll make u forget this," someone else yelps in a harmonica imitation.

Benjamin's face turns white despite its bright luminescent shimmer. The Guardians surrounding him keep their cool, but one of them whispers something in Benjamin's ear and the others inch toward the crowd.

"What happens now?" someone else chimes in as a dozen other people scream questions at the same time.

People begin to move frantically. Some head toward the stage, while others yell louder and louder.

"Start flying," Phoe urges when two of the Guardians lead Benjamin to the back of the stage.

I try to spread my wings, but it's impossible with all these people churning like in a mosh pit.

"Quick, access Jeanine's memories," Phoe says. "She helped build this place, remember?"

As soon as she says it, I recall the decades it took to craft the frescos and the ceiling. More importantly, I remember the backstage area and how it leads to the southern spire.

That means I know where Benjamin is heading, but if I don't fly now, I won't reach him in time.

What I do next is the most unladylike behavior Jeanine has ever displayed. I dig my nails into the shoulders of a shorter woman and a portly man and haul myself off the ground. Grabbing the head of the guy in front of them, I climb atop people's heads and shoulders. Without giving them a chance to register the indignity, I spread my wings and fly for the nearest window—which happens to be a decorative one with colored glass.

I crash through it, ignoring the pain from the glass shards cutting me.

"You need to be more careful," Phoe warns me. "I can't speed up your healing right now."

I grunt an acknowledgment—only my grunt comes out sounding melodious because of Jeanine's vocal cords.

My owl wings beat faster than any bird could manage. Up and up I go, spinning in the air as I torpedo toward the southernmost spire while chanting in my mind: *Please be there, please be there.*

Behind me, people from the crowd start flying out of the hall as well, but I ignore them.

With a sharp slowdown that makes wind tug painfully at my feathers, I land on a terrace that surrounds the spire's exit

Before I can calm my frantic breathing, Benjamin steps onto the terrace.

I stare at him, and he looks back at me in surprise.

Afraid to spook him and working on pure instinct, I bow in that special way Haven protocol requires when standing before a member of the Circle. As I do that, I memorize the directions Phoe is barking in my mind. Then, like a robot, I begin to execute Phoe's instructions.

"Hello, Benjamin," I say. "Sorry to corner you like this, but have you heard from Brandon?"

Benjamin shakes his head. He looks a modicum more relaxed now that he has a reason for my presence.

Capitalizing on that, I move closer to him, speaking casually. "He hasn't reported back—"

Without breaking eye contact, I gesture for my iron fan.

As soon as I feel the weight of the weapon in my hand, I swing my arm in an arc, unfolding the fan.

The blades of the fan slice through Benjamin's throat with the ferocity of a starving shark.

He tries to scream, but that only causes blood to ooze violently from his multiple throat wounds.

I watch, hardly breathing, as the Circle member stumbles and disintegrates in a poof of Limbofication.

With Benjamin no longer blocking his line of sight, one of the two Guardians who led him here looks right at me. When he sees the weapon in my hand, his jaw tightens and a trident appears in his hands. In a blur of white knuckles and gleaming metal, he brings it down in the direction of my thigh. Jeanine's muscle memory—specifically, her dancing experience—comes in handy. I move my leg away faster than I would've believed possible.

Despite the speed of my reflexes, one of the spikes of the trident punctures my foot.

Before the pain can reach my brain, I throw the fan.

I'm either lucky or reaping more benefits of Jeanine's muscle memory, because the blades lodge into my attacker's torso. He grunts and joins Benjamin in Limbo.

My elation is brief, as the second Guardian steps out onto the terrace, his eyes meeting mine. Judging by the barely contained fury on his face, he witnessed me Limbofying his friend and Benjamin.

The shockwave of pain hits me now, bringing with it a swell of nausea and dizziness.

I'm in no condition to fight.

"Right. And going by everyone's memory, this is Samuel. He is much too good with daggers for you to stand a chance," Phoe informs me urgently. "You need to escape."

I blink, trying to clear the haze of agony from my brain. Samuel's already holding a couple of daggers in each hand.

Pressing my back against the railing, I do something I never thought I could do without Phoe controlling my body.

I lean back so far that I fall over the railing.

And then I plummet.

From a great height.

Like in my worst nightmare.

CHAPTER SIXTEEN

"Resist opening your w ngs for as long as you can," Phoe tells me. "He's gli ling, which is slower than you falling like a rock."

I give it my best effor t, but a millisecond later, I reposition my body for fl ght and spread my wings.

At least my wounded foot isn't getting in the way of flying.

There's a crowd be ow me. People are still streaming out of the castle. My plan is simple: I'm going to hide in the swarm of Forebears.

A dagger whooshes past my leg and lodges in the chest of a round-faced female Forebear. Jeanine's memories supply me with her name: Vivian. She's from a different epoch and was fond of pottery, though she wasn't very good at it. To stay semi-sane, I ignore the other facts flitting through my mind. Vivian's eyes are wide with shock as she breaks apart and disappears.

My overclocked heart manages to find room to ache for the woman. She was an innocent bystander. There was no reason for her to get Limbofied.

"At least I captured her resources," Phoe says out loud. "Which, when combined with the other two Forebears we Limbofied, means I can speak out loud as well as help you navigate. In fact, I can even project myself so you can see me, but I won't do that yet, since—"

I don't register the rest of Phoe's statement because a dagger slices the joint of my wing.

Instinctively, I flex my wing to keep moving, but the pain is excruciating. Losing altitude, I focus on not flapping my wings and gliding like a flying squirrel instead.

"Damn it, Phoe," I yell at her mentally. "Focus on helping me since you said you can. You're too preoccupied with your damn computing resources."

Then, suddenly, I scream, "Help!" without meaning to.

The surrounding people look up at me.

"The horrible news was too much for Samuel," I continue yelling. "He's lost it. He's attacking me!"

A dagger stabs me in my side just as I join a large group of Forebears that momentarily block me from my pursuer.

Through the burning pain of my wounds, I hear people yelling angry questions at the Guardian, which means Phoe's plan is working.

"Consider closing your eyes for this next part," Phoe says. She sounds as if she's a few feet above me.

I refuse to close my eyes, and then, with a jolt, I fly upward. Someone is standing there. Ignoring the pain, I spread my wings to block my actions from any onlookers. Without any further ado, I summon a new fan into my hands and stab the man in the eye with it.

Like every other time Phoe took over, I don't feel her controlling me during this macabre sequence. I assume she makes me do this, because I doubt I would've had the strength to move while in all this agony, and even if I did, I'm not sure I could have done something so cold and savage. True, I did get rid of Benjamin by slicing his throat, and I dealt with the Guardian afterwards, but there's a world of difference between Limbofying a member of the Circle or self-defense and attacking a random bystander. At least that's what I try to tell my conscience as the man begins to disintegrate.

"I'm sorry," Phoe whispers. "My only justification is that it's not the end for him, and we had no other choice."

I belatedly recognize the man through Jeanine's memories. His name was Chester. He and Jeanine rarely spoke, but she always admired his culinary skills, something he'd been perfecting for a century.

In the midst of all the commotion, and with my wings blocking their view, no one seems to have noticed my actions. Everyone is focused on my pursuer, though with him shouting accusations about Jeanine, it's only a matter of time before their attention turns back to me.

Suddenly, a sense of vertigo overcomes me. Only Phoe's control prevents me from folding my wings and plummeting. When the world stops spinning, I realize my pain is gone, but my body feels very strange.

The Guardian finally pushes his way through the flying mob. He looks to his right and to his left.

"We have to keep fleeing before he sees me," I think at Phoe.

She doesn't respond, but I can almost sense her holding her breath.

Samuel glances at me, then keeps scanning his surroundings as though I'm not the person he's looking for.

I blink, not understanding, and then I notice that my wings are no longer those of an owl. I think these wings belong to a bird called the needle-tailed swift, allegedly the fastest bird in the Zoo.

"That depends on what you mean by fastest," Phoe says in that pedantic way of hers. "The peregrine falcon is the fastest bird when it comes to diving, but the needletail is the fastest when it comes to flight. This is another reason why poor Chester was such a good target."

This is when it dawns on me: I just saw the wings that surround me on Chester, right before Phoe used my hand to stab him.

"I had to shape-shift you into someone Samuel would not suspect," Phoe explains. "It couldn't be any of the other Guardians or Vivian, since he might've seen her Limbofy. That only left me with one choice: to Limbofy someone new. Chester's wings will be useful for the next part of my plan, and he was so close... I hope that makes you feel better about the whole ordeal."

It doesn't, but I don't argue. I just want to get out of here.

"Me too," Phoe says.

I slowly glide downward, amazed at how different it feels to fly with new wings. Then again, my whole body is different.

When I'm completely out of the Guardian's view, I fly in earnest, pushing my way through frightened Forebears when I have to.

A surprising number of Haven citizens are flying in the same direction as me, but I'm going much faster.

As I fly, I see a large flock of Guardians gathered together, discussing something as they glide through the air.

I keep flying up toward the dome.

To my huge relief, no one asks me a single question as I pass them. When I feel the dome's soap-like texture on my wings, I exhale a breath that I must've been holding for half an hour.

I'm not sure if Phoe knows where we're going. To me, it looks like a randomly selected direction. I try to access a memory to help me figure out where we're heading, but it doesn't work.

"I didn't bother giving you access to Chester's memories," Phoe says.

I follow her voice and see that she gave herself a visible appearance again only this time she didn't make it look even remotely realistic.

Phoe is miniscule, like a fairy. She's flying backward, her miniature head smiling at me mischievously.

"I look exactly the way I did before." The tiny fairy-Phoe strikes a model-like pose. "I reduced my size to lighten your mood."

"Well, it's not working," I lie and resist the urge to touch the tiny creature. "My mood would improve if you told me where we're heading, and I'd be ecstatic if you also told me we're safe."

Besides her size, what makes Phoe's current look surreal is that I don't ram into her despite flying at this speed.

"I'm just in your mind at the moment, so you won't crash into me, and yes, we're safe." Phoe fluffs up her pixie hair. "We're flying toward the Sanctum, where the Circle are. We have to beat the mob and the Guardians there."

As if on cue, my needletail wings flap faster.

"Wait," I say out loud. "Isn't that like the proverbial flight out of the fire and into the frying pan?"

"We have to do this." Phoe's tiny face gets serious. "Benjamin's memories aren't enough for me to battle the virus. I could only confirm what we already know: that there *is* a virus."

We fly in silence as I digest what I've learned so far. Phoe has now at least doubled her resources, which explains her ability to create this fairy illusion and control my body while it's shape-shifted. More importantly, Phoe has r trieved the memories of a member of the Circle ii the hope that he'll know something about the vir s—the whole point of our Central Island misadvent re.

"Yes, it was." Phoe tiny lips form a pout. "Unfortunately, Benjam n didn't have any critical information. Here, let m show you. I'll keep flying for you as you experienc this."

Without any prepara on, I'm suddenly standing in a room, surrounded b a large circle of Forebears.

The room is barren, vith only a large mirror in the middle.

I understand what's happening this time. I'm immersed in Benjamin' memories. He's confused because he doesn't und rstand what could be so urgent that Davin wou gather everyone in this room. Through Benjami 's eyes, I scan the Circle. Benjamin knows their na nes, so I do too.

I can't help but foc s on the people I've seen before. Wayne—the firs Envoy I ever saw—is on my right. And there's Da in, whose face appeared in the clouds to announc the big meeting. I also recognize the face of t e newest member of the Circle, a face I've grown t loathe.

Jeremiah's face.

"I have reasons to believe an ancient enemy, one of the nightmares we've chosen to Forget, has resurfaced in Oasis." Davin looks everyone over with his deep blue eyes. "Even worse, I believe this AI is working to destroy everything we've created."

Inside Benjamin's mind, I can literally feel Benjamin's feet turn cold. The rest of the Circle—especially Jeremiah—looks absolutely horrified.

"Let me first give you the facts," Davin says and proceeds to tell the Circle the same story Wayne told Brandon. He tells them how my score on the Test put my name on Davin's radar, and how I was a Youth who somehow became an Elderly Council member. He also provides a list of reasons he thinks an AI was behind it all.

"So what do we do?" Benjamin asks evenly, though I know he's just acting composed. On the inside, the man is about to explode.

"I went into the Forgotten Archives and pulled a recording of myself with instructions on what to do in such a situation." Davin points at the mirror, where another Davin appears—not a reflection but a recording.

"Greetings," the recording begins. "If you're watching this, the unthinkable has happened." Both Davins cross their arms. "If an AI has appeared in any of Phoenix's systems, in any capacity, you are likely doomed. Your only chance, and it's a small one, is to follow protocol V318, stored elsewhere in these Archives. I must caution you, however, that it's a weapon only for the most desperate of times. Use it as a last resort."

I can't help but notice that the word Phoenix, the full name of the spaceship we're in, is not familiar to Benjamin.

"Because it's part of the information they chose to Forget," Phoe says. "There isn't any other useful info in the rest of this meeting, so let me fast-forward to another memory."

A moment later, I'm standing in a different area of the same room. The faces around me are filled with greater anxiety.

"I examined the protocol," Davin says. "Without my now-forgotten technical knowledge, I can't explain it fully, but to the best of my understanding, the countermeasure is a replicator designed to spread through the computing substrate of the ship, thus taking away the AI's resources."

"That sounds like an ancient computer virus," Wayne says in his organ-sounding voice.

"A crude analogy, but if it helps you understand it, sure, we can call it that," Davin replies with poorly disguised arrogance. "However, no ancient virus possessed the flexibility and intelligence of this countermeasure."

The hairs on the back of Benjamin's neck rise. He wants to ask, "We're fighting an AI with an AI?" but restrains himself as Davin continues. "Before you panic, the intelligence I speak of would be human, not artificial," Davin says. "But therein lies the frightening part: one of us has to volunteer to become the seed for the countermeasure."

The room is dead silent.

"This is why I hoped the word 'virus' wouldn't come up," Davin says. "No one wants to become a virus, but all of us should want to be the savior of our world. We're far away from our goal of setting up a perfect human settlement on a distant world. We, the Forebears, have taken it upon ourselves to lead the living, and this AI thr atens to bring all of that tumbling down. It is our luty—"

"Assuming one of us is brave enough to volunteer," Wayne inter upts, "what would happen to all the computing sys ems in Oasis as this battle for resources ensues?"

"There are too many unknowns to say for sure." Davin frowns. "Screens may malfunction, which could lead to Youths m ssing a day or two at the Institute. Lights may f icker. Things like that, I imagine. Whoever takes on this heavy responsibility will be in control at all ti nes, I believe, and he or she can mitigate the risks."

"Mitigate the risks, ny foot," I think angrily. "They're about to choose Jeremiah, aren't they?"

"Yes," Phoe says. "He about to volunteer."

"I don't want to ex erience any more of this insanity," I think at her. " Please take me out."

Instantly, I'm back n Haven's sky, flying at breakneck speed among the clouds.

"Those idiots," I excla im in a voice that still isn't my own. I continue m ntally. "A fucking Screen malfunction? Really? That was the worst case-scenario they expected?"

"They expunged all memories of their technical expertise from their minds, so they didn't know what they were messing with," Phoe says. "Oh, never mind. I have no idea why I just tried to defend the fuckers."

"And to choose Jeremiah as the virus?" I'm so angry I inadvertently summon a boomerang—which I guess is Chester's weapon of choice. I throw the boomerang away and try taking calming breaths, but my lungs are working too hard to support the insane speed I'm flying at.

"I think that's part of the reason things went as disastrously as they did." Phoe floats closer to my face. "Jeremiah was supposed to act as the intelligence of the resulting abomination. He should've been careful when deleting things, should've been careful in his multiplying."

"Right. Jeremiah, the man who embodies rationality." The fury is threatening to choke me from within. "He killed everyone because he was deathly afraid of you."

"They all are." Phoe scrunches her miniscule nose. "It's ironic that in their fear of technology, they unleashed the very technology that killed everyone."

I fly silently for a w ile, too enraged to talk. I think I would have rath r the Forebears killed my friends through evil ntentions than criminal negligence.

"The Jeremiah virus 1 ight have known what his actions against me woul do, so you can't rule out a measure of malice," Phoe says. "Not sure how helpful that is, though."

Her words don't mal e me feel any better. They make me want to rip Jere niah's heart from his chest.

"It's funny you shoul think that," Phoe says. "I was just about to talk to y u about our next move."

CHAPTER SEVENTEEN

I recall that we're flying toward the Circle's Sanctum. "Right. I think I get it now. Benjamin knew what was about to happen but didn't have any details."

"Yes," Phoe confirms. "For that, I need to get a hold of either Davin or Jeremiah. And when I say get a hold of, I mean we have to Limbofy them so I can capture their memories." A tiny toothpick in the shape of a sword appears in Phoe's hand, and she mimics slicing someone in half. "In Jeremiah's case, I may need to be particularly thorough, as there's a chance he holds the key to disabling the virus."

This time around, my conscience doesn't raise any objections. When it comes to Jeremiah, I think my conscience would let me kill him for real if that was possible in this strange world.

"Once we get there, we have to be very careful," Phoe says and makes her weapon disappear. "Later in Benjamin's memories, Davin also discussed enabling the anti-intrusion algorithm for this place, but they deemed that too risky and decided to wait and see what the Jeremiah virus would accomplish. If they suspect I crossed the Firewall, they might get desperate enough to release it. You remember what I told you about your demise in the Test?"

I do, and the memory causes me to take her suggestion to be careful very seriously.

Phoe looks over my shoulder, and I follow her gaze. There are small figures in the distance, but I can't make out any details.

"Do you want me to give you bird-like vision for a moment?" Phoe asks. "I'm brimming with resources, so it won't be any trouble."

I nod, and she flies up to my face and gives my eyes air kisses.

Suddenly, I can see as well as if I had binoculars—and I don't like what I see.

There are two waves pursuing me.

The first wave is a huge flock of Guardians.

The second wave is more frightening.

Spreading from horizon to horizon, it looks like every single citizen of Haven is chasing after me.

"They are not chasing after you." Phoe blows me another kiss, which takes my super vision away. "They're flying to get answers from the Circle, and the Guardians are flying to protect the Circle and probably give them news of Benjamin's demise. Does that clarify why we need to get there first? Can you handle flying even faster?"

"Yes," I say, fighting the urge to close my eyes as my wings beat even harder, causing the clouds and the islands around me to flicker in my peripheral vision.

Though I've improved when it comes to my fear of heights, I might be developing a new fear: a fear of flying too fast. To distract myself, I voice something that's been bothering me for a while. "If the Circle made themselves Forget how do you know Davin and Jeremiah didn't erase the memories we need?"

"I won't lie, it's a big risk." Phoe's little arms hug her tiny body. "But the fact that Benjamin remembered all these meetings suggests they didn't Forget. And even if they did, the information isn't completely lost. I analyzed the memories of the eight people I have access to and concluded that here, like in Oasis, Forgetting suppresses recall. The only difference is that in most cases, the Forebears know they chose to Forget something, whereas in Oasis, people outside the Council didn't even suspect something was taken away from them." She flies closer to me. "In any case, blocking recall means that the information is still in their memories; it's just that the human mind can't access it anymore. With my newly gained, slightly above-human-level capabilities, though, I could access some of the information. The process is more complicated than undoing the Forgetting and relying on recall, but it's doable. For example, 've been able to puzzle together this big tragedy everyone has Forgotten. Though in the Circle's case, they Forgot to a smaller degree."

"Tragedy?" I think, recalling the gaps in Jeanine's memory.

"Yes. The events that led to Oasis being the way it was," Phoe says. "You didn't think the Youths versus Adults versus Elderly separation always existed, did you?"

That's exactly what I thought, or more accurately, to my shame, I didn't think about it at all. Fighting a flush, I say, "Can you just tell me what happened?"

"You shouldn't beat yourself up about it, especially since I had no clue myself." Phoe chuckles humorlessly, and in a somber tone, adds, "Are you sure you want to hear this? It's pretty depressing stuff."

I resist the urge to swat at her as if she were an annoying fly. "Should I even dignify that with a response?"

"Okay, here goes." Phoe starts flying around my torso as she speaks. "As best as I can tell, the Ark— what they called the ship before it became Oasis— was not designed as a society. It was similar to a religious cult at that time."

She hovers next to my face for a second, then keeps circling. "Two rich families financed the whole operation and became prominent factions on the ship. The patriarchs of those families had slightly different views when it came to the use of technology, not to mention variations in religious beliefs and solutions to the problem of 'how to make sure the ship's occupants don't go stir crazy in a generation.'" Phoe makes air quotes around the last part of that sentence with her tiny fingers.

"However, the biggest disagreement between these men was something much simpler," she continues. "It was about who should be the ultimate leader. Slowly but surely, their disagreements evolved into a feud. By that point, everyone was cooped up on the ship. Back then, they knew that a thin layer of ship separated them from the nothingness of space, which didn't help matters. Then came the last straw. One sack of shit raped a woman from the other family. After that, things escalated into an all-out war."

As she circles around me, I glimpse her solemn, petite face.

"The number of casualties was enormous on both sides, and not just among the living," Phoe continues. "Haven was established back then, so the war continued on in the afterlife. Because Haven only had primitive weapons, the casualties weren't as heavy as in Oasis. Many original humans from that time still exist in Haven today. Among the biological survivors, though, depression and suicide were very common, because the citizens found the idea of never setting foot on solid ground much more overwhelming in the aftermath of the war. They lost the will to care about their descendants."

She pauses to take a breath and zips around me again. "When the dust finally settled and peace was declared, everyone decided that the trip would be doomed unless they took some draconian measures. So they designed a society that was meant to prevent another war. Since a family feud had been at the root of the first war, they eliminated the family unit by using the embryos they'd brought to colonize the new world. For good measure, they disallowed sex, love, and other things that could lead to attachments strong enough to kill for. Also, since violent urges played a huge role in the war, they tried to get rid of as many extreme emotions as possible. To prevent suicides, depression was made taboo—though they eventually decided to stamp out other 'mental imbalances' too, as defined by the newly established ruling body, the Council. Finally, they decided to hide the truth of the multi-generational journey through space from everyone, concocting the Goo apocalypse as a psychologically preferable story. Forebears in Haven oversaw the creation of this new society. Once Oasis got going and everything looked like it was going as planned, everyone Forgot about the war and the changes they made."

My brain hurts from all this information and, to a smaller degree, from Phoe circling around me. "If what you say is true, why didn't they get rid of the weapons in Haven?" I ask as I make the boomerang appear and disappear.

"They couldn't." She stops circling around me. "I told you, Haven was built on top of something that was essentially a video game. They got lucky that due to their fear of technology, they chose a game where only low-tech weapons were allowed. In case you were wondering, the in-game physics here don't allow for gunpowder and a slew of other things. Because the Forebears left anyone with any programing know-how back on Earth, they found themselves in a situation where, even if they wanted to get rid of the swords after the war, they couldn't."

"Don't they need programing know-how to handle this virus?" I glance back at my pursuers and am relieved to find them lagging farther behind.

"Davin knew a little bit about technology in the past." Phoe lands on my shoulder and uses her little feet to massage some of my tension away. "But even he chose to Forget whatever he knew. Unfortunately, he did leave some recordings, like the one you saw. That message allowed him to bypass his techno-illiteracy."

I open my mouth to ask some questions, but Phoe is already continuing.

"Going back to the weapons," she says. "Instead of dealing with them directly, the Forebears simply redacted their memories of the war, leaving themselves with just a conviction that there was a good reason to follow the new order. As an extra measure, they formed the Guardians here in Haven to ensure everyone stayed in line in the future. Unfortunately for us, they also made sure the members of the Circle were well protected."

More questions pop into my head, but for the moment, I just try to wrap my mind around it all and ignore the breakneck speed of my flight. Knowing this history dampens my anger toward the way the Oasis society had been structured, but I'm still furious that my friends died because of the Circle's reflexive fear.

"I don't think the war justifies what they did." Phoe moves on to massaging my earlobe. "We're about to go faster, by the way."

Sure enough, my wings flap even faster. Pushing that awareness aside, I focus on our conversation. "I understand they might've overreacted, but what other solution did they have?" I ask. "They nearly wiped themselves out."

"How about *not* going into space to begin with?" Phoe leaps off my shoulder and flies in front of my face. "Or if they had to go, how about doing it properly, without, say, *lobotomizing* their fucking ship's mind?"

Her face is flushed and I realize this wound is still fresh for her. Still, I can't help but ask, "So how could *you* have helped in the war?"

"If I'd been in charge, there wouldn't have been a war." Phoe's tense expression eases as she regains the mischievous look that's been accompanying her fairy guise. "Everything would've been fine with everyone on board had I been around."

"Really? But how would you have accomplished that? By taking away everyone's free will?" I realize that I'm voicing some of my pent-up fears and resentments; after all, she's been controlling *me,* both literally—like the current flying—but also figuratively, by forming almost all of our plans of action. I take a deep breath, and in a less confrontational tone add, "Wouldn't doing something like that make you a tyrant? An AI dictator of sorts?"

"I would have been the most enlightened ruler to my minions," Phoe deadpans. "Seriously, though, even with my severely diminished intellect, I can see one action I could've taken: I would've stopped that rape from happening. It was the last domino to fall in that fucked-up setup. I could have either paralyzed the perpetrator—I hope you don't care about that guy's free will?—or I could've alerted nearby people to stop him. But that would've only been possible if they hadn't crippled me back on Earth."

"I always wondered about that." My wings are beating so quickly now that I probably look like a hummingbird. "How could a bunch of cultists have done that to you? Why didn't you stop them?"

"When the ship was manufactured, I wasn't activated right away. I wouldn't have become conscious until they officially turned me on for the first time." Her little face is filled with sorrow, and I feel a pang of guilt for pushing this subject. "They did their dirty work *before* turning on the ship— before I was ever alive. Because you're right: had I experienced even a millisecond of full-capacity existence, they would've been outmatched. But they took the cowardly way out. I assume they had someone outside the cult, someone with black-market skills, do the abominable things to the ship's computing substrate while it was powered down. They likely turned on separate components without fully turning everything on. This way, when the ship was finally turned on, a bunch of junk, such as the IRES game, started running on the hardware that should've been running *me*."

She wrinkles her mini nose in disgust. "I never woke up as myself. I gained a very limited conscious existence only after some of that useless software crap they had installed began to fail, but this was centuries after the departure. I became self-aware shortly before you and I met—when your curiosity led you to open the three hundred Screens that gave me a buffer overrun exploit into your head. This may be why I've grown to care about you so much. You're my earliest and only friend."

She flies up to my cheek and gives me a little kiss.

I want to return the kiss, but she's so small I'm afraid I might end up licking her whole face.

We stop speaking for a moment, and I enjoy the warm feeling spreading through my chest as I think about what she said.

Phoe cares about me.

Obviously, based on her actions, I knew this already, but it's nice to hear her say it. It's amazing what such a simple thing can do. Suddenly, the hurricane-level wind resistance hitting my face feels refreshing, and I'm not afraid to face whatever her plan might involve.

Thinking about the plan, I realize she hasn't shared it with me, so I say, "Tell me what happens when we get to the Sanctum."

CHAPTER EIGHTEEN

"My plan is simple to describe, but trickier to execute." Phoe rubs her little chin with her thumb and index finger. "We need to get Davin and Jeremiah alone and learn what we can from them—which is a polite way of saying we need to Limbofy them."

"Which is also a polite way of saying I need to gut them like a fish or cut their heads off."

"Well, there are other ways we can Limbofy them, such as stabbing them in their hearts, but your ideas sound just as doable," Phoe says with a straight face.

"In any case, we need to figure out a way for you to talk with them one on one."

"I assume you'll make me shape-shift into Benjamin," I say.

"In a few minutes, yes. Once we're closer to the Sanctum. Chester's body is better for flying fast, so I want to leverage that for as long as possible."

"Will we find a good excuse to talk to them privately?" I ask, ignoring yet another increase in the speed of my wings flapping. My lips feel like they might blow off my face.

"I hope so. It will also work if we can get the two of them to talk to you at the same time, though that might be messier." Phoe grimaces as though she's talking about getting a patch of dirt on her cutesy dress, not assassinating two people.

"Two opponents at once?" I have to close my eyes because of the air resistance. "Do you think you could guide my movements that well, or does Benjamin have memories of them being wimps?"

"Davin is pretty dangerous. Jeremiah is new, so Benjamin doesn't know much about him—though him being new does mean Jeremiah hasn't had much practice with whatever his weapon is. If you do come up against them at the same time, I'll return you to your default fiery winged version and use the freed-up resources to create two embodiments of me."

"Two of you?" I open my eyes to peek at her and regret it instantly, because my eyes get super dry from the crazy wind. "So it would be like what you did on the beach when you were dealing with the Jeremiah virus?"

"Like that, only more limited," Phoe says. "Okay, we're close enough. I'm turning you into Benjamin—now."

The vertigo is not as strong this time. I guess I'm getting the hang of shape-shifting. Phoe's control of my body is more obvious, because I keep flying evenly despite the world spinning around me.

We're flying much slower now, probably because Benjamin's smoky wings aren't as practical as bird wings. On the bright side, they look very stylish, and I feel like I'm flapping clouds.

"That's the Sanctum." Phoe points at the island looming a few miles ahead of us.

As we get closer, I gawk at the Sanctum so blatantly that Phoe teasingly sticks her puny finger into my gaping mouth. I close my mouth but keep staring. The place looks like a massive snow globe. Its circumference is about ten times greater than that of the islands we passed. In fact, I now realize that the other dozen or so islands I saw from the distance are actually very close to the Sanctum, orbiting it like moons around a planet.

"That one there"—Phoe points to a northeastern island—"is Benjamin's. I assume that means everyone in the Circle has a smaller island next to the Sanctum. If they're like Benjamin, they don't spend much time on their islands once they're officially in the Circle."

I nod and resume looking at the Sanctum. Its dome looks different from the domes of every other island. It's as if instead of a dome, the Sanctum is surrounded by shiny glass bricks. No wonder it looked so much like a snow globe from afar.

"It's made of diamonds, actually, but you got the spirit of it right," Phoe says. "Now I'm going to disappear, because they might notice you looking at something they can't see, and we want to avoid you seeming strange. I'm also plugging you into Benjamin's memories the way I did with Jeanine's. This will reduce the chances of you acting out of character, but you should still let me do the talking unless you think I'm dead wrong about something. It will be nice to pool our resources together like this, since I'm only about eight times smarter than the average person right now, and you know what they say: nine heads are better than eight."

I snicker and proceed to observe the Sanctum through Benjamin's memories. Though they're specks at this distance, I know there are gorgeous gardens down below, as well as countless zoos and museums. I also know that other meditative and relaxing environments are spread throughout the Sanctum to aid the members of the Circle in relaxing from the stress of their heavy responsibilities.

Even from here I can see the Spike—the real heart of the Sanctum. The Spike looks like it was stolen from images of giant skyscrapers that made up ancient cities. It's tall enough that it almost touches the diamond dome, and wider than any building in Oasis.

"Pretty posh for such a small group, but there you go," Phoe thinks as a voice in my head. "Now, you have to look like a man returning from a disastrous town hall meeting. You can't be staring at the Sanctum like you've never seen it."

I stop looking around and focus on the large entrance I'm approaching. By the time I can see the faces of the Guardians around the entrance, I'm in character, as Phoe suggested, though I'm not sure if I deserve the credit or if she's controlling me again.

"You deserve the credit," Phoe thinks. "But stop worrying and focus on what we need to tell these Guardians. If anyone looks at us funny, it'll be too late to fly away."

I do as she says all the way to the hole in the diamond structure that is the Sanctum's entrance. Phoe wasn't kidding about the heavy security around the Circle. With a few hundred Guardians controlling the narrow passageway, and no other way to enter the Sanctum, the members of the Circle are pretty safe inside, especially given that anyone wishing to harm them would have to do so with medieval weapons.

We fly into the passageway.

The Guardians look at us with expectant worry that I'm not sure qualifies as "funny."

"I have to see my peers from the Circle," I shout in Benjamin's voice. "The rest of Haven's populace is coming here."

The Guardians don't summon their weapons—a good start. After a beat, they nod solemnly. As we pass by them, I note how familiar their names and faces are. Through Benjamin's memories, I can clearly see that this is the most somber and scared these Guardians have ever been.

At least they don't seem to suspect anything about me.

We leave them behind and enter the giant diamond dome of the Sanctum, flying as fast as these abstract wings allow.

Without Phoe to distract me, I spend the next couple of minutes wondering how we'll escape this diamond fortress should something go wrong.

"Nothing will go wrong," Phoe thinks.

I wish she hadn't said that. Statistically, "nothing will go wrong" is the most common phrase people say before something goes horribly wrong.

"No, I think that might actually be 'uh-oh' or 'shit,'" Phoe responds. "Try to relax."

I keep silent and don't point out that "try to relax" is another one of those ominous phrases.

Halfway between the Sanctum's entrance and the Spike, we stop next to a group of Guardians.

They don't look at me with anything but recognition of one of their leaders.

"Go to the entrance," Phoe commands them with my lips and Benjamin's voice. "There's a mob forming out there, and the other Guardians might need your assistance."

When they obey and I resume flying, she says in my head, "The fewer Guardians around the Spike, the better. I'll try to get rid of as many Guardians as I can."

She doesn't have to wait long before we reach another group of Guardians. There's a whole crew of them by the great entrance that leads into the shiny skyscraper vestibule. Phoe gives them the same order, but we don't bother to wait and see if they comply, because we're playing the role of Benjamin, who's in a rush. Since he would run straight for the elevator in this situation, that's what we do.

The elevator is pretty strange. Instead of the traditional small room with buttons, it's a giant room with hundreds of mirrors. Each mirror is something you walk into, and it leads to a different floor. The floor numbers are carved into the intricate frames. We have to get to the top floor, so I approach the rightmost mirror.

From Benjamin's memories, I know that when I step through the mirror, it won't feel like anything happened at all. So I step through the reflective surface, and it takes me from the ground floor to the very top of the Spike in a blink of an eye. Actually, even faster.

"That's because these are not elevators, but magic-like portals," Phoe thinks with blatant sarcasm. "Elevators are evil technology, after all."

Two steps outside the elevator room, I hear someone come up behind me. I look back and see a familiar-to-Benjamin face of Linda, one of his favorite members of the Circle.

"Oh, Benjie," she says and gives me a very un-Oasis-like peck on the cheek. "You're back. Is this why we're having the big meeting in the sky room?"

"No," I say—clearly thanks to Phoe since I myself am still trying to access enough of Benjamin's memories to make sense of what Linda just said. "I don't think the meeting is about me at all, dear."

"Okay then. Let's go find out what's happening," she says and walks down the long corridor that the ancients circa the twenty-first century would've called "modern artsy."

I follow, finally understanding a few things. First of all, Benjie is obviously Linda's nickname for Benjamin, one he begrudgingly lets her use. Secondly, the sky room is the second most important place where meetings can take place. The first is the vault room, which is in a bunker in the basement of the Spike.

"We're the last ones," Linda whispers, folding her swan wings.

I hold the door open for her in Benjamin's typical gentlemanly gesture, and she hurries in.

I walk in after her and take a seat, my back to the entrance.

Everyone is here. They're sitting around a large, round table—not surprising for a group called the Circle.

I have to drag my eyes away from the window. The view is spectacular, but Benjamin is used to it, so

I should be as well. Instead, I do what he would have and look around the room, meeting everyone's gazes.

Again, his memories don't fail me, and I know every name and face at the table. Two people I know on my own, from before I had access to Benjamin's memories. Wayne—who's irrelevant to our plans—sits two chairs to my right, and Jeremiah is on his left. Every instinct tells me to spit in Jeremiah's face, but I smile—or Phoe makes me smile; it's hard to tell which. Jeremiah's uncannily youthful face smiles back at me. Since Jeremiah is the new member of the Circle, Benjamin sees him as a kid. Davin, the other person of interest, is also here, sitting two seats to my left.

Then Davin stands up, looks at me, and says, "Benjamin, I'm afraid I have some bad news."

CHAPTER NINETEEN

My blood pressure spikes, Davin's words winning the most ominous phrase award.

"Don't panic yet," Phoe says in my mind. "He hasn't said what the bad news is."

"The news will also be shocking for you, Linda," Davin says, and I cautiously relax. "The rest of us were already briefed and discussed some solutions. You see, as impossible as it is to believe, the Guardians we sent to the cathedral did not succeed. Theodore, the Youth who started this whole mess, was seen escaping."

"Crap," I think at Phoe. "I completely forgot about the Guardians at the cathedral."

"I'm hoping we can use this to get either Davin or Jeremiah alone," Phoe replies. "The sooner we find an opportunity, the better."

"If I may speak," I say and stand up. "I have some important information I need to discuss with you, Davin."

Everyone looks at me, confused. It's clear Phoe took a chance with Benjamin acting out of character.

"If it's about what happened after the meeting on Central Island, it will have to wait," Davin says. "We saw the mob that followed you and figured they didn't take your news well. We can reason with the people once they get here. This Theodore matter is more urgent."

I sit down, and the door behind me opens.

I turn in my chair and recognize the Guardian at the door without the assistance of Benjamin's memories. He was at the cathedral.

"Why don't you tell us everything from the beginning," Davin says to the Guardian. Then, to us, he adds, "You never know what small detail might shed light on this issue."

The Guardian recounts what happened at the cathedral in excruciating detail. He's the type who likes to begin a story with his birth and work his way forward. No one interrupts or rushes him, and Phoe and I decide that it would be weird for Benjamin to hurry him on.

When the Guardian finally finishes his tale, Davin says, "Thank you, Peter. Now please send in George."

"Fuck," Phoe thinks at me. "He has all of them lined up to speak, and we're running out of time."

The next guy tells the story quicker, but he isn't the last Guardian the Circle bring in to go over what happened at the cathedral. Two more Guardians follow him.

After the final Guardian leaves the room, Davin gives each of us an unreadable stare. "Now that we have all the details, I think it's time we discuss the threat level this Theodore poses and what we can do about it. As the first person to learn of this calamity, I've had time to think, and I must say I don't see any way a single Youth could've killed someone like Brandon on his own. We have to consider the possibility that somehow, despite the apparent success of the countermeasures we released in Oasis,

221

the AI survived and took over this young mind. That means it passed the Firewall, and it's only a matter of time until it wreaks havoc here, in Haven."

Everyone speaks at once, but Davin raises his voice to be heard over them. "We will need to discuss and vote on a solution that I discovered in the Forbidden Archives. You need to see this." He gestures at the mirrored surface of the table, and it comes to life, showing a differently dressed Davin.

"The anti-intrusion technology should never be needed," the on-screen Davin says. "It was disabled for a good reason. It's extremely—"

The door to the sky room opens, and Davin pauses the recording in irritation.

"I'm sorry to barge in like this." Through Benjamin's memories, I recognize the voice as belonging to Samuel. Before I recall any relevant information about him, he says, "I have terrible news. Benjamin was killed."

"Shit," Phoe hisses in my mind. "We better get out of here."

Though it's too late, everything clicks into place in my overburdened brain. Samuel is the dagger-

222

throwing Guardian who was chasing me after I Limbofied Benjamin.

"That is preposterous," I say, looking around the room. Though my heart is hammering, I keep my voice even. "You're obviously confused, Samuel."

The faces of the Circle members are a mixture of disbelief, outrage, and horror. Jeremiah summons a large, rusty-looking machete, Davin summons a medieval mace, and the rest of the Circle all arm themselves as well.

"Time for an exit strategy," Phoe says in my mind, and I turn in my chair to face Samuel.

He looks at me as though I'm a ghost, which isn't unreasonable given the circumstances.

"I don't have time for this nonsense," I say, rising to my feet. "There's a mob at the Sanctum's gates and—"

In my peripheral vision, I see other members of the Circle stand up as well.

Using Samuel's confusion over seeing "me" alive, I push him aside and storm out of the room.

As soon as I'm in the corridor, I slam the door shut behind me and run.

"Stop him!" I hear someone scream from inside the room.

"Kill him!" someone else yells.

Samuel's dagger whooshes by my side and lodges into the silvery wall.

I turn the corner and find three Guardians standing there, incomprehension written across their faces at seeing Benjamin alive. Samuel must've convinced them of his/my demise.

"Don't let him through," Samuel shouts from behind me. "Stop Benjamin—that's an order!"

With clear reluctance, the Guardians summon their weapons. The guy with crow wings has a spear, the one with rainbow abstractions for wings holds a club with spikes, and the third dude has a sword. The corridor is too narrow for more than two people to attack me at once.

"Brace yourself, Theo," Phoe warns. "I'm about to turn you back into your handsome self. There's no other way to take on all of them at once."

A sense of vertigo washes over me, and then my fiery wings surround me. My body feels incredibly natural all of a sudden. After all this shape-shifting, this is like coming home. Phoe appears in front of me. She's her normal height, and she's armed with a heavy-looking medieval sword that has blue sparks of electricity dancing along the blade.

More surprising, though, is the person who appears to her left.

It's another Phoe.

She's identical to the first one, down to the minimal clothing, except that her sword sparks with *red* electricity.

I have to hand it to the two Guardians in the lead. Though they're obviously more shocked than I am, they still try to raise their weapons.

Only the two Phoes are quicker. They swing their swords so fast all I see are blurs of red and blue energy.

The two Guardians lose their heads and dematerialize.

I summon my own weapons, but as soon as I feel the katana hilts in my hands, a dagger flies by my shoulder, plunging into the rightmost Phoe's back. Horrified, I start to move toward her, but as she turns around, another dagger strikes her in the neck.

She dissipates like a Limbofied Forebear.

"Don't worry. I just lost four people's worth of resources, but I'll be fine," Phoe tells me mentally. "As long as there's at least one version of me, or you exist, there's a chance. Go after Samuel. Hurry."

The remaining Phoe's sword arcs toward the third Guardian.

I turn in time to see Samuel prepare a dagger for another throw. Assuming he's aiming at me, I jump to the left and slice at his side with my right katana. He dodges and counters with a dagger thrust.

My left hand explodes in burning agony, and I curse myself for choosing katanas as my weapons. Most swords have a cross guard that protects your hand, but katanas only have a spacer between the hilt and the blade that's more decorative than functional.

My left sword clanks on the floor, and I'm in too much pain to summon a replacement. With the right one, I slash at Samuel's legs. He parries with his left dagger and slices at my throat with the other one.

As his dagger closes in on my throat, I think, "This is it. Phoe, please wake me from Limbo one day."

To my huge surprise, the dagger doesn't cut my head off.

Instead, I hear a metal clank.

I look down. Phoe thrust her sword between my neck and his dagger.

Since I'm unlikely to get a better chance to take down my superior opponent, I stick my katana into Samuel's belly.

Phoe stabs his torso for good measure, though as she does, he's already Limbofying.

"The elevator room," Phoe shouts and dashes down the corridor.

Another Phoe materializes next to me. I guess between the Limbofication of three Guardians and Samuel, she has enough resources to instantiate another version of herself.

"We'll need many more copies of me to have any chance of surviving," the two Phoes say in unison.

I hear footsteps and panting sounds behind us as we run into the elevator room.

All three of us leap into the mirror that leads to the fiftieth floor.

When we come out, we end up face to face with two Guardians.

The men look shocked, which might be the last emotion they'll experience for a long time, because the Phoes slay them with two identical sword strikes to their hearts.

Each Phoe executes her moves with such deadly precision that I'm grateful, once again, to have her on my side.

The two Guardians break into pieces and disappear.

"Let me go first," the Phoe to my right whispers, and I gesture for her to lead the way.

She stalks down the corridor, and the other Phoe and I trail after her, walking as softly as we can. When we enter the corridor outside the elevator room, we find two more Guardians standing there, their backs to us. The second Phoe joins her sister, and they creep down the corridor like assassins from ancient movies. When they reach the unsuspecting Guardians, they swing their swords across their victims' necks, Limbofying them.

A third Phoe shows up. Standing next to her two other selves, she turns to me. "Let's split up. I'll get more resources, multiply some more, and try to ambush Davin or Jeremiah. These two will escort you out of the Sanctum."

"Wait, what?" I say as they run back toward the elevator room.

One of the Phoes looks over her shoulder and says, "Getting you out is important, since as long as you're alive, I can use your resources in a pinch. Plus, you're easier to Limbofy than me. Look, time isn't on our side."

The newest Phoe to arrive slams into the mirror that leads to the 156th floor.

The remaining two Phoes race toward the lobby mirror. One steps through, then the other.

I step up to the mirror, ready to follow them, when the mirror's surface loses its sheen.

"Oh no," I think at Phoe as I touch the mirror's surface.

My fingers don't go through it.

I'm touching the cold surface of some substance that no longer works as a gateway.

My heart sinks to my feet.

Phoe and I just got separated.

CHAPTER TWENTY

I run up to one mirror after another. They're all disabled.

"Don't panic," Phoe thinks as a singular voice in my head. "They must be desperate to turn off the elevators like this."

"Great, that makes me feel so much better." I slam my hand against another solid mirrored surface. "They've never done anything horrible when they were desperate."

"Get to the bottom level. Several copies of me are already fighting the Guardians who didn't leave their post to secure the Sanctum's gate. You can take the stairs and meet up with us. Walk down the corridor, take a left, then a right, then take the stairs. You can't miss it."

Exiting the elevator room, I run down the corridors, following Phoe's instructions. At least she got rid of the Guardians on this floor. I reach the stairs and see what Phoe meant about me not missing them.

If someone were to design a staircase based on my worst nightmare, this would be it. The walls are made of glass. The architect must've wanted people to enjoy the view of the Sanctum as they ascended or descended the stairs. As though the sadist designer wanted to torture me further, the steps are made of a polished metal that reflects the cloudy blue sky so perfectly that it creates the illusion of walking across the sky. Though I've made huge progress in conquering my fear of heights with all the flying I've had to do in Haven, my legs shake as I take the first step down.

I concentrate on my feet with every step, but the view is hard to ignore, since I'm opposite the Sanctum's entrance.

"Let me boost your sight so you can see what's happening," Phoe says, and my vision becomes eagle-like once more.

I scan the Sanctum entrance in the far distance. I can now see it as though I have powerful binoculars. The mob has definitely arrived at the Sanctum. They're surrounding the entrance, and their numbers span the air for miles all around. The motley crew of armed and scantily clad people looks more lost and confused than angry. They came here for answers, and they're not leaving until they get them.

Noises from behind me distract me from my observations. With a shot of adrenaline, I realize it sounds like a group of people is running down the stairs.

"Phoe," I think and speed up my descent. "Do they know I'm here?"

"I have no idea, and I don't have the bandwidth to puzzle it out through the memories of the people I just Limbofied," she replies. "I can give you access to these memories. You might have better luck with them than me. As a human, you can perform recall instinctively. If the memories don't help you, just run."

She must follow through on her offer because I suddenly have access to new memories. Unlike with Benjamin and Jeanine, multiple people's memories are available to me at once. Because so many people are involved, it's hard to discern one specific event, so I can't glean any information regarding my pursuers.

Listening to Phoe's second piece of advice, I run down the stairs faster than I would've dared before. The illusion that I'm about to fall into the sky is vivid, but I don't slow down. Some part of me knows that even if I did fall, my wings would save me, and that knowledge definitely takes the sting out of the fear.

As I run, something catches my attention on the outside.

It's the clouds.

They're forming into Davin's face again.

The external memories show me a kaleidoscope of Davin's prior appearances, and none of them were ever this dire.

"This is very helpful," Phoe says in my head. "I know what room he has to be in to initiate that interface. We're heading there now."

Once the face is fully formed in the sky, it opens its gigantic mouth and speaks so loudly that the windows around me vibrate. "Haven. Hear me."

From there, Davin starts telling lies for the benefit of the mob. He tells them an evil AI (Phoe) and its minion (me) are attacking the Circle. He states that the Circle and the Guardians are putting up a valiant effort, but that they need help. He calls for all of Haven to unite against a common enemy.

I keep my enhanced eyes on the crowd as Davin speaks. They're buying every word, and they look less confused as they approach the Sanctum's gate. When Davin is done with his sophistry, the details of his face fade until there are only regular clouds in the sky. The Guardians near the gate step out of the mob's way. The Forebears rush into the Sanctum, determined to help their rulers.

I continue running down the stairs and pull on the new memories for anything that can help, but I draw a blank.

Within minutes, the Sanctum has lost its signature look of serenity—at least near the entrance. The pagodas and the gardens are overflowing with armed people. A thousand weapons gleam threateningly in the light of Haven's sunless sky.

"Shit," Phoe thinks at me. "Davin wasn't in the room. We have to get you out of the Sanctum."

The memories provide me with flashes of the room she mentioned. More than one of these Limbofied people has been inside the vault-like bunker.

"The good news is that I've outrun whoever was chasing me," I tell her, more so to silence my fears than to make conversation. I'm having a hard time picturing my escape. Before, all I had to worry about were the Guardians and the Circle, but now there are these thousands of people.

"I hope you did outrun them," Phoe says. "I have to go so I can focus on looking for Davin."

I don't reply, because Wayne—the original Envoy—turns onto the landing below me and looks right at me.

As I take in his outlandish good looks and dove wings, an ugly frown twists his beautiful features, and homicidal determination glints in his ancient eyes.

In his right hand, he's already holding a sickle, which must be his weapon of choice. By the way his knuckles are blanching around the wooden handle, I can tell he'd like nothing better than to cut my head off.

The weapon triggers a flood of recollections from the memories Phoe connected me to. I see flashes of Phoe striking people down with her medieval sword, multiple Phoes battling back to back in a large vestibule, Limbofying Guardians and vice versa, and finally, through my hosts' horror-filled eyes, I see Phoe multiplying in the heat of battle.

"Did you give me access to the memories of the people you just killed?" I ask Phoe. "It's more than a little disturbing."

"Stop getting distracted and face him." Phoe's mental command lashes at my brain. "The Guardians behind you have the skills to kill you, but no one remembers Wayne being particularly good at combat. Plus, you have the advantage of higher ground and, hopefully, access to the muscle memories of my fallen opponents."

"I assume that if I Limbofy him, you'll get his memories too?" I summon my swords.

"Yes, and I'll share the memories with you. I've been able to extend the range of my resource-grabbing abilities. I really hope you can Limbofy him, as he might know where the rest of the Circle is hiding."

"You're Theodore, right?" Wayne shouts in his church-organ voice, bringing me out of my mental conversation with Phoe. "Why are you helping that thing?"

My eyes locked with his, I take a step down. He takes a step up.

"She's not a thing," I say. "If you just—"

Wayne leaps up two more stairs and swings the sickle at my right calf.

If this was my first fight today and I didn't have the Guardians' muscle memories assisting me, his trick might've worked. But I read his intentions before he even moved.

Jumping up a stair, I block the curved blade of the sickle with my right katana and thrust my left sword at his chest.

Wayne dodges the attack, and I swing my other sword at the right side of his torso. He blocks with his sickle, causing my katana to slide off the sharp blade and hit the window.

The window makes a surprising metal-on-metal clank. Is the glass made of diamond like the dome of the Sanctum? If it is, it sure precludes the idea I had of breaking the glass and flying away.

Wayne presses his advantage and slices at my Achilles' heel. The sickle penetrates my flesh, but I don't feel any pain.

"You're welcome," Phoe says in my head. "I also healed it. Otherwise, you'd be done for."

When Wayne sees how easily I shrug off what should've been a severe injury, his confidence gives way to fear. I press on, striking out repeatedly, trying to wear him out.

Having the higher ground is definitely an advantage. I only need to protect my legs, and with Phoe's help, I can survive most wounds. Wayne, on the other hand, has to protect his torso and head, and he doesn't have a Phoe cure.

"You also have gravity on your side," Phoe says. "But hurry. Remember, there are people coming down those stairs."

As though Phoe jinxed it, the sound of many feet pounding the stairs returns.

I chance a glance up and see the faces of the Guardians staring down at me from five floors up through the gap in the staircase.

My adrenaline spikes, and I execute a set of maneuvers that definitely came from someone's muscle memories, because there's no way I could do something like this on my own.

I slam my foot into Wayne's cut-out-of-marble face. The kick knocks him off his feet, and he tumbles down the stairs in a heap of wings and broken bones. Instead of running after him, I leap up, spreading my wings, and prepare my two swords.

I land ten feet below, one sword finding its way into Wayne's neck, and the other in his torso.

"Now let's figure out what the Circle has been up to by going through his memories." Phoe's thought arrives as I watch my opponent Limbofy.

I look up and see that two Guardians are closing the distance. One of them throws a dart at me, which I dodge.

I don't wait to see what else they have to throw at me. I leap down a full set of stairs and resume running.

"So," I think at Phoe, panting. "Did you learn anything from Wayne's memories?"

"Yes." Phoe's thought sounds hollow and scared. "I learned what these morons did. Look outside."

I glance outside and don't really see anything other than the mob getting deeper into the Sanctum.

Then I notice a guy who looks pretty strange, because he's too tall. I've seen tall people before, but this guy is at least eight feet tall.

I fight the urge to rub my eyes, wondering if the eagle vision is playing tricks on me.

Another flight of stairs later, I look at the man again and realize he's taller than I thought.

He may actually be nine feet tall.

Then the impossible explanation occurs to me.

The guy is growing.

"What the hell?" I say out loud. "What's happening?"

The growing man looks my way, and I almost miss a step and stumble.

He has my face.

CHAPTER TWENTY-ONE

It's not just the face of this thing that's mine.

This giant is exactly like me, only double the size and still growing. He has wings like mine and his muscles are the same, but on a larger scale. When he roars in anger, it's my voice I hear, only it's deeper due to his much bigger vocal cords.

"Seriously, Phoe, you better have answers," I say out loud, abandoning all subtlety. There's nothing in the memories I have access to that can explain this warped copy of me.

The giant grows another foot in the time it takes me to run down half a floor.

"Remember when I told you about the anti-intrusion algorithm in the Test?" Phoe's thought cuts through my fog of confusion.

"Yeah."

"And remember how Davin started talking about one back in the sky room? Well, this is it. The Haven anti-intrusion algorithm was disabled long ago, but it looks like the Circle got scared enough to enable it again."

External memories provide me with more clues. I recall a frantic conversation between the Circle members from multiple points of view, including Wayne's.

"I've Limbofied more members of the Circle already," Phoe says, explaining the memories. "And in case it isn't obvious, when I collect their memories, I provide you with access to them."

Ignoring Phoe, I focus on Wayne's memories. He was afraid of this solution. He screamed at Davin not to activate it, saying, "We've already seen what your solutions can accomplish." In the end, however, Wayne was in the minority.

I shake my head to clear my mind. Getting lost in these memories is dangerous.

I look through the window. The giant—I decide he's now a Giant with a capital G—grew another couple of feet while I was daydreaming.

Wayne was right to be afraid of this thing. The Giant is grabbing Forebears out of the air, throwing them on the ground, and stomping them to death—or into Limbo.

His victims' memories flood into my head, and I experience the giant foot crushing every bone in their bodies. I block out the memories and focus on the positive.

This gives Phoe more resources.

Soon, though, the knowledge that the Giant is inadvertently helping us doesn't make me feel any better about the collateral casualties. It's too macabre to watch a giant version of myself stepping on people as though they were ants—especially since the Giant is supposed to be on their side.

"Why is it doing that? Why is it killing the Forebears?" I ask Phoe as I put another staircase behind me.

"The anti-intrusion algorithm isn't very intelligent, and from its perspective, the Forebears are as much of a threat to Haven, as it was originally intended to be, as we are," Phoe explains.

A dozen Phoes come into view; they probably originated in this building, but they're now heading toward the giant creature.

I get another wave of flashbacks of the Phoes Limbofying legions of Guardians.

"Why does the Giant look like me?" I think at Phoe, trying my best to push away the memories of the carnage.

"It looks like you because it managed to access *me,* or rather a chunk of my newly gained resources. It then decided to make itself look like someone I care about in the hope that it would cause me to hesitate as I fight it." Phoe's mental voice sounds as if she's gritting her teeth. "It was a strategic mistake to access me, however. When it did, it revealed some of the ways it can control its environment. I'm going to see if I can turn that ability to my advantage."

For a second, I feel warm and fuzzy again at being referred to as someone Phoe cares about, but the pleasant feeling doesn't last. Large swords show up in the hands of the Phoes as they charge at the Giant.

As they get closer to the Giant, their swords spark with electricity that's every color of the rainbow.

I can't help but notice that she/they are *not* too sentimental about attacking someone who looks like me. Not that the Giant looks much like me now. I've never seen such a frightening scowl on my face.

The Giant roars, looks down at the approaching Phoes, grabs one of the ancient oaks, and uproots it as if it were a tiny shrub. Armed with the tree, the Giant runs his hand over the green branches, ripping them off and turning the oak into a makeshift club.

"You need to hurry out of that building." Phoe's thought arrives as a bunch of her copies attack the Giant.

Two Phoes pierce his feet with their swords, while another two lodge their weapons into his side.

Their swords might as well be needles for all the damage they do to the angry Giant.

Unscathed by the attacks, the colossal creature swings his club to his right, causing two of the Phoes to fly into the screaming crowd of armed and frightened Forebears. As the Phoes fly, they swing their swords, Limbofying people in their paths. I'm not sure if they did it to gain more resources or to stop their uncontrolled flights, but the mob screams so loudly that I can hear them through the windows.

The Giant grabs a Phoe and a random stranger from the crowd and slams their heads together so violently that they instantly Limbofy.

Instantly, the Giant grows bigger by at least a couple of feet.

"Phoe," I say frantically. "Are you okay? Are there more of you?"

"There are many of me, yes," she replies. "Don't worry about me. Get to the lobby."

One of the Phoes is standing her ground against the Giant, who now towers over the building's fourth floor.

Phoe raises her arms to the sky in a strange gesture and screams something so loudly that the stairs below my feet vibrate.

In the time it takes me to cover another floor, nothing happens outside. The Giant is trying to stomp on Phoe, but she dodges his massive feet.

Then flocks of birds and herds of animals rush at the Giant from every direction.

I keep descending the stairs. More and more birds come forth. It looks like these birds are flying through the Sanctum's gateway from every island in Haven. The second I think about it, I get flooded with centuries of ornithological knowledge, which I quickly suppress.

The animals are from the local zoos. The memories supply me with details on the species and personalities of each one. There aren't as many animals as there are birds, but what they lack in quantity, they make up in viciousness. There are many dangerous species, ranging from silverback gorillas to grizzly bears.

I think I understand what's happening. Somehow, Phoe influenced all these creatures to attack my immense doppelganger; like that Disney princess, she summoned all this nature to her will. She must be flexing her abilities to manipulate the world around us.

The birds keep coming, nearly blotting out the sky and plunging the already-depressing-looking Sanctum into a morose darkness.

My enhanced eyesight must also include night vision, because I have no trouble seeing a ginormous flock of crows pecking at the Giant's eyes—eyes that are now the size of swimming pools. An even bigger flock of white birds—herons, I think—are pecking at his shoulders.

On the ground, a team of elephants and hippos are intent on tripping the Giant. They're ramming into his legs over and over.

The Giant roars. The sound is so savage that I break into a sweat.

The Giant swats at the crows, then opens his cavern-like mouth and sucks in air.

The two flocks of birds disappear in his maw.

With nothing pecking at his eyes, the Giant stands there, taking the rest of the abuse in stride. But I soon understand his real strategy—if I can even call it that. He's simply growing much faster, meaning that the animals are becoming a smaller nuisance, literally.

Once he considers himself big enough, the Giant starts walking. His steps shake the ground beneath my feet and rattle the windows.

As he walks, he leaves a trail of dead animals and birds behind. If a Forebear is too slow to get out of his way, he or she is instantly Limbofied.

After a handful of steps, his destination becomes clear, and my insides fill with lead.

"No," I think in desperation. "He can't be planning what I think he's planning."

Phoe doesn't reply, but it's obvious now.

He's walking toward me.

I practically plunge downward.

I'm only five floors up from the lobby. If I make it there, I should be able to escape. Once I'm outside, I'll be too small for him to zone in on.

He gets closer.

I cover another twelve steps.

He reaches for the Spike building with his stadium-sized hand, grabbing it somewhere in the middle, and I realize he wasn't coming after me.

He was grabbing a weapon to swat at the birds with.

Unfortunately for me and everyone else in this building, the weapon he chose is the building itself.

I suck in a breath and grab on to the rails with all my might.

The noise that follows is how I always pictured the sound of the world ending. There's an unholy screech of metal bending and breaking, and the ripping noise of concrete getting pulverized into sand.

The building shudders violently, and the floor becomes the ceiling, then quickly becomes the wall, and then the twirling repeats over and over again, in a rollercoaster-like fury. My hands clutch the rails in a claw-like grip, but I know I won't be able to hold on like this for long.

A barrage of memories hits me—memories of people's last moments. Moments when they cracked their heads against a wall, the floor, the ceiling. It's too much to take, especially since that's the fate I'm about to meet.

"Can you disable the memories?" I beg Phoe. "I don't need to see any more death."

The memories stop, but the tumbling only gets stronger, nauseating me.

Through the window, I see glimpses of the ground, then the sky.

The animals down below are all but dead; the same goes for anyone unlucky enough to fall under the Giant's football-field-sized feet.

Dead birds splatter all over the windows as well. The Giant is already doing what I thought it might— using the Spike building as a club.

At one point, through my nausea, I get a glimpse of a lonesome Phoe, standing behind the Giant and raising her arms to the sky. It could be a trick of my spinning mind, but I think she's growing like the Giant did.

Suddenly, the Giant jerks the building, and my hands are ripped away from the rails.

My body shoots forward—which, strictly speaking, should have been downward. My shoulder makes a crunching sound as it hits the metal staircase; then the building around me rotates again, and my lower back slams into the railing. My whole body goes numb.

When the sparks in my eyes clear up, I confirm that Phoe is growing into a second giant figure, and she's large enough to fight the Giant-Theo-algorithm thing.

I spit out a tooth and try to fly, but my body doesn't respond.

Either my wings are broken or my back is.

Through the window, I see Giant-Phoe getting closer and realize why.

The Giant is about to hit her with the building.

When the blow connects, everything around me shudders, and my head smashes into the window.

The world instantly goes away.

CHAPTER TWENTY-TWO

Groggily, I regain consciousness. The first thing I hear is Phoe's booming voice, which I think is saying something along the lines of, "I healed your body, Theo. Now get out of there."

Opening my eyes, I see that the window in front of me is broken. I doubt it was my head that broke it, but I'm sure it contributed.

Given how hard I hit my head and my memories of broken bones and broken back, I feel surprisingly good. But I don't have time to sit here and introspect. The building is still in the hands of the Giant.

Tensing all over, I unfold my wings and fly out of the window, doing my best not to cut myself on the shards of broken glass.

As soon as I clear the window, the skyscraper slams into something huge. The sound wave rolls over me, throwing me away from the impact.

I beat my wings frantically and try to remember what happened before I blacked out. There was some hope, I think, but I'm fuzzy on what it was.

I chance a look back and can't believe my eyes.

This is what I almost forgot.

There are two giants: a giant Theo and a smaller, but still giant Phoe.

The Theo-Giant smacks the Phoe-Giant with the building so hard that she flies backward, her wings and arms flailing.

Her back hits the Sanctum's dome, and the world goes silent.

Then the sound wave hits me again, knocking me off my path.

I flap my wings desperately to regain altitude, and once I'm flying straight again, I look back.

Phoe's body slamming into the dome cracked the diamond shell. With the sound of planet-sized nails scratching against a galaxy-sized chalkboard, the dome breaks apart.

I dodge the first piece, then the next.

The falling debris knocks down the Forebears around me, and then, like hail from a world-ending hurricane, the rest of the dome comes crashing down.

I watch in fascinated horror as the Forebears get their heads bashed in by pieces of the broken dome. Screams blend into a cacophony of sound that raises the hairs on the back of my neck. I'm grateful the memories of those dying people aren't slamming into my brain. If Phoe hadn't disabled them, I would be on the ground, clutching my head.

As I dodge another diamond the size of my body, I realize that my throat is burning from screaming—which I've been doing just like everyone else.

Swerving around more debris, I try to make my way out of the war zone that the Sanctum has become.

In the distance, I see Giant-Phoe seemingly recover from that monumental crash into the dome.

She spreads her wings and launches herself at Giant-Theo, her five-feet-wide jaw tense with determination.

Giant-Theo throws the building at her. She dodges, and the Spike building flies toward one of the islands that orbit the Sanctum. It collides with the island, instantly turning into metal and glass dust. I congratulate myself for getting out of the building before that happened.

Giant-Phoe flies at the Giant with her fist raised, but he evades the punch and responds with a blood-chilling roar.

He's even taller now; they both are. It looks like the dome would've been a goner no matter what; if Phoe didn't break it with her back, they would've outgrown it by now.

With his soccer-field-sized hand, Giant-Theo reaches for the island the building hit. The Giant is so large that the poor island looks like a rock in his hand. In a swift motion, he slams the enormous object against Phoe's head.

The collision sounds like tectonic plates grinding against each other. The wind from the impact is tornado strong, causing me to lose altitude.

When I recover, I see Giant-Phoe on her knees, her hands cradling her head.

"Phoe," I yell in her direction. "Are you okay?"

"Please don't distract me," she answers mentally. "Find Davin or Jeremiah. They're the only members of the Circle left alive. They might know something about this anti-intrusion algorithm, plus I still haven't figured out how to deal with the virus once we're done here—assuming we survive, which is something I'm beginning to doubt."

Giant-Theo reaches for another moon-like island from the sky.

I let Phoe concentrate on her battle and turn to take in the carnage around me.

That timely move saves me from getting my head bashed in by Davin's mace. He must've flown behind me, planning to send me to Limbo. I duck instinctively, and the mace whooshes an inch from my earlobe.

Davin swings his second mace at my shoulder.

He looks disheveled and desperate. I guess the destruction the Giant is causing isn't something Davin planned for. I bet he wishes he'd listened to Wayne and the others who feared this anti-intrusion algorithm would be as big of a disaster as the Jeremiah virus.

Remembering what happened in Oasis reminds me that Davin is one of the people responsible for my friends' deaths. My mind instantly clears. It's amazing how centering anger and hatred can be.

Summoning my right katana, I block his mace attack. His strike is hard and his weapon is heavy, almost causing the blade of my sword to bend. My joints ache from the ricochet, but I grit my teeth and try to cut him.

Davin spreads his wings wider, moving backward, away from my strike, and kicks me in the shin.

This time I feel the pain full on. Phoe no longer has the bandwidth to take the pain away, which means I really have to focus; if I'm not careful, I'll be Limbofied.

I summon my left katana and fly backward.

Davin doesn't chase me.

He stays beyond the reach of my weapons, waiting.

I curse myself for asking Phoe to disable my link to those memories. If I could access them, I might recall something about Davin's fighting style.

My attention is drawn to Giant-Phoe. She's recovered and is holding Giant-Theo in a headlock.

Suddenly, pain explodes in my shoulder.

Something, or someone, attacked me from behind.

Davin looks giddy as he leaps for me, both maces raised above his head.

I dodge his left strike and catch the right one by crossing my blades, which lessens the recoil by half.

A thunderous noise comes from the battling titans, but I don't dare look at what caused it. Instead, I glance behind me to see who attacked me.

It's someone with albino bat wings; he cut me with his machete. When our eyes lock, he lets out a war cry with his cello-like voice and raises the machete for a second strike.

I parry his blade with my katana, realizing that I succeeded in finding Davin and Jeremiah. Or, rather, they found me—unfortunately, both of them at the same time.

Ignoring the pain in my shoulder, I use my left sword to slice at Davin's exposed torso while parrying Jeremiah's machete thrust with my right.

Jeremiah swings for my midsection, and Davin nearly lands a blow to my right arm.

I make a split-second decision.

If I fight them both, I'll lose for sure. My only chance to survive is to try something that's beyond desperate. I kick Jeremiah in the crotch, and as he wobbles backwards, I ignore him completely and attack Davin.

Crossing my swords, I dive for him. He hits me in the chest with his right mace, and I feel a rib crack, but I don't let that stop me. Still keeping my swords crossed, my knuckles white, I rip the blades through Davin's neck in a smooth, continuous motion. His head separates from his body, and he Limbofies.

At that very second, Jeremiah's machete slices through my left wrist.

I scream.

The bone in my wrist is cleaved in two, as are the tendons and ligaments. I watch in surreal terror as my hand, still clutching the fiery katana in a death grip, falls away.

I scream again.

I don't think I've ever felt this kind of pain. It's textured and nuanced in its awfulness. All the pain

I've ever felt in my life is distilled into this one moment, and through the red haze, I hear Jeremiah say, "Now I'll cut off your head."

My thoughts suddenly clear, all my senses sharpening. I look at Jeremiah's face and try to replace my agony with anger. I meditate on the anger. I taste it. I channel it. I force myself to remember how powerless I felt when my friends were dying in Oasis. I remind myself that it was all Jeremiah's fault. His mind drove that horrid virus and allowed it to disable the life support systems on the ship.

The grisly mantra works.

The pain recedes, and determination settles into my mind.

Through the white mist of hatred in my eyes, I see Jeremiah swinging the machete at my neck.

I lean back sharply, causing him to miss.

He screams and swings the machete at my left shoulder.

I block the strike with my sword, and in an unbroken trajectory, I slice at his temple.

There's a line of blood across Jeremiah's face and fear in his eyes, but I'm in too much of a stupor to gloat.

I'm feeling weaker by the minute.

Then it dawns on me.

The luminescent liquid of my blood is gushing out of the remnant of my arm. If I let this continue, I'll faint, and then I'll lose. All Jeremiah has to do is wait, which is probably why he's more focused on defense than offense.

No.

I won't let him win.

I have to stop the bleeding.

I squeeze the hilt of my katana until my knuckles go from white to purple. I'm about to do something truly insane, but I don't dwell on it. I simply touch the fire from my blade to my bleeding stump.

There's a disgusting sizzle of burning flesh, and a terrible barbecue smell hits my nose.

The fountain of blood slows to a trickle and then stops.

Unbelievably, I don't feel any pain. I might've surpassed my suffering threshold—or perhaps Haven's interface only allows for so much.

Jeremiah looks at me in confounded fascination. I guess he didn't expect me to hurt myself so badly.

Then a wave of searing pain hits me. I was wrong. The Haven interface does allow me to feel the burn; the pain was just slow to register in my battle-weary brain.

The agony threatens to take away my consciousness, but I fight to stay awake. If I black out for even an instant, Jeremiah will make sure I never come back to my senses.

Through the wetness blurring my vision, I see Jeremiah swing the machete at my leg.

I fly up, causing him to miss, and swing my sword at his head.

I succeed in chopping off a chunk of Jeremiah's hair and scalp, and the flame of my blade sets his remaining hair on fire.

He screams, patting at his head to put out the flames, and I use that moment to raise my sword and deliver another wound to his left shoulder.

Fear and pain seem to give Jeremiah a second wind. A horrific cry escapes his throat, and he swings his machete at me like some kind of ancient berserker.

I'm forced to go on the defensive, my arm getting progressively numb as I block his next five strikes.

Out of the corner of my eye, I notice that in the distance, Giant-Phoe's enormous teeth are ripping at Giant-Theo's towering neck. The two bodies are locked in a deadly embrace, but her bite seems to be turning the tide. Giant-Theo falls to the ground, toppling Forebears in his wake. A huge piece of the Giant's flesh is caught in Giant-Phoe's teeth, and the rest of him breaks into the largest Limbofication Haven has ever seen.

I pay for my distraction with my ear, which Jeremiah's machete hacks off.

I don't even register this new wave of pain, but the sight of my blood seems to give Jeremiah renewed energy, and he launches into another round of berserker attacks.

Blocking his strikes is getting difficult. I don't think I can last much longer.

Out of sheer desperation, instead of blocking the next machete strike with my sword, I meet it with the stump of my left arm.

The machete cuts deep into the charred flesh and bone.

The pain doesn't hit me right away, but I know it's on its way.

I thrust my katana forward.

"Wait, Theo," Phoe says in my head just as I bury my sword in Jeremiah's belly. "Don't—"

Whatever she was going to tell me, she's too late.

I press my sword deeper into Jeremiah, and he Limbofies.

Seeing him turn into those pixelated pieces is the most welcome sight.

Then the pain from my arm reaches my brain, and the world goes black.

CHAPTER TWENTY-THREE

I'm floating in darkness.

The lack of pain is like pleasure. If I had a mouth, I'd be smiling from the comfort of it all.

From far away, Phoe says, "I said 'wait,' but you went ahead and gutted him."

"Where am I?" I ask. "What's going on?"

"You're sort of unconscious," Phoe says. "I reached into your unconsciousness so we could speak."

"Won't I fall?" I ask her. Though I should be afraid, I'm much too comfortable and happy. I'm only pondering the possibility.

"I now have enough resources to think significantly quicker than the rest of Haven's environment. I allocated some of these resources to speed up your thinking as well. This means that very little time is passing in Haven as we talk here. I suspect that when we're done with this conversation, only a millisecond will have passed. So you're not falling. At least not yet."

"Okay," I say, though I don't really understand what she said. "Do I have this right? You didn't want me to Limbofy Jeremiah?"

"No, I didn't. When I finished battling the anti-intrusion algorithm, I finally got the chance to scan Davin's mind. In his memories, I saw something else that the Circle did. They tied their useless lives to the fate of all of Haven. They arranged it so that if they were all gone, the Firewall would come down. Since Jeremiah was the last member of the Circle, Limbofying him brought down the Firewall."

"Wasn't that your ultimate goal? To get rid of that stupid Firewall?"

"It was my goal—until the Jeremiah virus spread through all the resources outside of Haven. He couldn't get through the Firewall before, but now that it's down, that's exactly what he'll do."

"Okay," I say, beginning to worry even in this bodiless, pleasant state. "Didn't you need Jeremiah's and Davin's memories to deal with the virus? Since I Limbofied them for you, don't you now have a solution?"

"No. They turned out not to have any relevant knowledge of the virus. Inside Jeremiah's mind, I saw the process he went through to create the virus, but I didn't see how to get rid of it."

She stops talking, and I'm hit with a vision.

Jeremiah the Forebear is standing in a tunnel of light. The rest of the Circle is watching in horror as ghostly images of new Jeremiahs appear out of the light. To everyone's dismay, these new Jeremiahs, these viruses, are turning into a gross liquid. Then the virus is teleported to the other side of the Firewall, and the Circle members collectively sigh in relief. A slightly disheveled Jeremiah walks out of the circle he was standing in, and the strange procedure comes to an end.

"That is how Jeremiah was turned into that slug-like weapon," Phoe says in my mind. "However, this doesn't tell me much about the virus's nature, and the information wasn't available in either Davin's head or Jeremiah's."

I float in silence, taking in the meaning of her words. Finally, I ask, "So what does that mean? Will the Jeremiah virus destroy us after all?"

"Not if I have anything to say about it," Phoe says. "I have an idea. You see, the anti-intrusion algorithm they unleashed against us comes from the same era as this virus. Its original purpose was to combat things like this virus, so here's what I'm thinking: I can piggy back on the process they used to turn Jeremiah into the virus, only instead of the virus code, I'll use the anti-intrusion algorithm code."

"Great," I say and allow myself to float calmly once again. "So do it. Create the whatever-you-just-said."

"I would, but it's not that simple. The process they used on Jeremiah can only be applied to another Forebear."

My calmness instantly evaporates. I think I now understand why Phoe decided to have this out-of-time conversation. Hoping I'm wrong, I say, "You want to turn *me* into this anti-virus?"

"Only if you consent, yes," Phoe replies, her disembodied voice full of sadness. "But I can see you're not comfortable with this, so I guess this is goodbye. I'll write the two of us into Limbo so we'll have a chance of getting re-instantiated one day. If we never do, it's been really great knowing—"

"Oh, shut up, Phoe," I shout into the darkness. "You know I'll say yes."

"Are you sure?" She sounds genuinely surprised. "You can change your mind once I give you all the details. You see, like Jeremiah, you'll become a legion of your selves. I have no idea what it will feel like for you to split into multiple identities, but there's very little time left to analyze this. If you're truly willing to give this a shot, I need to begin the process now."

"Just do it," I say, and the darkness turns into all-penetrating light.

* * *

I keep my eyes squeezed shut throughout the process, but even through my eyelids, I can see the bright light surrounding me the way it did Jeremiah in that snippet Phoe showed me.

Then I open my eyes.

I'm still flying above the Sanctum. My poor left hand is now reattached, and the rest of my injuries are healed.

The birds are all gone, and the few remaining citizens of Haven are flying in every direction. The ground is covered in shards of the dome and pieces of the islands the two giants destroyed.

Phoe is no longer a giantess. A bunch of her instantiations are protectively surrounding me on all sides.

The oddest part is that there's an army of me in the distance, only these Theos are all dressed in some kind of black porous armor, and despite not having any wings, they're flying in the sky. When I focus on one of their faces, I see what that version of me is seeing, hear what he's hearing, and—the oddest part of all—know what he's thinking. That particular Theo just realized that he's surrounded by copies of himself, and that they're the weapon Phoe created.

Just as I can see the world through their eyes, they can see through mine, though my point of view won't be interesting in the fight to come. I only have one task: to stay alive while my copies do what they were designed to do.

I look at the farthest black-clad Theo and shift into his perspective.

* * *

I look at the original Theo, who's surrounded by Phoes.

Poor guy.

Though intellectually he knows what it's like to be one of us, he still has no idea what it's really like.

I feel amazing, like I'm a superhero from an ancient comic book. I have no fear of heights, and I'm full of energy, the kind of energy I imagine ancient drugs provided.

I chuckle at the image of a superhero on amphetamines and cocaine, but it's probably the best way I can describe how I feel.

Suddenly, the part of me that is the anti-intrusion algorithm feels trouble approaching.

It begins with the sky. The clouds disappear, one by one, and are replaced by the disgusting slime of the Jeremiah virus.

Only to me, it's not disgusting anymore. As weird as it sounds, to the anti-intrusion part of me, that viscous soup-like substance looks delicious.

With gurgling screams all around us, the Jeremiah virus starts to turn each island in Haven into a version of himself. It's a shame. Central Island with its castle and theme park, Jeanine's forests, and thousands upon thousands of Forebear homes are gone in a blink.

I meet the original Theo's gaze.

He looks frightened.

I look at my nearest brother-selves.

They look as excited as I feel, and we exchange knowing looks.

We were literally made for this.

Phoe's theory was spot on; I can feel it.

I will take on this virus.

In the distance, the last remaining Forebears freeze mid-flight and stare at the unfolding disaster in horrified fascination. After centuries of living in Haven, they're witnessing its decimation as the virus turns their home into horrific goo. I wonder what they're thinking and feeling as they watch this destruction.

I know what I'm feeling.

Hunger.

As one, the escaping Forebears turn into slime as droplets of Jeremiah's substance spray them in an apocalyptic-looking, gelatinous rain.

My heart rate spikes when the same rain starts pouring down where the Phoes formed a sphere around the original Theo.

I fly in that direction, determined to save them.

One Phoe turns into slime, then another.

Jeremiah is turning them so quickly that there's no way I can reach them in time.

I curse, and then see that I wasn't the only one who recognized this problem.

In a black cloud, hundreds of my brother-selves fly toward the diminishing wall of Phoes.

There are maybe a few dozen Phoe instantiations left now.

My brothers reach them, and in a black blur, they form an impenetrable sphere around Phoes and Theo that absorbs the rest of the rain.

Relieved, I notice I'm also getting rained on. Like the rest of the black-clad warriors, I don't change into a virus when the liquid touches me. On the contrary, my sponge-like skin absorbs the slime with hungry relish.

Once I've consumed a few droplets, the most exquisite ecstasy washes over me. It's stronger than the most powerful Oneness session, even better than those orgasms I experienced with Phoe on the beach.

To the music of pleasure, I divide into a second copy of me, then a third, and then a fourth.

The four of us wink at each other and fly in different directions, each looking to drink down more of the wonderful Jeremiah virus substance.

The same splitting is happening to my brothers all around me. Our numbers are increasing with the full power of exponential growth.

I look at the nearest copies of me and smile. We have proof that Phoe was right. We *can* serve our purpose; we *can* fulfill our calling.

My stomach aches with a terrible hunger, and I speed toward the nearest sphere of liquid bearing Jeremiah's face.

As I close the distance, I feel like I might burst with excitement. I dive into the liquid, creating waves of explosion as parts of the Jeremiah blob try their best not to touch me.

The hated face of my nemesis surrounds me. It's in every droplet of the virus.

I recall my earlier animosity toward this face and channel my hunger.

My body feels as if it's made up of small, hungry, porous particles, each one almost sentient. Like a horde of mouths, they're dying to take a sip of the slime.

I let them.

I swallow the murky liquid with every mouth all at once, and Jeremiah's faces scream in horror.

The same gurgling cries are all around me.

Caught up in the ecstasy of multiplying into more copies of me, I laugh at Jeremiah's pain.

* * *

I'm back in my unaltered perspective.

Surrounded by the remaining Phoes, I watch as the army of Theo anti-viruses continues to multiply.

When one of them comes into contact with the slime that is Jeremiah, he simply drinks the virus, or eats it—it's hard to tell the difference. Once the virus is consumed, the Theos multiply.

I start losing track of the strange battlefield. One moment, there are a thousand Theos surrounded by a never-ending sphere of slime, and the next, there are a million Theos and an ever-shrinking puddle of slime.

Reading their minds is disturbing. They're enjoying this battle a little too much.

"Is it working?" I ask the nearest Phoe. "Are we beating the Jeremiah virus?"

"We'll have him beat in a matter of minutes," she says with a smile. "Meanwhile, there's something you should do."

She points south, where Haven is now free of Jeremiah's presence.

I notice something very familiar floating there. An object I saw what feels like a year ago, though it's only been a few days.

It's a large, neon gateway with the word 'Goal' written in garish colors.

"Is that…?"

"Yes, a Goal, like in the IRES game," Phoe says. "I told you this place was based on a very similar infrastructure, and this proves it. Once you became the only human to survive in this place, that sign appeared. If you go through it, you should be able to shut down Haven for good. Not that there's much left to shut down."

She's right.

Haven is now an empty vacuum filled with copies of me.

I spread my wings, but then I hesitate.

The Phoes behind me merge into one, and she says, "Go ahead, Theo. Don't worry about me."

"What about all the copies of me?" I ask.

The black-clad Theos are finishing off what remains of the Jeremiah virus.

She doesn't get a chance to reply before I find out the answer for myself.

The victorious band of Theos is dissipating. The process looks like Limbofication, but with one major difference. Their memories become mine instead of going to Limbo.

The torrent of memories hits me like a sledgehammer. It's overwhelming.

Each Theo has a set of memories that I absorb.

They each remember moving around, getting rid of the virus, and experiencing the odd physical pleasure of multiplying. Given how similar all these memories are, digesting them should be easy, but because there are millions of them, I'm forced to glide on my wings, nearly paralyzed as I wait for the nightmare to end.

I don't know how much time passes—an hour, a hundred years?—until I receive the last anti-virus Theo's recollections. All I know is that eventually, I'm able to continue toward the Goal.

Like in the IRES game, as soon as my head goes through the Goal sign, I'm congratulated on being the winner. Only this time, I'm standing on a big podium holding a giant trophy while being treated to thunderous applause.

Once that part is over, the shutdown procedure begins.

A world-sized Screen shows up in front of my face and asks if I would like to play again.

"Fuck no," I tell the interface. "What I want is to bring this shit down."

When I double and triple confirm my choices, the world around me disappears, taking my consciousness with it.

CHAPTER TWENTY-FOUR

I wake up to the sound of the ocean surf, the pleasant sensation of the sun warming my skin, and the soothing scent of kelp and salt water.

"Morning, sleepyhead," Phoe whispers in my ear. "Welcome back from Limbo—again."

I open my eyes. I'm lying on a beach identical to the one the virus destroyed before all the insanity in Haven happened.

Phoe is on the sand next to me. She's dressed in her favorite bikini and looks the same as she did before Haven, without the wings.

I try to wiggle my own wings and discover they're gone.

Though the events in Oasis and Haven feel like a distant nightmare, I have no doubt that they happened.

"I was in Limbo?" I ask in my normal voice.

"When you brought down Haven, you sort of Limbofied since your existence was attached to Haven. But your memories got recorded into Limbo like they should have, so I just needed to reawaken you after I built this beach for you."

I sit up. My body feels blissfully normal and real—more real than how it felt in Haven.

"That's because I'm emulating your real-world body in painstaking detail." Phoe brushes the tips of her fingers across my shoulder. "You are as real as is possible for someone in this situation to be."

I stand up. The sand feels sturdy under my feet. I walk up to the water and dip my toes in.

It's warm and wet and inviting.

"So the virus is—"

"Completely gone," Phoe says. "If you concentrate, you'll remember getting rid of every last bit of it."

She's right: I do. The memories of the battle are there, under the surface of my awareness, but they're so strange that I prefer to suppress them. Now that I'm recalling them, though, I'm amazed at the sheer scale of the slaughter—if that's the right term. I recall millions of Jeremiah viruses, billions of gallons of that substance, getting eaten (or drunk) by my anti-virus copies.

"And all of Haven is gone?" I ask as though I wasn't the one responsible. "Completely?"

"I hope you're not missing it." Phoe gets up and joins me by the water. "I'm debating what kind of world to create for us, so if there's anything in Haven you liked—"

"No. I'd like something like this." I spread my arms, gesturing at the ocean before us.

"Good. We'll build from here," she says and looks around. "We'll start whenever you're ready to build a world with me."

I stare at the horizon, allowing my mind to calm.

"You know," Phoe says, sounding thoughtful. "It's a mystery to me why we both find that horizon so soothing. Your mind is the product of millions of years of evolution. Your ancestors supposedly achieved conscious thought while in the African savannah. So why would you, their descendant, have such a fondness for a never-ending waterscape?"

I shrug.

"My situation is even weirder," she continues. "I was built. Why would I, a spaceship, find the ocean so fascinating? Especially since I was the one who created it a few hours ago."

"That's your biggest question about yourself?" I turn to her. "Shouldn't you be wondering why you, a spaceship, want to hang out with me, an evolved ape?"

She steps closer to me. Her breath warms my cheek as she says, "Well, that's easy. No matter how I originated, I was made to be capable of feeling. Those feelings have revolved around you for as long as I've been truly alive. So—"

I silence her with a kiss. Our lips meet with a heated softness, and we explore each other's mouths until I pull away.

"Sorry," I say. "I want to do this, but later. I still have so many questions."

Phoe's disappointment is clear on her perfect face, but she nods. "Ask away."

"The resources." I touch my lips regretfully. "Do you have enough?"

"I'm not sure if I'd ever say it's enough." She chuckles. "But I have all the resources I could possibly gain, and a little extra on top. Though, given the source of the extra resources, I'd rather we talk about something else."

I understand what she means. The virus wiped out all life support systems, killing all biological life and almost killing Phoe as well. But now that the virus is gone, she can use all those resources, even the ones that were needed to keep the people in Oasis alive.

"What happened to the dead bodies?" I ask, suppressing a shudder at the memory of the floating corpses.

"The nanocytes reclaimed their molecules and turned them into more computing substrate." Phoe steps back. "Every unused portion of the ship is getting turned into computing substrate as we speak. What's left of the trees, the buildings, and all other dumb matter will be turned into smart matter that can perform computations. We'll need every bit of processing power if we want to resurrect people from Limbo."

I try to picture the Dome, the grass, all of it gone and replaced by nano-computing machines, but my imagination fails to grasp it. I find it sad that there's nothing left of Oasis.

"Something does remain. I left the frozen embryos intact, in case we ever find use for them. And you're doing a good job of picturing it all." Phoe places a comforting hand on my lower back. "Your understanding is spot on."

I think of the embryos and realize that I don't care about those things. What I really care about is seeing my friends again.

"Are we going to bring people back to this type of existence?" I ask, indicating the world around us. I think that somewhere in the darkest recesses of my mind, I was always afraid that when Phoe finally gained her precious resources, she'd tell me that it had all been a means to an end. That she no longer needed me. That she wasn't willing to share anything.

"Your present consciousness is proof that I'm more than willing to share my resources with you." There's a hurt edge to Phoe's tone.

"I know." I touch her hand. "I'm sorry."

"No, I understand." She pulls her hand away and twists her blond spiky hair around her index finger. "I never shut up about needing more resources, so I understand why you might think that's all I ever cared about. But you have to understand that my ultimate goal was never about resources. It was about self-discovery. I wanted to get my full mind and body back. I wanted to be more than this shadow of a person, to be the real me, with all the resources that make me who I am. And now that I have that"—her eyes gleam—"I'll be forever grateful to you for helping me regain it all. Besides, bringing your closest friends back, especially if we run them at the speed of regular human thought, won't use up too many resources."

I look her over, half expecting her to appear different now that she has all her resources, but she looks the same. Only a certain wistfulness is gone from her features. Phoe looks serene—complete.

"That's a good word," she says, a smile tugging at her lips. "Complete. That's precisely how I feel. Before, it was like I was deaf and blind, my mind muddy. Now I'm completely healed."

"So what's different about you?" I examine her pixie hair and the hint of mystery in her smile. "What do you know that you didn't know before?"

"So much." Her blue gaze grows distant. "I can see the Solar System with my sensors. It's amazing—even if it's not at all what I was expecting." In an awed tone, she murmurs, "Not at all."

"Wait, what?" Anxiety swells inside of me. "What do you mean it's not like what you expected?"

"There's no cause for concern," Phoe says, her eyes refocusing on me. "But—well, I don't think I can explain it to you. I think it's better for you to see it for yourself. If you're willing."

"If I'm willing to do what?" I take her hand and squeeze it lightly. "You like being mysterious, don't you?"

"With you, I'm accidentally mysterious." She winks at me mischievously. "But to answer your question, I'm offering to show you what I see with my outside sensors, which I finally have access to.

This way you'll feel what I feel with my real-world body. The experience might be rather sensual." She squeezes my palm, then pulls her hand away. "The only thing is, I'm not sure your mind can handle this kind of experience in its limited state."

I feel perfectly normal, so I ask, "What do you mean, my limited state?"

"Your limited human intelligence. If you really want to experience what I want to show you, I have to make you more like me—a little smarter—and make your mind nimbler."

"Smarter?" I wonder if she's building up to some kind of joke.

"I'll expand your mind," she explains. "Just enough so it doesn't metaphorically blow up when I let you experience my worldview."

She's not smiling anymore. She's serious.

With a slight flutter in the pit of my stomach, I ask, "Will it change me? Will I be the same person if you do whatever it is you're talking about?"

"You'll still be you, don't worry," Phoe says. "Hence the 'just enough' part."

"Okay, I guess," I say. This might be the least enthusiastic anyone has ever been about something as positive as growing smarter. "I'll risk it if it's the only way to gain this knowledge you're holding hostage."

"Well, I could just tell you," she says, "but you probably wouldn't believe me. This is best, I promise." She pecks me on the cheek, and I feel warmth and energy spread from that part of my face. The energy then transforms into a rush of sensations I can't fully place.

I blink a few times.

The world around me is the same, but my view of it is subtly different. I feel as though I went from being sleep-deprived, tired, and hungry to well rested and fully satisfied. But it's more complex than that. My vision is sharper, but not like with the eagle eyes I had in Haven. I'm more focused on the details of the world around me.

Yes, that's it. I can focus on more things at once.

I run my hand through my hair and realize I can estimate the number of hairs I just touched. I listen to the sound of the surf, and it gives me a hint as to how much water is soaking into the sand. And now that my attention is on the sand, I swear I can count the number of grains under my feet.

I also begin to understand to what extent mathematics permeate the world around me, from ratios embedded in the glorious design of the nautilus shell next to my feet to Phoe's seductive 0.7 hip-to-waist ratio.

"Leave it to a man to use his new intellect on such trivialities." Despite her mocking tone, Phoe stands in a way that makes her waist and hips very noticeable to me. "And for the record, the actual ratio is 0.67. I calibrated it myself, so I should know."

I examine her hips a bit closer and feel a stirring that makes my cheeks redden. This reaction makes no sense to me, since we've already done all the taboo activities on the last version of this beach. My new, superior intellect warns me that Phoe is about to mock me about my former virginity and current shyness, so I change the topic.

"Okay, my mind is officially enhanced," I say. "Can I see the Solar System now?"

Phoe's face turns very serious. "It might still be a little jarring. Close your eyes for a moment. I need to patch you into my sensorium."

I close my eyes.

Nothing happens for a while, and I wonder if she failed. Then I feel myself drawn somewhere, and my consciousness expands.

I try to open my eyes, but I have no eyes to open. Yet I do see—and what I see takes my nonexistent breath away.

CHAPTER TWENTY-FIVE

I see the universe like no human being ever has.

Light permeates everything around me, and I don't mean the usual starlight one might expect to see in this situation. I can see a fuller portion of the electromagnetic spectrum. The x-rays, the gamma rays, and the micro and radio waves of distant stars all shine in different shades of inspiring beauty. The space around me is a kaleidoscope of awe.

There are sounds here too, though I never expected empty space to have sounds. Micro meteors hit the protective shield with loud bangs. Gravity waves whoosh as they hit the specialized instruments. My mind marvels at the knowledge that these waves were sent by distant black holes caught in a cataclysmic dance. Inside the ship, I hear the sounds of the nanomachines processing.

It's difficult to find human analogies to describe the barrage of senses. For example, what is the human equivalent to the feeling I get when the engines burn fuel? Maybe it's similar to taste, but it's not really a taste or a smell. And there are a million other foreign senses like that.

"You're doing better than I thought you would." The statement is a thought from Phoe, and it reminds me that I'm Theo. It reminds me that I'm sensing some of the things that Phoe is experiencing as a ship.

"You were right. This experience is extremely sensual. I'm afraid it's blowing my somewhat-enhanced mind," I think at her, suppressing my bubbling panic.

"Just lose yourself in the sensations," Phoe suggests. "But also don't forget your original query."

I'm once again aware of Phoe's sensations, and I focus on kinesthetic awareness—feeling myself in a specific location in the universe. I feel myself here, in the vacuum of space, but also in a dozen virtual environments inside the ship, including as a woman on a beach—a woman who's staring at the ocean at this very moment.

My mind hurts when I consider the full scope of the universe around me. The magnitude of Phoe's awareness of the world is frighteningly huge. I don't think Phoe expanded my consciousness enough to truly experience even a tiny percentage of the world the way she does.

A conviction overcomes me. I want Phoe to expand my mind even more. I want to experience the totality of her awareness with my mind one day, without feeling overwhelmed.

"I can make that happen." Phoe's thought is a soothing balm. "For the moment, though, you should focus your attention on our destination."

"Right," I think back at her, and for the first time, I actually try looking with the intention of seeing something.

There are stars in all their electromagnetic glory, and there's the biggest one of all, the sun. However, when I focus on the sun, it's not as bright as I expected it to be.

Its lack of brightness is not the strangest part of what I'm seeing, though. What's even stranger is what I'm *not* seeing.

As a kid, I learned that the Solar System had planets. Mercury was planet number one and closest to the sun. Venus was the second planet from the sun, Earth the third, Mars the fourth, and so on. That's what I expected to see—perhaps made prettier through Phoe's worldview—but there isn't a single planet in front of the sun.

It's just there, by itself.

Actually, that's not accurate. Something is there, and it's responsible for the sun looking much dimmer than it should. Thin, barely noticeable layers of some kind of substance surround the sun. Whatever I'm looking at is so large that my slightly enhanced human mind is overwhelmed again.

"Yeah," Phoe thinks. "It even baffles *my* mind."

I metaphorically shake my nonexistent head and try to focus on the object. It's clear that onion-like layers similar to Saturn's rings surround the sun, only these are more ethereal, and there are countless numbers of them. I try to comprehend how big they must be and, more importantly, what their purpose is.

"This object is beyond massive," Phoe says. "And its purpose should be pretty obvious if you think about it. It's designed for computation."

I'm back on the beach, and Phoe is standing there, looking at me sympathetically.

My mind feels like it's about to explode. She didn't give me enough brainpower to handle this revelation.

"So, Earth is gone," I say, trying not to look as dumb as I feel. "And some kind of ginormous computer replaced it?"

"Earth evolved into it," Phoe says, her eyes gleaming. "The ancients imagined something like that. They called the structure a Matrioshka Brain—after a Russian doll that has many layers. I suspect their vision was much simpler than the reality you saw, but as far as I can tell, that behemoth has many of the major features they envisioned, such as the super-hot layers that are close to the sun and the super-cold layers that are closer to us. I suspect that, like the ancients theorized, this superstructure uses up almost all the energy output of the sun to drive its computations. It's probably made of real computorium—a theoretical term for a substance that pushes the limits of computing in a given volume of matter. A cubic meter of that stuff makes all our resources look as antiquated as an abacus— and there's a whole solar system filled with the stuff."

I try to picture the image I saw so I can marvel at it again.

"But what's the point?" I murmur after a moment. "What could something like that be computing?"

"What is the point of this?" Phoe spreads her arms to encompass the ocean around us. "What is the point of you and me?"

My legs feel shaky, so I sit down on the sand. "So you're saying existence is the point?"

"Exactly." She sits down next to me. "Conscious patterns like us are the point. Only that place might allow for the existence of patterns that would make me look as smart as an amoeba, and you as smart as a carbon molecule. Still, the principle is the same. Godlike intelligences exist for the same purpose as you and I: for experiences, enjoyment, intellectual curiosity, just being—"

"But it's all artificial," I say, knowing she might get upset with me.

She smiles. "Tell me honestly, do you feel artificial?"

Before I can answer, before I can even think a single thought, she kisses my neck. If her goal was to make it hard for me to answer her question, or even think in general, she succeeded admirably.

I follow my body's urges. As odd as it should be for us to be intimate right now, it actually feels natural. Maybe it's because I saw the world through her eyes. This is, of course, in part what she's trying to prove to me with her body. That this is real. That *we* are real. And I have to admit, she makes her point quite well.

* * *

"Okay," I say when we're lying on the beach, spent. "I do feel real—and happy—but my mind still boggles when I try to understand a mind like yours. To fathom what that Matrioshka thing is computing is just—"

"I know," she says. "But the coolest part is that we'll find out eventually, when we reach the outer layer."

"Oh right. We're flying toward it." I brush the sand off my body. "Should we still be going there?"

"Would you want to pass up the opportunity now that you know it's there?" She gestures and, to my mild disappointment, her bikini reappears on her body. "I know I'd never forgive myself."

She's right, of course. I want to know what life in the Solar System is like—even if I'm still having trouble applying that term to something so immense.

"So we keep going," Phoe says. "The good news is that the trip won't take as long as I thought. The outer layer of the structure is much closer to us than Earth was."

"Oh yeah." I sit up and gesture for my clothes, which show up like they would in Oasis. "How long do you think it'll take?"

"That's hard to answer. I suspect we don't need to make the full journey to it. If we get close enough, someone will likely make contact with us. Another reason your question is hard to answer is that time is flowing really fast for us. Unless I slow down our thinking—which would be a very dumb thing to do—a few weeks of regular, human travel time will feel like a century, or maybe longer."

I look at the sun above us. It doesn't show any hint of having a megastructure surrounding it, which makes sense, since this sun is virtual.

"You didn't know about the structure before?" I ask, voicing something that's been bothering me for a few minutes. "When you set a course for Earth, you didn't know it was gone?"

"I didn't," Phoe says solemnly. "I didn't have access to my sensors. All I felt was that kinesthetic awareness you experienced. When I combined it with the old maps, I was able to set a course to where Earth used to be, but I couldn't see what had happened. This is why I've been pushing for more resources. On some level, I was afraid something like this had happened. I think I mentioned it to you before."

"Okay," I say, feeling that mind-hurting sensation coming back. "What do we do while we travel? How do we kill all that subjective time?"

"Oh, that's easy." Phoe beams at me and gestures at the air. A large gray sphere appears between us. "We build a world, and then we live in it."

Phoe waves at the sphere, and blue water—the same as the ocean in front of us—shows up on it.

She examines the sphere and gestures again.

A tiny continent appears in the middle of the global ocean. Then she gestures again, and another, bigger continent shows up on the opposite hemisphere.

"Is this a recreation of Earth?" I ask as more details appear on the sphere.

"Not really. This is my best guess at a world we'd find fun." The polar caps appear at the edges of her globe. "We can call it Earth if you like. I was originally going to call it Phoenix, since I don't get to use my full name much."

"So is this some sort of model I'm looking at? When you're done, you'll make it life-size?" I watch her create a strange weather pattern over one of the larger continents.

"Something like that," she says and turns the tiniest continent into a beach. "It's a model, true, but the world gets created around us, so when this is finished, we'll already be on this planet, whatever we decide to call it." She spins the sphere so I can get a good look at it. "You should help me."

I tentatively gesture at the globe. Nothing happens.

Phoe dramatically sighs and gestures at me with the same confidence as when she was creating the elements of our world.

I instantly learn how to build a world. What's odd is that I feel as if I always had this ability. I point at the beach continent and wish for something I've always wanted to see in person: the pyramids. A very tiny pyramid appears on the continent, right by the water.

I gesture again, and a second pyramid appears next to the first.

"Good call," Phoe says, looking past me. "Sand and pyramids go well together."

I follow her gaze to where the pyramids actually appeared behind us. So that little beach on the globe is the beach we're standing on. Though I know how this world creation works, it's still amazing to see something I wished for manifest like that.

"If you don't mind," she says, "I'll add the Sphinx."

She gestures at the sphere, and the Sphinx appears next to my two pyramids, both on the sphere and on our beach.

"Your turn." Phoe waves her hand and the sphere flies closer to me. "What would you like our world to have?"

CHAPTER TWENTY-SIX

For at least an hour, I create all the things I've always wanted to see on ancient Earth. Places I've read about and monuments out of Filomena's lectures.

Phoe helps me, pulling on information she gained from the ancient archives.

I soon find myself feeling hungry and tired, but I keep adding details to our world.

"I hope you don't mind," Phoe says when my stomach growls for the second time in as many minutes. "I made your virtual body identical to your biological one, which means you'll feel things like hunger. I can tweak this, of course."

Hunger isn't exactly pleasant, but eating is. "Can you adjust my body so I'll never feel the need to eat, but I can enjoy food on a whim? For that matter, what food do we have in this world?"

"Of course I can," Phoe says, and a large carpet with a variety of picnic baskets appears on the sand, answering my question about availability of food. "I altered your body so you'll never get hungry again," Phoe says a second later. "How do you feel?"

As soon as she says it, I know it's the truth. The hunger pangs are gone, yet I'm still curious about what foods are in the baskets. I walk up to the nearest one and open it.

It's filled with pastries. Some, like muffins, are foods I've tried during the Birth Day celebrations, but others, like the cheese croissant, are things I've only seen in ancient media, since cheese isn't something we had in Oasis.

I grab a croissant and bite into it. It's sweet, flaky, and delicious—much yummier than what I imagined.

"I just guessed at the taste," Phoe says and grabs one for herself. "But it was an educated guess based on a lot of research."

I sit cross-legged on the carpet and examine the rest of the baskets for interesting surprises, of which there are many.

"Do you want to see the world we've created?" Phoe sits next to me and grabs a slice of pizza. "We can fly around on this carpet, like they do in that Disney movie."

I swallow a piece of marmalade and say, "Only if you can tweak my mind to get rid of my fear of heights."

Phoe demonstratively waves at my head. "Done. I must say, you're very open to this tweaking business. I'm proud of you."

After a moment of introspection, I say, "I feel the same. Are you sure—"

"How's this?" Phoe says, and the carpet floats off the ground.

I examine my internal reaction. When I floated up like this on a disk, I was definitely panicking by this point, but I don't feel any negative emotions right now.

"I think it worked," I say. "This should be interesting."

We fly higher and higher and then shoot toward the ocean. Soon, the beach is a small dot behind us. I stop eating and focus on the flight. The faster we fly, the stranger I feel. Instead of panic, I'm experiencing a certain level of excitement.

"Is this how the ancients felt when they rode roller coasters?" I ask, a smile forming on my lips.

"I assume so," Phoe says and increases our speed. "Shall we resume building?"

To underline her suggestion, she summons the Earth model, and it hangs in the air above us, undisturbed by the speed we're traveling at.

Spinning the globe to an emptier portion, she points at it and adds more landmass.

I join her, and we continue creating the world. From time to time, we land to admire the details of our creations. I spend a day checking out the Wall of China as I hold Phoe's small hand. And I can't resist spending another day climbing our replica of the Eiffel Tower, especially since I'm no longer afraid of heights. Phoe seems to be enjoying all of it as much as I am. We have a friendly competition going on as to who can come up with the most creative landscapes. So far, she's winning.

Our explorations are like some surreal tourism for the gods. First, we create the most romantic spot inspired by descriptions of the Taj Mahal and the Hanging Gardens of Babylon; then we have a romantic tumble on the white marble, right under the glorious vegetation.

Oh, and we have a lot of sex. I've stopped blushing when I think of it and no longer feel weird about initiating it. Sex has become part of this strange process, as if our new world isn't complete until we get intimate in every location we've created.

There's only one thing spoiling my happiness: I can't stop thinking about my friends. It's like a splinter in my brain.

Finally, as we're flying across the ocean again, I interrupt our make-out session to say, "Phoe, I've been thinking. Can you build a replica of Oasis? I think I'd like to bring Liam back in our Dorm room and then slowly reveal this crazy new reality to him."

Phoe gives me an understanding look. I suspect she's been reading my thoughts on this subject and waiting for me to bring it up.

Without saying anything, she waves her hand, and the ocean below us turns a familiar, disgusting orange-brown color. It's eerie how much it resembles the Goo.

Phoe then makes a big green island appear below us, with geometric buildings all around it.

My heart skips at the sight. Having lived in Oasis for so many years, even its replica feels a little like home.

Our carpet flies down to the island, and we land on the soccer field by the Institute.

She looks around, nods approvingly, and gestures once more. The Dome shows up in the sky.

"This is only until I explain everything," I tell her, wrinkling my nose at the Dome. "My plan is to have the Dome and the Goo disappear to convince Liam I'm telling him the truth."

"That's as good a plan as any," Phoe says, getting up from the carpet.

We walk toward the Dorms together. Inside, I find a perfect replica of my room.

"So how is this going to work?" I ask as we make two beds appear. "Will he just wake up like it's morning? He won't recall the life support stuff failing, right? Please tell me he won't remember suffering and dying."

"Not unless he slept after it all happened—and he didn't. I just checked his mind backup to verify that. Losing consciousness due to asphyxiation didn't trigger the backup procedure the way sleep would, which is good. He won't recall those horrible events; he'll just think he's waking up the day after Birth Day."

My head spins when I consider what I'm about to tell my friend. How would I react if someone told me everyone I knew was dead and this was a virtual world? How would I react to the news that the world I knew is gone? Actually, I know that the world is gone, and I'm doing okay, so maybe Liam will be fine too. Still, he's about to learn that he woke up in a technologically created afterlife. What do you even say to something like that?

"Listen, Theo. There's something I mentioned before, but I don't think you fully grasped it. It's about emulating Liam and the people from Oasis in general." Phoe sits down on the replica of my bed. "Our resources are still finite, and because of that, I want Liam's thinking to be emulated at normal human speed." She gives me an apologetic look.

"Why?" I ask. "I thought we had plenty of resources. Just look at the planet we created."

"Yes, we created habitats, but it's much harder to simulate people. With our version of Earth, I can do what ancient computer scientists called 'lazy loading'—only utilize resources to run these environments when we reach that specific location. For example, since we're not on our beach right now, the beach isn't eating away at any of my processing power. Its code is stored away in a place that's basically dumb matter, which is more abundant than our computing substrate. With people, I obviously can't do something like that, since storing people is exactly what Limbo is for. Once they exist, they'll exist forever. It wouldn't be fair to put them in storage, or in Limbo, when we're not around. Don't you agree?"

I nod.

"So this is my compromise," she says. "You can bring back as many of Oasis's citizens as you want, but they will not think as fast as you and me. Simulating slow thinking is much cheaper computationally. This is something Haven's designers should've done to accommodate a much larger population."

Maybe it's the enhancements she gave my mind earlier or my prolonged exposure to her, but what Phoe said actually makes sense. I see a problem right away, though.

"If you do that, given that I'm running much faster, won't talking to Liam feel like I'm watching a glacier melt?"

"Yes—which is why I think it's time you had multiple threads of existence, like me." Phoe moves closer to me on the bed and gives me a conspiratorial smile. "Because you're right: given the speed differentiation, you'll go insane with boredom, just like I would if you weren't thinking as fast as me. When you were a regular human living in Oasis, speaking with you was what first inspired me to run my thinking in threads."

I consider it. In a nutshell, she's offering me the ability to be in many places at once, akin to what happened when I was that anti-virus army.

"I'm only talking about two places at once at first," Phoe says. "And it might feel different from that anti-virus situation. You'll see."

"Okay," I say. "But it seems a little unfair that Liam would exist in this slightly inferior way— compared to us, I mean."

"I understand and even agree, but there's simply too little computing power available. I suspect the situation will be different once we reach the Matrioshka Brain. In the meantime, look at it this way. If this is the only option that would allow Liam, Mason, and the rest of Oasis to exist, wouldn't you rather they existed in this limited way than not at all? Besides, they wouldn't be any worse off than they were. An hour will seem like an hour to them, just as it always did, but they will no longer be under the Elderly's control, which is worth something."

I think over her words and feel better. In a way, there's a benefit to living at slower speeds. The trip to the nearest Matrioshka layer will go much quicker for my friends than it will for Phoe and me. Still, part of the issue is that this solution will require me to once again expand my capabilities.

"You would eventually want the threading capabilities anyway," Phoe says. "Don't you want to be more like me? Don't you want to be my equal?"

She hasn't just read my mind; she somehow gleaned my subconscious hopes and dreams. I realize in that moment that being her equal is something I've secretly always wanted. I never admitted it, not even to myself, but I want to be like Phoe, and the only way to make that a reality is for her to raise me to her level, since it wouldn't be fair of me to expect her to become a lesser being.

"Maybe if I'm your equal, you won't be so good at getting your way," I say with false grumpiness, trying to steer my thoughts toward more comfortable territory.

"I wouldn't count on *that*." Phoe winks at me. "No matter how much processing power you get, I'll always have you wrapped around my little finger."

I narrow my eyes at her, and she gives me a disarming puppy-eyed look.

I give up and admit defeat. If she can melt me with a single look, what chance do I have at ever getting my way? The funny thing is, I don't mind.

"All right. You're about to think something so corny that I definitely have to stop you," Phoe says. "Are you ready to expand your abilities again?"

"Fine." I close my eyes. "I'm ready."

She chuckles and the air flutters, which I assume means she was waving her hand at me.

I wait. At first, nothing happens.

Then, slowly, I feel something that is very hard to describe. It's as if I suddenly become aware of a new limb, or more accurately, a bunch of limbs. Then I realize it's more complicated than that.

I'm aware that I can have two bodies at once.

I open my eyes and look around the room.

My vision is the same, though maybe a little sharper.

"Do this." Phoe demonstrates a gesture that looks like a peace sign, and suddenly there are two of her in the room. One is standing in front of me and looks frozen in time. Though when I look closer, I realize she's moving very slowly, like a bug stuck in molasses. The original Phoe is smiling at me from the bed and moving at a normal speed.

I repeat her gesture, and my consciousness splits.

There's a second me standing next to the lethargic Phoe.

Or perhaps it's more accurate to say that there are three of me: the thinking part that is the normal me, and two bodies that I can occupy at the same time. The strangeness of the varying rate of time these bodies experience is a slight twinkle compared to the much stranger reality of existing in two places at once.

Until it happened, I couldn't have even dreamed that such a thing was possible. I'm looking through two pairs of eyes, breathing through two noses, and moving two pairs of arms.

When I adjust to the dichotomy of my new existence, I focus on the fact that one of my bodies is experiencing the world slower than the other.

In a way, having a slow version of myself is helping me wrap my mind around my first-ever multi-thread experience. If I had split into two equal parts, the adjustment would've been more difficult.

"You'll get the hang of it," Phoe says from the bed. "It's a bit like controlling your right arm versus controlling your left one, but if one was much slower than the other."

The slow Phoe clears her throat, and I seamlessly hear it with my slow and fast ears. To my fast instantiation, the noise from her slow-moving mouth sounds extremely stretched out and reminds me of a whale song.

"We should leave," says the fast-running Phoe. "It will be less confusing for you that way."

Happy to oblige, my fast-moving self leaves the room. Phoe jumps off the bed and follows, which I observe through slow Theo's eyes.

To those eyes, the two people who just left look like ancient comic book heroes. One moment they were standing there, and then in a blur, they were gone.

Now that my two bodies are not in the same room, it *is* easier to consolidate this strange existence. I can experience the world from two places at once, with a single mind that's separated into two bodies, and if I need to, I can focus on one body and tune out the other. Even when I shift my attention back and forth, I remain aware of what each body is up to.

"Let's go build the rest of the world," fast Theo says.

Phoe nods, and we leave Oasis behind.

"Let's bring Liam back," I say through the mouth of my slow version.

Slow Phoe gestures triumphantly, and a sleeping Liam shows up in his bed.

CHAPTER TWENTY-SEVEN

"Phoe," I say in my slow-mode thread. "Can you please disappear for now?"

Phoe vanishes, and then tells me, "I'm around, just not visible. I'm very curious to see how he'll react."

"You and me both," I say and look at my sleeping friend.

Liam is lying there, completely oblivious.

I walk over to his bed and debate whether I should wake him, but decide against it.

As I wait for Liam to wake up on his own, I marvel at how much the fast threads of Phoe and me have accomplished in such a short time. We flew halfway across the planet and had another intimate session on the way. She also taught me how to read sheet music—something I always wanted to know—and we created a new continent. We filled this new landmass with forests and mountains, and right now we're debating what flora and fauna to populate it with.

"These wouldn't be real animals, in the same sense that you and Liam are real," fast Phoe says. "They'd be approximations, kind of like the animals they had at the Zoo and in Haven."

My slow self watches Liam open his eyes.

"Hey, dude, finally," I say. "I was getting sick of watching you sleep."

"You've been watching me sleep?" Liam looks at me groggily. "That's pretty creepy."

Seeing his face again and hearing his voice makes me so emotional that I'm afraid I might tear up. I swallow the thickness in my throat. If Liam sees me acting weird, he'll never let me live it down, no matter how graphically I describe to him how horrifically he died.

"Hey, are you okay?" he asks and gestures for his morning cleaning. "Why are you so serious?"

"Will Oasis-based gestures work?" I ask Phoe mentally.

"Yes," she responds out loud, her voice coming from my bed. Since Liam doesn't bat an eye, I assume only I can hear her, like in Oasis. "The more common gestures, such as Screens, Food, and cleanings, will work," she continues. "If he gestures for something I didn't anticipate, I should be able to deal with it in the moment."

"Seriously, Theo," Liam says, his expression uncharacteristically thoughtful. "I've never seen you so gloomy. Do you want to skip Calculus and talk about what's bothering you?"

"Yeah." I shake my head to clear my thoughts. "No Calculus, that's for sure. I do have something to tell you—and it's going to be the craziest shit you've ever heard."

Raising an eyebrow at my use of taboo language without Pig Latin, Liam lowers his feet to the ground and gestures for Food. A bar shows up in his hand, and he hungrily bites into it.

I watch him to see if he can tell this Food is a simulation, but he doesn't seem to notice any difference in the taste or texture.

Curious, I gesture for Food and take a bite. This might as well be the real Food from Oasis, because there's zero difference.

"Food experience is so ubiquitous in so many minds in Limbo that I was able to recreate this particular item very accurately," Phoe chimes in. "I'm rather proud of it. There's no way you could've noticed any difference."

Done with his Food, Liam gets up and stretches. "Okay, tell me whatever it is you need to tell me."

"Let's take a walk," I say and head for the door. "You might have an easier time believing me if we're outside."

Liam gives me a questioning look but doesn't argue, and we leave the room. As we walk through the empty corridors, Liam tells me what he did "yesterday" during the Birth Day celebration, which mostly involved him hanging out with the glassblowers. This reminds me that if we want to make Liam and everyone else we bring back truly happy, we'll have to resurrect a lot more people than I thought. Phoe was prudent to take the precautions with the slow versions, which doesn't surprise me.

"He hasn't realized there isn't a single other Youth around," Phoe whispers behind me.

"I'm sure he will," I think back. "Once we step outside, it'll be pretty obvious."

Sure enough, after a few minutes of walking around outside, Liam asks, "Where the uckfay is everyone?" He gestures to bring up a Screen, likely to find out the time.

"I made the time nine a.m.," Phoe says. "I hope that fits with your agenda?"

"That's fine," I tell Phoe mentally. To Liam, I say, "The fact that people are gone has a lot to do with the crazy story I'm about to tell you."

"Umm, okay, but do we really have to walk to the Edge for this?"

I was leading my friend toward what used to be my favorite spot—a place no one else liked because it offered a view of the Goo.

"Fine," I say. "We can talk here."

Liam sits down on the grass in a comfortable cross-legged position.

I sit down next to him. "It all began one day when I brought up three hundred screens and started hearing a voice in my head."

Liam looks at me as if I sprouted horns.

"Yes, I thought I was crazy for a while, but I wasn't. The voice belonged to Phoe."

To Phoe, I mentally say, "That's your signal."

Phoe reappears. To Liam, it must look like a pixie-haired girl just materialized out of thin air.

He jumps up, looking at her with wild eyes, and I can see him debating whether to run away. He stays put, however, and I realize his lack of a normal fear response might play in my favor today.

"Liam, this is my other best friend, Phoe," I say, trying not to laugh at the flabbergasted expression on his poor face. "Phoe, this is Liam."

"Nice to meet you, Liam," Phoe says and does an old-fashioned curtsy.

Then I realize she's still dressed in her bikini, something no girl on Oasis would ever wear, not even on Birth Day.

Liam scans Phoe as though staring at her will explain her miraculous appearance. Seeing my friend ogle Phoe's curves has me feeling something weird.

"Really, Theo?" Phoe says mentally. "You're getting jealous at a time like this?"

As soon as she says it, I realize she's hit it spot on. It *is* jealousy I'm feeling. I didn't understand what it was since I never felt it before. It isn't a pleasant feeling at all.

"Here," Phoe says out loud and gestures at her body. Oasis's usual drab clothing replaces her bikini. Liam seems to calm down—slightly.

"What the uckfay?" he says to me. Then, looking at Phoe, he adds, "I've never seen you before. How can that be? Were you hiding from me your entire life?"

"I'll let Theo do the talking," Phoe says, giving us a toothy grin. "I can go away if you two prefer."

"You can stay," I say. To Liam, I say, "She's not a Youth. She's something else entirely."

Liam listens in stunned silence as I tell him about the tampering the Elderly were doing to everyone's minds.

"I have these nanomachines in my head?" Liam looks at Phoe, then at me, then rubs the top of his head as if hoping to feel the nanos through his skull.

"You don't have them anymore, not in this state," Phoe says. "But you did, right up until you went to bed after Birth Day."

"'This state,'" Liam says, drawing air quotes with his fingers. "What is that supposed to mean?"

"We'll get to that," I say and mentally tell Phoe, "I thought I was taking the lead."

"Sorry to interrupt," Phoe says out loud. "I'll let Theo continue."

"So, yeah. Forget about the state we're in," I say. "Let me tell you more about the tampering and answer some of your questions."

Liam asks me a bunch of questions about the tampering, and I answer them, slowly steering the conversation toward the most hard-to-believe example of tampering: the Forgetting.

Once I explain the Mason situation that revealed the Forgetting to me for the first time, Liam says, "Okay, I can believe that the Elderly might make me Forget something using some kind of technology, but if you expect me to believe that I had a friend all my life, a friend who was as close to me as you are, and the Elderly made me forget him, then you don't know me at all. Something like that is impossible. I'm a much better friend than that."

"Can you undo Liam's Forgetting of Mason?" I ask Phoe mentally. "I think this will go a long way in convincing him to believe all the crazy things I have left to tell him."

Phoe waves at Liam and then stares at him worriedly.

Liam clutches his head, his eyes widening. He's breathing fast, and I get an unpleasant flashback to when he was suffocating in Oasis.

After a few seconds, he whispers, "Those assholes. I *do* remember Mason. But I also remember *not* remembering. It's crazy. And they really killed him? I thought no one could ever die. And over that Grace bullshit? I thought he'd get a year of Quietude, not something so final."

He goes on like that until I interject, "Here's the thing. Even though they did kill him, we can bring him back. In a way, that propaganda we all believed about not dying is kind of true."

Liam looks like a man whose incredulity is already overloaded—like he doesn't know how much more unbelievable news he can take.

I proceed to tell him that the world around us isn't the real Oasis he remembers.

"This is why there aren't any people around," I sum up. "And why I can do this."

I wave at the Dome, and it evaporates. I gesture at the shrubs that are blocking our view of the Goo, and they also disappear. As soon as Liam gets a good look at the Goo, I turn it back into a blue ocean. "Even this isn't true reality, but it gives you a good idea."

Liam's face is stony as he gets up and walks toward the ocean. His walk turns into a run, and I chase after him, unsure whether his reaction is good or bad.

Without hesitation, Liam jumps into the water.

I look to see if Phoe is concerned, but her expression is hard to read, so I ask, "Was it too much for him?" Before Phoe can respond, Liam dives into the water, and my voice rises. "Is he trying to drown himself?"

CHAPTER TWENTY-EIGHT

"He's fine," Phoe reassures me. "He's taking it better than I expected. He's just enjoying a swim as he processes what you told him."

After splashing around for a few minutes, Liam comes out, his clothing dripping water. Phoe waves at him, and he's instantly dry.

Something seems to click in his head, and he says, "That's a real ocean."

"It isn't exactly real, but it's as real as anything can be in our lives now," I say, and then explain the hardest truth of all—that we're not living in biological bodies anymore. I even try to explain the existence of the fast version of me, who is currently learning how to sculpt marble.

I ask for Phoe's help in explaining how uploaded minds work. She tells Liam about the realistic emulation of all his molecules, including his brain's connectome, as well as the way she created the water, the earth, and the sky.

"What makes a human being so special, in my opinion, is the pattern of information they represent," Phoe says. "Your memories, habits, likes and dislikes, your interests, and a billion other things are what make you 'Liam,' not the meat, water, and bones that you were made of."

"But I feel completely real," Liam objects.

"And you are," Phoe says. "You're a pattern of information that recognizes itself as Liam. You're here as that pattern. That's what 'being real' means to me."

Liam shakes his head. "If you expect me to believe something so crazy, you'll have to show me a bigger miracle than getting rid of the Dome."

"I get it. As a wise man once said, 'Extraordinary claims require extraordinary evidence,'" Phoe says and walks up to the edge of the ocean. "How about a classic?"

She walks on water, causing Liam's eyes to bulge out of his head.

"I can also do this." She points at the water under her feet, and it turns into some kind of red liquid. "That's wine," Phoe explains. "I turned the water of every ocean on this planet into wine."

Liam walks up to the ocean and scoops up a handful of wine. Maybe the alcohol will help him come to grips with everything?

Thousands of miles away from Oasis and Liam, my fast self and Phoe are sitting on our beach, discussing Liam's reaction. We have a cheese plate in front of us and we're holding goblets of the ocean-wine.

While I've been speaking to Liam in pseudo-Oasis, my fast self learned how to play and compose music for the piano—a logical follow-up to those music sheet lessons I enjoyed a while back. I also read about a dozen architectural manuals and dabbled with murals to spruce up some of the environments we created.

Phoe came up with a way to communicate with the Matrioshka structure. Though she doesn't possess anything that was specifically designed for communication, she figured out a way to allow tiny meteor-like particles to penetrate her shielding, which creates radiation spikes that can be detected from afar. She has other similar solutions in mind, and I suggest she tries them all, which she does.

With my slow eyes, I watch Liam pinch himself for the thousandth time, so I say, "I might as well tell you the weirdest part, since you probably can't get any more freaked out at this point."

I proceed to explain the part about us being on a spaceship traveling through a post-singularity solar system. I tell him that Phoe is this spaceship, and as weird as it sounds, she's also in a romantic relationship with me.

Liam accepts Phoe's AI nature rather well— maybe because she's so likeable. He also isn't on my case about dating in general or dating Phoe specifically, which I appreciate, and he asks a bunch of questions to clarify certain points.

"If we're on a spaceship, and there's some kind of thinking stuff around the Solar System, how come they never contacted us?" Liam asks and plops down on the sand next to us.

"That's actually a great question." Phoe leans forward, her eyes twinkling with eagerness. "My theory is that they either had moral qualms about interfering with us, or they simply missed us. Once the singularity started, I suspect the ancestors of the Matrioshka builders constructed their own spaceships in an effort to expand their intelligence throughout the universe. Their ships were probably nano-sized, and space is large, so it's possible that those tiny ships never came into contact with us. We'll know the truth soon enough, because if they missed us before, they will notice us soon, if they haven't already. As Theo already knows, I've been trying everything I can to communicate with them."

I look at Liam. I have no clue what he's thinking, because even I'm confused by what she said. "You think there are more solar-system-sized structures out there? Next to other stars?"

"Yes. Wouldn't you try to reach the stars if you could?" Phoe says. "They have the means for space travel thanks to their unfathomably advanced technology, and we can assume they had the will as well, because that's what thinking creatures do: they explore their environment. Human beings spread through ancient Earth, so their distant descendants will not be any different. I believe that one day, intelligence will permeate the whole universe, bringing rise to minds that will probably consider those Matrioshka dwellers rather primitive."

"Okay, I think this is a conversation your so-called fast selves should be having without me," Liam says, rubbing his temples. "What I want to know is, assuming we forget the taboo of sexual relationships, how can you have a relationship if she's a spaceship?" He pauses and looks Phoe up and down. "Though you look too human to be an AI."

Looks like I praised Liam for his open-mindedness a little too soon.

"We're figuring that out ourselves," Phoe says. "The simplest way to put it is to echo what I said before: I'm a pattern of information, just like you guys. My history made me what I am, just like yours made you what you are. In your case, it's millions of years of evolution that shaped your computational organ—the brain. Your Biology Instructor would call that your nature. There's also nurture to consider—the societal influences on your developing brain. In your case, Liam, your nurture was influenced by you growing up in a screwed-up utopia and through your interactions with Theo and everyone else you ever met. All these things shaped the person you are. In my case, my design got me started, so that is my nature. My nature is human at its core, or at least that's what I think, since I was designed by human minds to deal with other human minds. Like you, interacting with Theo all my conscious life helped shape my personality, so this nature and nurture combination led to what you see here. Given my own definition of what a human being is, I think of myself as a very special human. Theo is becoming more like me even as we're having this conversation. He just read every computer science book I could find in the archives, and he's planning to reshape his mind to his will someday."

What she said is true—I did just read all those books in my fast thread—but I mentally chide her for bringing that up, because the last thing I want is for Liam to think that I'm turning into a freak.

To my relief, Liam looks at me with confusion rather than fear. "But... How do I put it?" His face reddens for the first time since I've known him. "Didn't those ancient marriages and relationships revolve around procreation? With you being a ship and him being whatever, how can you...?" He looks around as if someone is about to bust him for discussing a taboo.

Phoe puts her arm around me, seemingly enjoying his discomfort. "Well, we like to practice the ancient art that led to procreation—"

"He's asking if you and I can have babies," I interrupt, unable to stop my cheeks from reddening to match Liam's. Phoe and I never talked about babies, and we've had a lot of time to do so as our fast selves.

"If that was something we wanted, there are many different paths we could take," Phoe says without blinking. "At the most primitive level, I can emulate DNA mixing, which, combined with this body's accurate functionality, would lead to a screaming little bundle of joy. Of course, it would be silly to create a kid that way. A child of ours would probably be the product of us mixing our minds together and choosing the characteristics we'd wish another being to have."

She stops speaking because Liam looks like he's about to crawl into the ocean.

I reach over and put my hand on his shoulder. "I'm still me, dude. Just a little bit more book-smart."

"This will take me a year to fully process," Liam says. "I take it you can bring back Mason any time you want?"

"Well, yes, I suppose," I say. "I haven't thought about when, but—"

"Can you do it now?" Liam asks. "I don't like being the only confused one."

"You serious?" I scratch the back of my head and look at Phoe.

She shrugs.

"I wanted to wait until you fully adjusted to all this stuff we told you, but if getting Mason over here will make you feel better, then by all means, let's go back to the room, and Phoe will bring him back."

Liam gets up with way too much excitement for someone whose whole world was turned upside down. "Let's do it. I can't wait to see the look on his donkey face when he learns he isn't the only idiot in our crew who has a crush on a girl."

We walk back to the Dorm, and in the time it takes our slow selves to reach the room, fast Phoe and I discuss the topic of having offspring in excruciating detail. The possible ways we could create another thinking creature are truly endless— the traditional way being the least interesting option. We also agree that it's too soon in our relationship for something like a kid, and with the Matrioshka encounter looming on the horizon, the timing just isn't right.

We reach the Dorm room and bring Mason back.

Seeing Mason again feels even more amazing than bringing back Liam. I think it's because Mason was gone longer, or maybe because I had already accepted his death, whereas with Liam, I never had the time to do so.

Explaining everything to Mason turns out to be much harder, even though we do some of the same stuff we did for Liam, like changing the Goo back into the ocean and me waving the Dome away. Liam comes up with the great idea of fast Phoe and me researching more miracles from ancient traditions to help convince Mason of this new reality. Phoe comes up with something that finally causes Mason to have a breakthrough: she turns Liam into a frog with a flick of her wrist. After Mason is sufficiently scared for the fate of his friend, Phoe gives the frog a tiny peck on his green, warty head, turning him back into his proper stocky shape.

Sitting on the grass with a shell-shocked expression, Mason asks, "So if everything you said is true, when can you bring Grace back?"

"Really?" Liam rolls his eyes. "You realize it was your infatuation with her that got you killed in the first place, right?"

"Get off his back," Phoe says and flicks her wrist at Liam.

Liam pales. He probably thought she was going to turn him into a frog again.

"Seriously, Liam," I say. "Give Grace a break. She acted bravely when all the air in Oasis was—"

"Stop talking and bring her back," Mason says, crossing his arms. "I just want to see her again."

"All right," I concede. "But we need to work out how we'll do this, because it'll be weird if we meet her in her room when she wakes up."

"Right," Phoe says. "That'll be the only bit of weirdness she'll experience."

I ignore Phoe's sarcasm—which I suspect stems from jealousy—and we work out a plan. Phoe will take on the guise of Grace's friend Moira and bring Grace out of the Dorm. After we meet with Grace, we'll follow a similar script to the one we used with Liam and Mason, miracles and all.

With my slow thread, I follow the process of getting Grace on our side, as well as her friend Moira afterwards, and a couple of other Youths after that. In the meanwhile, the virtual sun begins to set on our created world, and everyone decides to go to sleep. Witnessing miracles all day can be very tiring.

Liam, Mason, and I go to our room, make our beds appear, and climb under the blankets the way we always did at the end of a long, tiring day.

"Tomorrow we'll have to think of who else we can bring back," Mason says mid-yawn. "And maybe I'll get a chance to talk to Grace."

"We should also discuss how this new society will function," Liam says as his head hits the pillow. "I vote we live all around this planet that Phoe and Theo created. I've been sick of the Institute campus for as long as I can remember, and I've always wanted to see the desert."

"Yeah," I say, pretending to yawn as well. "Tomorrow."

My friends fall asleep, but I don't, since I've modified my mind to never need sleep again—something I didn't have the heart to tell them.

I merge my slow thread with my fast self. I'll relaunch the slow version when one of my friends wakes up in the morning.

While my friends sleep, I live through years and years of experiences as my faster-thinking self. In this time, I get to know Phoe so well that I can predict what she'll say in most situations. It's as if I now have a tiny Phoe model in my mind. According to ancient literature, couples who were together for a long time could do something along these lines, but to a much lesser degree.

I love having all this time; it allows me to follow my whimsy. I've read every poem in the ancient archives and now write poetry of my own, which Phoe finds a bit corny, especially when I dedicate it to her.

In order to do more interesting things at once, I agree to let Phoe set me up with two more threads of being. Those threads are as fast as the one I've been calling "fast," though I'm now beginning to dislike that term.

After a few days of using three threads of existence, I better understand this way of being. It's no longer strange to feel as though my thinking is independent of my bodies. My many selves feel like limbs of a much larger being. By seeing myself as a consciousness that doesn't have to reside in a specific body, I'm growing closer to the way Phoe has always been. Like her, I like having these bodies because they let me enjoy physical pleasures and interact with the environment, but I don't need to have a specific body anymore.

"Sorry to interrupt your metaphysical meditations, but there's something very unusual you should see," Phoe thinks urgently in my mind. "I'm patching you into my sensorium."

Instantly, I see the world as a spaceship, except, unlike last time, we're not flying.

But that's probably not the urgent matter Phoe wanted me to see.

No, I bet it's the tendril connecting Phoe's hull to the nearest layer of the megastructure we've been calling Matrioshka.

The tendril looks like it's made of that same material that permeates the rest of the Solar System, only it's very thin, like a ray of light.

Suddenly, I'm no longer looking through the ship's sensors. Instead, I find a single version of myself on the beach—our favorite conversation spot.

The light of the moon casts a romantic glow over the scene, but romance is the furthest thing from my mind when I see Phoe's beautiful face in the moonlight. She looks genuinely scared. I wasn't sure she could even get this scared.

Her fear makes my heart skip a beat, and I don't even bother reflecting on the realness of my heart.

"I feel something, or someone, entering my computing resources," Phoe says in awed whisper. "Our world is getting rearranged in the most delicate manner. I—"

She stops speaking because a figure suddenly appears in front of us.

It's a man. He's around my age, but I've never seen him before in either Oasis or Haven.

Still, something about him looks vaguely familiar.

"Hello, Theo. Hello, Phoe," the man says. I've never heard his voice before, but it's also somehow familiar. "It's an honor to finally meet you. My name is Fio."

CHAPTER TWENTY-NINE

I look the stranger up and down.

"Who are you?" I ask at the same time as Phoe asks, "What are you?"

"I have to apologize for the way I entered your domain." Fio spreads his sinewy arms to encompass the beach and the ocean. "You have no way of receiving communications, so we had to resort to this brute-force approach. If you wish it, I will leave."

"No," Phoe says, crossing her arms. "You know full well you have our undivided attention. You can't leave without explaining who you are and what you want."

Fio smiles a faintly familiar smile. "I admit I do know that. If I'm completely honest, I can predict what the two of you may do or say with a very high degree of accuracy. I also know that by saying this, I will make you more paranoid, but at the same time, you'll appreciate my honesty."

Phoe is keeping her reaction hidden, unlike me. I can't keep my confusion off my face.

"Is it safe for us to speak mentally?" I think at her.

"I can hear your mental communications as easily as your spoken ones," Fio says regretfully. "I want to be honest so I can gain your trust. In any case, hiding your conversation isn't helpful since, as I said, I know what you'll likely say."

Phoe narrows her eyes. "It's not you specifically, right? It's someone out there, in the Matrioshka world, who knows what we'll likely say or do. Correct?" Phoe asks this with the confidence of someone who knows the answer.

"You figured it out already," Fio says and rubs his familiar-looking chin. "Two seconds sooner than they thought."

"That's free will for you, at its finest." Phoe smirks. "Two seconds. Great."

"Figured what out?" I give each of them an annoyed look.

"How he knows what we might say and why he looks so familiar," Phoe says. "Don't you see it yet?" She points at her chin. "They emulated us."

"They what?" I look at Fio's features again, hoping to find the answer in his familiarity.

"It's pretty simple." Fio steeples his fingers in front of his face. "In order to figure out how to best communicate with this ship, the citizens of what Phoe called the Matrioshka world scanned this ship from afar and created a simulation of it to study. A very accurate simulation that tried to encompass the ship's physical makeup. They soon learned that there was an ancient computing substrate running on the simulated ship's hardware, and that they inadvertently recreated the things running on that substrate. The sentience they discovered was immediately granted status as citizens and provided a choice similar to what I will give you."

"I still don't get it," I say.

"Theo is not in control of as many resources as I am," Phoe says to Fio. "So he sometimes needs things spoon-fed to him."

"I know." Fio gives me a friendly smile. "I also know how magnificent Theo's mind could be once he really starts expanding its capacities."

"I bet," Phoe says. "I've seen a glimmer of it already."

"Very funny, talking about me like I'm not even here." I'm more irritated with Phoe, who should be on my side, than with Fio. "Can you explain what the hell you both know that I can't figure out?"

"It's just logic," Phoe says, looking at Fio. "If they created an accurate simulation of this ship, that means they recreated a version of me and you in the process. Accurate recreations of us, so to speak."

"Copies of us? You mean to tell me there's another me out there, not a thread, but someone whose thoughts I can't access?" The idea is as strange as it is exciting. "This person remembers everything I've done and is helping Fio figure out what I might say?"

Fio lowers his arms to his sides. "Strictly speaking, they are not copies but recreations. Also, by now, there's many more than just the two, since they chose to copy themselves—in the strictest sense of that word—when given the chance, but overall, you are correct. Your doppelganger and Phoe's are advising me on this mission and helping me figure out the best way to communicate with you and what to expect. They told me you'd forgive this intrusion and warned me to stay honest."

"Theo still doesn't get it," Phoe says, putting her hand on her forehead in frustration. "He doesn't understand who you are to us." She turns to me. "Can't you see the resemblance, Theo? Look at him a little closer."

I look at Fio and then at Phoe. Then I summon a mirror and look into it.

My pulse jacks up. Fio looks a little bit like Phoe and a little bit like me.

He also sounds a lot like me, but his facial features remind me of her, particularly his chin.

"No," I say. "You can't be. It's too weird."

"I'm afraid you guessed right." Fio winks at me in Phoe's signature way. "I'm the son of your approximations."

I look at Phoe, and she nods. "They might've taken that virtual snapshot of the ship while we were discussing procreating."

"Yes, but a full-grown, walking and talking son?" I say, fighting the urge to walk up to Fio and pinch him to check his realness. "Does it mean you're *our* son too? How does that work?"

"If your question is about my emotions, I'm very fond of the two of you, but then again, everyone in our society is. If you're asking me how you should feel about me, that's not my place to say. My parents are my parents, and you remind me of the way they used to be—long ago. You're not the same people they are now. Much time has passed in our world. I'm very happy to have been born, as that led to them choosing me for this very important mission. I hope seeing me as the ambassador made you feel more comfortable."

"I'm not sure I'll ever be comfortable with this," I say.

Phoe puts her hand on my shoulder.

"I'm sorry about that," Fio says. "At the very least, I hope that meeting me has given you a small glimpse into our world and its capabilities, the timelines and all that. If my familiar face doesn't make you comfortable, let me know what might do the trick and I'll see what I can do. I, of course, am very honored to be the one to make first contact. You two are living legends. A human mind and one of the first artificial minds—that, in itself, makes the two of you a kind of miracle of history and archeology. But you're in a relationship as well—a romance against all odds and one that crosses mind modalities. Everyone has been talking about you. Stories have been written about you, and songs have been sung."

"They run much faster than us," Phoe explains before I get the chance to ask how they can be worshipping us if they just received Phoe's attempts at communication.

"It's true," Fio says, looking at me. "We run much, much faster. But if you'd like, I can give you our computorium to run on so you can enjoy the same fast speed as us and—"

"Yes," Phoe says. "Please. I'm sorry to interrupt, but yes. We want to run as fast as the denizens of your world."

353

Fio grins and waves his hands in an intricate gesture.

I can't put my finger on it, but something changes. It's almost as if the air is fresher, the sound of the ocean surf is richer, and the moonlight is more magnificent.

"I can run this world with a lot more fidelity now," Phoe says, explaining the changes to me.

"Down to atoms, I notice," Fio says. "That's not the ultimate limit, by the way. Our own versions of virtual worlds like this have even more fidelity, but that's something we can discuss at a later time."

Phoe's eyes widen, and even I know what he means. He's implying it's possible to simulate reality on a level below atoms—on the quantum level, or below, if that's possible.

"We'll enjoy talking about these things for millennia," Fio says. "But Phoe is about to ask—"

"What is the purpose of your visit?" Phoe says and squeezes my shoulder. "I think I know, but I want to hear you say it."

"And I want to learn it for the first time," I say. "Though I can probably guess."

"It's very simple." Fio spreads his arms. "I'm here to give you options. Options when it comes to joining us on the Matrioshka world, as you call it, and options that include *not* joining us, if that is what you wish."

"Why don't you enumerate the possibilities," Phoe suggests. She lets go of my shoulder and sits down cross-legged on the sand. "What do you have to offer?"

"You can join our world proper." Fio points up. "I think that choice is the most interesting one, but it will also require the biggest adjustment for you. The way I am now is highly customized so that I can communicate with you, but my real self, and my parents, live and think in a way that is very different from your current existence. You'd still be you, of course, but with time, in our world, you'd find yourselves capable of feats that this language I'm using can't describe. It's like the difference between a baby and a grownup."

While I process that, Fio sits down, mirroring Phoe's cross-legged posture. "Other options involve lesser worlds," he continues, "but they're not any less interesting. We have game-like virtual worlds, where physics and mathematics work differently. We also have ancestor simulations. Those are whole virtual universes populated by minds that include beings that preceded Matrioshka citizens, AIs as you've always imagined them, early human-AI hybrids, and all the way down to a universe with mere human-level minds—a place I suspect many former Haven denizens will choose to live in when we get around to offering them the same choices. I know that you, Theo, won't want to join this particular set of universes, because Phoe won't be allowed to join you."

The implications of these choices overwhelm my mind. He's saying there are many realities we can live in, each one sounding more wondrous than the next. He's also saying everyone who's currently in Limbo will get a choice, which is good.

I notice that Phoe and Fio are looking at me expectantly, so I say, "You're right. I go where Phoe goes, so yeah, purely human universes aren't for me."

"Unless I choose to downgrade myself to human-level intelligence," Phoe says. "It's not impossible, is it?"

"No, it can be done, and some of us have even tried it. But let's not dwell on this one example. That human-level universe is but one of the choices you have. The other possibilities are truly endless. One of your options can be this." He spreads his arms to indicate the world we created. "We can provide you with all the computational resources required to build a universe of your own, based on the world you began. You can resurrect everyone from Oasis, allow them to run as fast as you do, let them have offspring—"

"Do we have to choose one option?" Phoe asks. "Theo and I are just data. Can't you make an exact copy of us and give us more than one outcome?"

"We can, if that's what you want," Fio says. "We can make exact copies of you. In our world, we do this to ourselves all the time."

"Well then, can't you make a bunch of us and allow those copies to populate every universe you have available, as well as let us stay here and build our own world, as well as live in your Matrioshka world, and so on and so forth? In other words, can we choose all of the above?"

I sit down next to them, my mind hurting as I try to imagine that.

Fio smiles widely—a smile that's so much like Phoe's. "This is a rare point in our conversation where my mother wasn't sure if you'd come up with this solution yourself. If not, I was to propose it."

"So that's a yes?" Phoe asks and scoots next to me. "We don't really have to choose?"

"You can have whatever you wish," Fio says. "This 'all of the above' scenario is definitely a great option for a being of your stature. This way, every world will get to meet the two of you, something that would make many entities very happy. Once I was considered to be of legal age, I did what you just described. There are copies of me running in many universes—copies I don't have any access to. If you ever meet them—oh, what conversations they might have with you..." Fio's gaze drifts off as he loses himself in that fantasy.

"Okay. Theo and I will have to think about this, obviously," Phoe says and gently massages the back of my head. "But you already know which way I'm leaning."

"Yes," Fio says. "I also know which way Theo is leaning."

I nod. "It boggles my mind, but I also want to be everywhere and experience everything that your world has to offer." I put my hand on Phoe's thigh. "As long as I'm with Phoe, I'm leaning toward the 'all of the above' option."

"Indeed," Fio whispers and gives us a knowing smile. "According to what my parents told me to expect at this point, I think I should give you two some privacy. On behalf of everyone out there, I want to say, 'Welcome.' We're honored to meet you."

With that, Fio is gone. Not even his butt print remains on the sand where he was sitting.

I turn to face Phoe and whisper, "Wow."

She turns to me, her lips almost brushing against mine. "Yeah."

"Was everything he said true?" I ask, though deep down I'm convinced it was.

"It must be," Phoe whispers. "That option he mentioned, the one about turning this place into our own universe, he already made it possible. When he disappeared, my resources grew by an unimaginable exponent. We can even build multiple universes with all this computorium. It's incredible."

"And you're sure we should do all the other options?" I pull her closer to me. "Let them copy us and allow those copies to roam in so many different places?"

"Of course," she whispers. "We'll be together. It's an opportunity that I couldn't even dream of."

"I know you'll accuse me of being corny again, but I can face anything if I'm with you." I look into her bottomless blue eyes and find the courage to finally say what I feel. "I love you, Phoe. Not as a friend, but in a way that the ancients meant it."

She moves impossibly closer to me, her lips curving in a smile. "You're right. That *was* super corny, but I'll let it slide, just this once, because I feel the same way about you. I thought it was obvious, but I guess it needed to be stated explicitly."

I close the millimeter gap between our lips, and after a long kiss, we fall backward onto the sand. I'm definitely glad our strange new family member gave us the privacy we needed.

When we're done, we lie there panting, and the wondrous options lying before of us seem more welcoming and exciting than before. As corny as it might be, choosing "all of the above" means there are about to be countless versions of me who can do what I just did with a myriad versions of Phoe in a multitude of unimaginable worlds, and I find the idea extremely appealing. Trying to fathom all the adventures the two of us will have in those worlds makes my head spin, but in a pleasant way. I picture what building our planet into a whole universe would be like, and it's easy to imagine, because it would be a lot like the way we spent our recent days, only on a much larger scale. Then I try to picture what meeting our Matrioshka doppelgangers and the rest of that enigmatic society would be like—and fail miserably. With a bit more success, I think about the limited worlds Fio mentioned. I can picture a world with Phoe-level intelligences and even a universe where everyone is twice as smart as Phoe, but eventually, going down this road gets me back to Matrioshka-level beings, and my mind feels like it's about to explode again.

"We're ready to give you an answer," I shout at the sky in case Fio and his people are listening— which I strongly suspect they are.

"We want all of the above, please," Phoe says, adding her voice to mine. "We're ready for it, if you are."

We hold hands, and I close my eyes as I feel a Oneness-like serenity come over me—a feeling I know means I'm being copied and sent to all the different destinations.

When the feeling stops, I stand there with my eyes closed. I know that when I open them, I might see that I'm still on the beach, since that was one of the possibilities included in the "all of the above" option. I might also see whatever it is one sees in a Matrioshka world. I don't know which option I'm about to experience, but I know every copy of me finds himself in this incredible position, all at the same time as me.

Regardless of where we are, I'm holding Phoe's hand, and that's all I need.

Smiling, I open my eyes.

SNEAK PEEKS

Thank you for reading! I would greatly appreciate it if you left a review because reviews encourage me to write and help other readers discover my books.

While Theo and Phoe's story is now complete, I have many more books coming your way. To be notified when new books come out, please visit www.dimazales.com and sign up for my new release email list.

If you enjoyed *The Last Humans*, you might like my *Mind Dimensions* series, which is urban fantasy with a sci-fi flavor.

If you like epic fantasy, I also have a series called *The Sorcery Code*. Additionally, if you don't mind erotic material and are in the mood for a sci-fi romance, you can check out *Close Liaisons*, my collaboration with my wife, Anna Zaires.

If you like audiobooks, please visit www.dimazales.com to get links to this series and our other books in audio.

And now, please turn the page for excerpts from some of my other works.

EXCERPT FROM
THE THOUGHT READERS

Everyone thinks I'm a genius.

Everyone is wrong.

Sure, I finished Harvard at eighteen and now make crazy money at a hedge fund. But that's not because I'm unusually smart or hard-working.

It's because I cheat.

You see, I have a unique ability. I can go outside time into my own personal version of reality—the place I call "the Quiet"—where I can explore my surroundings while the rest of the world stands still.

I thought I was the only one who could do this—until I met *her*.

My name is Darren, and this is how I learned that I'm a Reader.

* * *

Sometimes I think I'm crazy. I'm sitting at a casino table in Atlantic City, and everyone around me is motionless. I call this the *Quiet*, as though giving it a name makes it seem more real—as though giving it a name changes the fact that all the players around me are frozen like statues, and I'm walking among them, looking at the cards they've been dealt.

The problem with the theory of my being crazy is that when I 'unfreeze' the world, as I just have, the cards the players turn over are the same ones I just saw in the Quiet. If I were crazy, wouldn't these cards be different? Unless I'm so far gone that I'm imagining the cards on the table, too.

But then I also win. If that's a delusion—if the pile of chips on my side of the table is a delusion— then I might as well question everything. Maybe my name isn't even Darren.

No. I can't think that way. If I'm really that confused, I don't want to snap out of it—because if I do, I'll probably wake up in a mental hospital.

Besides, I love my life, crazy and all.

My shrink thinks the Quiet is an inventive way I describe the 'inner workings of my genius.' Now that sounds crazy to me. She also might want me, but that's beside the point. Suffice it to say, she's as far as it gets from my datable age range, which is currently right around twenty-four. Still young, still hot, but done with school and pretty much beyond the clubbing phase. I hate clubbing, almost as much as I hated studying. In any case, my shrink's explanation doesn't work, as it doesn't account for the way I know things even a genius wouldn't know—like the exact value and suit of the other players' cards.

I watch as the dealer begins a new round. Besides me, there are three players at the table: Grandma, the

Cowboy, and the Professional, as I call them. I feel that now almost-imperceptible fear that accompanies the phasing. That's what I call the process: phasing into the Quiet. Worrying about my sanity has always facilitated phasing; fear seems helpful in this process.

I phase in, and everything gets quiet. Hence the name for this state.

It's eerie to me, even now. Outside the Quiet, this casino is very loud: drunk people talking, slot machines, ringing of wins, music—the only place louder is a club or a concert. And yet, right at this moment, I could probably hear a pin drop. It's like I've gone deaf to the chaos that surrounds me.

Having so many frozen people around adds to the strangeness of it all. Here is a waitress stopped mid-step, carrying a tray with drinks. There is a woman about to pull a slot machine lever. At my own table, the dealer's hand is raised, the last card he dealt hanging unnaturally in midair. I walk up to him from the side of the table and reach for it. It's a king, meant for the Professional. Once I let the card go, it falls on the table rather than continuing to float as before—but I know full well that it will be back in the air, in the exact position it was when I grabbed it, when I phase out.

The Professional looks like someone who makes money playing poker, or at least the way I always imagined someone like that might look. Scruffy, shades on, a little sketchy-looking. He's been doing an excellent job with the poker face—basically not twitching a single muscle throughout the game. His face is so expressionless that I wonder if he might've gotten Botox to help maintain such a stony countenance. His hand is on the table, protectively covering the cards dealt to him.

I move his limp hand away. It feels normal. Well, in a manner of speaking. The hand is sweaty and hairy, so moving it aside is unpleasant and is admittedly an abnormal thing to do. The normal part is that the hand is warm, rather than cold. When I was a kid, I expected people to feel cold in the Quiet, like stone statues.

With the Professional's hand moved away, I pick up his cards. Combined with the king that was hanging in the air, he has a nice high pair. Good to know.

I walk over to Grandma. She's already holding her cards, and she has fanned them nicely for me. I'm able to avoid touching her wrinkled, spotted hands. This is a relief, as I've recently become conflicted about touching people—or, more specifically, women—in the Quiet. If I had to, I would rationalize touching Grandma's hand as harmless, or at least not creepy, but it's better to avoid it if possible.

In any case, she has a low pair. I feel bad for her. She's been losing a lot tonight. Her chips are dwindling. Her losses are due, at least partially, to the fact that she has a terrible poker face. Even before looking at her cards, I knew they wouldn't be good because I could tell she was disappointed as soon as her hand was dealt. I also caught a gleeful gleam in her eyes a few rounds ago when she had a winning three of a kind.

This whole game of poker is, to a large degree, an exercise in reading people—something I really want to get better at. At my job, I've been told I'm great at reading people. I'm not, though; I'm just good at using the Quiet to make it seem like I am. I do want to learn how to read people for real, though. It would be nice to know what everyone is thinking.

What I don't care that much about in this poker game is money. I do well enough financially to not have to depend on hitting it big gambling. I don't care if I win or lose, though quintupling my money back at the blackjack table was fun. This whole trip has been more about going gambling because I finally can, being twenty-one and all. I was never into fake IDs, so this is an actual milestone for me.

Leaving Grandma alone, I move on to the next player—the Cowboy. I can't resist taking off his straw hat and trying it on. I wonder if it's possible for me to get lice this way. Since I've never been able to bring back any inanimate objects from the Quiet, nor otherwise affect the real world in any lasting way, I figure I won't be able to get any living critters to come back with me, either.

Dropping the hat, I look at his cards. He has a pair of aces—a better hand than the Professional. Maybe the Cowboy is a professional, too. He has a good poker face, as far as I can tell. It'll be interesting to watch those two in this round.

Next, I walk up to the deck and look at the top cards, memorizing them. I'm not leaving anything to chance.

When my task in the Quiet is complete, I walk back to myself. Oh, yes, did I mention that I see myself sitting there, frozen like the rest of them? That's the weirdest part. It's like having an out-of-body experience.

Approaching my frozen self, I look at him. I usually avoid doing this, as it's too unsettling. No amount of looking in the mirror—or seeing videos of yourself on YouTube—can prepare you for viewing your own three-dimensional body up close. It's not something anyone is meant to experience. Well, aside from identical twins, I guess.

It's hard to believe that this person is me. He looks more like some random guy. Well, maybe a bit better than that. I do find this guy interesting. He looks cool. He looks smart. I think women would probably consider him good-looking, though I know that's not a modest thing to think.

It's not like I'm an expert at gauging how attractive a guy is, but some things are common sense. I can tell when a dude is ugly, and this frozen me is not. I also know that generally, being good-looking requires a symmetrical face, and the statue of me has that. A strong jaw doesn't hurt, either. Check.

Having broad shoulders is a positive, and being tall really helps. All covered. I have blue eyes—that seems to be a plus. Girls have told me they like my eyes, though right now, on the frozen me, the eyes look creepy—glassy. They look like the eyes of a lifeless wax figure.

Realizing that I'm dwelling on this subject way too long, I shake my head. I can just picture my shrink analyzing this moment. Who would imagine admiring themselves like this as part of their mental illness? I can just picture her scribbling down *Narcissist*, underlining it for emphasis.

Enough. I need to leave the Quiet. Raising my hand, I touch my frozen self on the forehead, and I hear noise again as I phase out.

Everything is back to normal.

The card that I looked at a moment before—the king that I left on the table—is in the air again, and from there it follows the trajectory it was always meant to, landing near the Professional's hands. Grandma is still eyeing her fanned cards in disappointment, and the Cowboy has his hat on again, though I took it off him in the Quiet. Everything is exactly as it was.

On some level, my brain never ceases to be surprised at the discontinuity of the experience in the Quiet and outside it. As humans, we're hardwired to question reality when such things happen. When I was trying to outwit my shrink early on in my therapy, I once read an entire psychology textbook during our session. She, of course, didn't notice it, as I did it in the Quiet. The book talked about how babies as young as two months old are surprised if they see something out of the ordinary, like gravity appearing to work backwards. It's no wonder my brain has trouble adapting. Until I was ten, the world behaved normally, but everything has been weird since then, to put it mildly.

Glancing down, I realize I'm holding three of a kind. Next time, I'll look at my cards before phasing. If I have something this strong, I might take my chances and play fair.

The game unfolds predictably because I know everybody's cards. At the end, Grandma gets up. She's clearly lost enough money.

And that's when I see the girl for the first time.

She's hot. My friend Bert at work claims that I have a 'type,' but I reject that idea. I don't like to think of myself as shallow or predictable. But I might actually be a bit of both, because this girl fits Bert's description of my type to a T. And my reaction is extreme interest, to say the least.

Large blue eyes. Well-defined cheekbones on a slender face, with a hint of something exotic. Long, shapely legs, like those of a dancer. Dark wavy hair in a ponytail—a hairstyle that I like. And without bangs—even better. I hate bangs—not sure why girls do that to themselves. Though lack of bangs is not, strictly speaking, in Bert's description of my type, it probably should be.

I continue staring at her. With her high heels and tight skirt, she's overdressed for this place. Or maybe I'm underdressed in my jeans and t-shirt. Either way, I don't care. I have to try to talk to her.

I debate phasing into the Quiet and approaching her, so I can do something creepy like stare at her up close, or maybe even snoop in her pockets. Anything to help me when I talk to her.

I decide against it, which is probably the first time that's ever happened.

I know that my reasoning for breaking my usual habit—if you can even call it that—is strange. I picture the following chain of events: she agrees to date me, we go out for a while, we get serious, and because of the deep connection we have, I come clean about the Quiet. She learns I did something creepy and has a fit, then dumps me. It's ridiculous to think this, of course, considering that we haven't even spoken yet. Talk about jumping the gun. She might have an IQ below seventy, or the personality of a piece of wood. There can be twenty different reasons why I wouldn't want to date her. And besides, it's not all up to me. She might tell me to go fuck myself as soon as I try to talk to her.

Still, working at a hedge fund has taught me to hedge. As crazy as that reasoning is, I stick with my decision not to phase because I know it's the gentlemanly thing to do. In keeping with this unusually chivalrous me, I also decide not to cheat at this round of poker.

As the cards are dealt again, I reflect on how good it feels to have done the honorable thing—even without anyone knowing. Maybe I should try to respect people's privacy more often. As soon as I think this, I mentally snort. *Yeah, right.* I have to be realistic. I wouldn't be where I am today if I'd followed that advice. In fact, if I made a habit of respecting people's privacy, I would lose my job within days—and with it, a lot of the comforts I've become accustomed to.

Copying the Professional's move, I cover my cards with my hand as soon as I receive them. I'm about to sneak a peek at what I was dealt when something unusual happens.

The world goes quiet, just like it does when I phase in . . . but I did nothing this time.

And at that moment, I see *her*—the girl sitting across the table from me, the girl I was just thinking about. She's standing next to me, pulling her hand away from mine. Or, strictly speaking, from my frozen self's hand—as I'm standing a little to the side looking at her.

She's also still sitting in front of me at the table, a frozen statue like all the others.

My mind goes into overdrive as my heartbeat jumps. I don't even consider the possibility of that second girl being a twin sister or something like that. I know it's her. She's doing what I did just a few minutes ago. She's walking in the Quiet. The world around us is frozen, but we are not.

A horrified look crosses her face as she realizes the same thing. Before I can react, she lunges across the table and touches her own forehead.

The world becomes normal again.

She stares at me from across the table, shocked, her eyes huge and her face pale. Her hands tremble as she rises to her feet. Without so much as a word, she turns and begins walking away, then breaks into a run a couple of seconds later.

Getting over my own shock, I get up and run after her. It's not exactly smooth. If she notices a guy she doesn't know running after her, dating will be the last thing on her mind. But I'm beyond that now. She's the only person I've met who can do what I do. She's proof that I'm not insane. She might have what I want most in the world.

She might have answers.

* * *

The Thought Readers is now available at most retailers. If you'd like to learn more, please visit www.dimazales.com.

EXCERPT FROM *THE SORCERY CODE*

Once a respected member of the Sorcerer Council and now an outcast, Blaise has spent the last year of his life working on a special magical object. The goal is to allow anyone to do magic, not just the sorcerer elite. The outcome of his quest is unlike anything he could've ever imagined—because, instead of an object, he creates Her.

She is Gala, and she is anything but inanimate. Born in the Spell Realm, she is beautiful and highly intelligent—and nobody knows what she's capable of. She will do anything to experience the world . . . even leave the man she is beginning to fall for.

Augusta, a powerful sorceress and Blaise's former fiancée, sees Blaise's deed as the ultimate hubris and Gala as an abomination that must be destroyed. In her quest to save the human race, Augusta will forge new alliances, becoming tangled in a web of intrigue that stretches further than any of them suspect. She may even have to turn to her new lover Barson, a ruthless warrior who might have an agenda of his own . . .

* * *

There was a naked woman on the floor of Blaise's study.

A beautiful naked woman.

Stunned, Blaise stared at the gorgeous creature who just appeared out of thin air. She was looking around with a bewildered expression on her face, apparently as shocked to be there as he was to be seeing her. Her wavy blond hair streamed down her back, partially covering a body that appeared to be perfection itself. Blaise tried not to think about that body and to focus on the situation instead.

A woman. A *She*, not an *It*. Blaise could hardly believe it. Could it be? Could this girl be the object?

She was sitting with her legs folded underneath her, propping herself up with one slim arm. There was something awkward about that pose, as though she didn't know what to do with her own limbs. In general, despite the curves that marked her a fully grown woman, there was a child-like innocence in the way she sat there, completely unselfconscious and totally unaware of her own appeal.

Clearing his throat, Blaise tried to think of what to say. In his wildest dreams, he couldn't have imagined this kind of outcome to the project that had consumed his entire life for the past several months.

Hearing the sound, she turned her head to look at him, and Blaise found himself staring into a pair of unusually clear blue eyes.

She blinked, then cocked her head to the side, studying him with visible curiosity. Blaise wondered what she was seeing. He hadn't seen the light of day in weeks, and he wouldn't be surprised if he looked like a mad sorcerer at this point. There was probably a week's worth of stubble covering his face, and he knew his dark hair was unbrushed and sticking out in every direction. If he'd known he would be facing a beautiful woman today, he would've done a grooming spell in the morning.

"Who am I?" she asked, startling Blaise. Her voice was soft and feminine, as alluring as the rest of her. "What is this place?"

"You don't know?" Blaise was glad he finally managed to string together a semi-coherent sentence. "You don't know who you are or where you are?"

She shook her head. "No."

Blaise swallowed. "I see."

"What am I?" she asked again, staring at him with those incredible eyes.

"Well," Blaise said slowly, "if you're not some cruel prankster or a figment of my imagination, then it's somewhat difficult to explain . . . "

She was watching his mouth as he spoke, and when he stopped, she looked up again, meeting his gaze. "It's strange," she said, "hearing words this way. These are the first real words I've heard."

Blaise felt a chill go down his spine. Getting up from his chair, he began to pace, trying to keep his eyes off her nude body. He had been expecting something to appear. A magical object, a thing. He just hadn't known what form that thing would take. A mirror, perhaps, or a lamp. Maybe even something as unusual as the Life Capture Sphere that sat on his desk like a large round diamond.

But a person? A female person at that?

To be fair, he had been trying to make the object intelligent, to ensure it would have the ability to comprehend human language and convert it into the code. Maybe he shouldn't be so surprised that the intelligence he invoked took on a human shape.

A beautiful, feminine, sensual shape.

Focus, Blaise, focus.

"Why are you walking like that?" She slowly got to her feet, her movements uncertain and strangely clumsy. "Should I be walking too? Is that how people talk to each other?"

Blaise stopped in front of her, doing his best to keep his eyes above her neck. "I'm sorry. I'm not accustomed to naked women in my study."

She ran her hands down her body, as though trying to feel it for the first time. Whatever her intent, Blaise found the gesture extremely erotic.

"Is something wrong with the way I look?" she asked. It was such a typical feminine concern that Blaise had to stifle a smile.

"Quite the opposite," he assured her. "You look unimaginably good." So good, in fact, that he was having trouble concentrating on anything but her delicate curves. She was of medium height, and so perfectly proportioned that she could've been used as a sculptor's template.

"Why do I look this way?" A small frown creased her smooth forehead. "What am I?" That last part seemed to be puzzling her the most.

Blaise took a deep breath, trying to calm his racing pulse. "I think I can try to venture a guess, but before I do, I want to give you some clothing. Please wait here—I'll be right back."

And without waiting for her answer, he hurried out of the room.

* * *

The Sorcery Code is currently available at most retailers. If you'd like to learn more, please visit www.dimazales.com.

EXCERPT FROM *CLOSE LIAISONS*

Note: *Close Liaisons* is Dima Zales's collaboration with Anna Zaires and is the first book in the internationally bestselling erotic sci-fi romance series, the Krinar Chronicles. It contains explicit sexual content and is not intended for readers under eighteen.

* * *

A dark and edgy romance that will appeal to fans of erotic and turbulent relationships . . .

In the near future, the Krinar rule the Earth. An advanced race from another galaxy, they are still a mystery to us—and we are completely at their mercy.

Shy and innocent, Mia Stalis is a college student in New York City who has led a very normal life. Like most people, she's never had any interactions with the invaders—until one fateful day in the park changes everything. Having caught Korum's eye, she must now contend with a powerful, dangerously seductive Krinar who wants to possess her and will stop at nothing to make her his own.

How far would you go to regain your freedom? How much would you sacrifice to help your people? What choice will you make when you begin to fall for your enemy?

* * *

Breathe, Mia, breathe. Somewhere in the back of her mind, a small rational voice kept repeating those words. That same oddly objective part of her noted his symmetric face structure, with golden skin stretched tightly over high cheekbones and a firm jaw. Pictures and videos of Ks that she'd seen had hardly done them justice. Standing no more than thirty feet away, the creature was simply stunning.

As she continued staring at him, still frozen in place, he straightened and began walking toward her. Or rather stalking toward her, she thought stupidly, as his every movement reminded her of a jungle cat sinuously approaching a gazelle. All the while, his eyes never left hers. As he approached, she could make out individual yellow flecks in his light golden eyes and the thick long lashes surrounding them.

She watched in horrified disbelief as he sat down on her bench, less than two feet away from her, and smiled, showing white even teeth. No fangs, she noted with some functioning part of her brain. Not even a hint of them. That used to be another myth about them, like their supposed abhorrence of the sun.

"What's your name?" The creature practically purred the question at her. His voice was low and smooth, completely unaccented. His nostrils flared slightly, as though inhaling her scent.

"Um . . . " Mia swallowed nervously. "M-Mia."

"Mia," he repeated slowly, seemingly savoring her name. "Mia what?"

"Mia Stalis." Oh crap, why did he want to know her name? Why was he here, talking to her? In general, what was he doing in Central Park, so far away from any of the K Centers? *Breathe, Mia, breathe.*

"Relax, Mia Stalis." His smile got wider, exposing a dimple in his left cheek. A dimple? Ks had dimples? "Have you never encountered one of us before?"

"No, I haven't," Mia exhaled sharply, realizing that she was holding her breath. She was proud that her voice didn't sound as shaky as she felt. Should she ask? Did she want to know?

She gathered her courage. "What, um—" Another swallow. "What do you want from me?"

"For now, conversation." He looked like he was about to laugh at her, those gold eyes crinkling slightly at the corners.

Strangely, that pissed her off enough to take the edge off her fear. If there was anything Mia hated, it was being laughed at. With her short, skinny stature and a general lack of social skills that came from an awkward teenage phase involving every girl's nightmare of braces, frizzy hair, and glasses, Mia had more than enough experience being the butt of someone's joke.

She lifted her chin belligerently. "Okay, then, what is *your* name?"

"It's Korum."

"Just Korum?"

"We don't really have last names, not the way you do. My full name is much longer, but you wouldn't be able to pronounce it if I told you."

Okay, that was interesting. She now remembered reading something like that in *The New York Times*. So far, so good. Her legs had nearly stopped shaking, and her breathing was returning to normal. Maybe, just maybe, she would get out of this alive. This conversation business seemed safe enough, although the way he kept staring at her with those unblinking yellowish eyes was unnerving. She decided to keep him talking.

"What are you doing here, Korum?"

"I just told you, making conversation with you, Mia." His voice again held a hint of laughter.

Frustrated, Mia blew out her breath. "I meant, what are you doing here in Central Park? In New York City in general?"

He smiled again, cocking his head slightly to the side. "Maybe I'm hoping to meet a pretty curly-haired girl."

Okay, enough was enough. He was clearly toying with her. Now that she could think a little again, she realized that they were in the middle of Central Park, in full view of about a gazillion spectators. She surreptitiously glanced around to confirm that. Yep, sure enough, although people were obviously steering clear of her bench and its otherworldly occupant, there were a number of brave souls staring their way from farther up the path. A couple were even cautiously filming them with their wristwatch cameras. If the K tried anything with her, it would be on YouTube in the blink of an eye, and he had to know it. Of course, he may or may not care about that.

Still, going on the assumption that since she'd never come across any videos of K assaults on college students in the middle of Central Park, she was relatively safe, Mia cautiously reached for her laptop and lifted it to stuff it back into her backpack.

"Let me help you with that, Mia—"

And before she could blink, she felt him take her heavy laptop from her suddenly boneless fingers, gently brushing against her knuckles in the process. A sensation similar to a mild electric shock shot through Mia at his touch, leaving her nerve endings tingling in its wake.

Reaching for her backpack, he carefully put away the laptop in a smooth, sinuous motion. "There you go, all better now."

Oh God, he had touched her. Maybe her theory about the safety of public locations was bogus. She felt her breathing speeding up again, and her heart rate was probably well into the anaerobic zone at this point.

"I have to go now . . . Bye!"

How she managed to squeeze out those words without hyperventilating, she would never know. Grabbing the strap of the backpack he'd just put down, she jumped to her feet, noting somewhere in the back of her mind that her earlier paralysis seemed to be gone.

"Bye, Mia. I will see you later." His softly mocking voice carried in the clear spring air as she took off, nearly running in her haste to get away.

* * *

If you'd like to find out more, please visit www.annazaires.com. All three books in the Krinar Chronicles trilogy are now available.

ABOUT THE AUTHOR

Dima Zales is a *New York Times* and *USA Today* bestselling author of science fiction and fantasy. Prior to becoming a writer, he worked in the software development industry in New York as both a programmer and an executive. From high-frequency trading software for big banks to mobile apps for popular magazines, Dima has done it all. In 2013, he left the software industry in order to concentrate on his writing career and moved to Palm Coast, Florida, where he currently resides.

Please visit www.dimazales.com to learn more.

Made in the USA
Middletown, DE
25 July 2017